The Storm That Broke The World

Tim Slocum

Aolan Publishing
United States of America

For my son, Jackson—
whose colors he may not always be able to control,
but who shines brighter than any storm.

For my wife Shannon,
for her unwavering support and belief in me.

And for Jace and Madison,
whose childlike excitement and encouragement lit
the way.

Contents

Prologue

Recovered Field Journal — Sgt. Luka Varga
Carpathian Front, Ground Zero — Three Days Before
the First Surge.

Day 1

The sky forgot how to end.
It started over the ice fields. A sunrise that bled into
itself. Now every night the horizon glows, green,
violet, bruised, restless. We all went outside to watch.
Even the captain. The light clung to the snow and
turned our rifles to glass.

Command keeps insisting its atmospheric interference.
They issued a memo this morning telling us not to
"sensationalize optical distortions." The memo didn't
explain why the air thins in my lungs when the colors
rise, or why it feels like something inhales with me.

It's beautiful. It's wrong. They've begun calling it
resonance, light that feeds on feeling.

Rule One (scribbled hastily):
Emotion remembers the storm.
It didn't bring power; it woke it. The resonance
crawled into everything that could feel, air, water,

blood. You can hear it now, faint and steady, when the camp goes quiet. Almost like it's waiting.

Day 2

No one's sleeping. Private Anton cried during roll call, said he didn't know why. The laughter that followed didn't sound real. Animals are acting strange. Crows fly at night; the dogs stay silent. I keep hearing a low tone when I close my eyes. It's not a sound, more like pressure behind my teeth.

The snow looks different, too bright, too alive. I keep thinking of my sister's last letter. She asked if the snow was beautiful here. I can read her words, but I can't remember what "beautiful" feels like.

A report came in over the radio before the static swallowed it. Something about villages in the valley seeing the lights too. If that's true, it isn't contained to us anymore.

Rule Two (half-crossed out):
Emotion becomes matter when it moves.
Stillness is safe. Motion turns feeling into shape. The air takes note of anger. The ground shifts when fear runs. Some lights cling, some lash out. Some dim. Some burn. Feels like they want different things.

Day 3

This morning, the first fight broke out. Two men over rations, nothing new. But when Corporal Danyel's anger hit, I saw it, red light crawling under his skin. He hit harder than he should have. The other man's arm snapped. After that, everyone shouted. You could feel it spreading, fear, rage, bouncing between us like static.

When Danyel panicked, something inside me stirred in answer, like his fear was feeding mine, like the light itself was hungry for it.

I caught my reflection in the mess tent window; my eyes were glowing faint blue.
Didn't write that down right away. Didn't want it to be true.

Part of this page is torn. It looks like I started writing, *"If it spreads to the—"* but the rest is missing.

Rule Three (smudged at corners):
Resonance takes the path of least resistance.
It breaks through the fractures we try to hide guilt, rage, love, whatever won't stay buried. Resonance gathers fastest where emotions run unchecked.

Day 4

Tonight, the sky came down.
A shimmer rolled across the ridge first, like heat above metal. Then colors thicker than fog swept through camp. Radios died mid-transmission. The lieutenant tried opening that new containment crate Engineering sent us—the one made of metal that doesn't ring when struck, but it locked itself. Or jammed. Or *hesitated.*

Private Danyel changed first, his veins lit red, body swelling, breath steaming like furnace smoke. He screamed until his voice broke.

Then it wasn't his voice anymore.

He tore through the tents like paper. Others followed, not all red. Some glowed blue, some pale green, trembling, whispering apologies even as their skin cracked open. Some of us started shooting, but the bullets slowed when they hit them, like the air had turned to syrup. Like it remembered.

The ground lurched once, bracing for something we couldn't see.

Rule Four:
What one feels, all nearby remember.
A single scream can stain the air for miles. A crowd's grief can darken the sky.

Sometimes I think it listens. Sometimes I think it's learning.

Final Entry

Half the camp is gone. The rest are changing. We've started naming the colors—rage, grief, despair, hope. None of them save you. The light hums all the time now. It's not outside anymore. It's in the barracks walls, in the metal cot frames, in us.

I don't know how long I have before it finds the rest of me.

(Below this entry, written in a steadier hand):
Recovered near Sgt. Varga's pack during post-event sweep.
Filed by Recon Unit B.

Chapter 1

The veins came first, thin turquoise filaments tracing Elena's wrists like rivers seen from orbit. They brightened when she breathed too deep; her thoughts and actions all seemed to have a trace of curiosity driving them. It wasn't pain. It was persuasion, soft and relentless, urging her to pay attention to every detail, every shift in the world around her.

Elena steadied the scanner against her arm. Numbers slid across the glass, beautiful but indecipherable. Each spike hinted at something she couldn't explain yet. The house whined lightly, as if the drywall had a throat.

Outside, Detroit wore a spill of wrong-colored light. The sky had been doing that for two days now, auroral seams that shimmered with the shifting hues of the northern lights. Emerald, violet, and sapphire danced across the sky, painting the windows in liquid waves of color. Sirens sang out, their pitch warped and stretched, as if the storm's magnetic pulse rewrote the city's frequencies. Somewhere nearby, the radio in her neighbor's garage slipped between stations, voices folding into static and melody. She thumbed her recorder on because habit could hold a person together when nothing else did.

She lifted the recorder, thumb shaking only slightly. "Current observations suggest possible patterns," she murmured. "Red aligns with anger or aggression. Blue with grief or memory. Gold with affection or connection. Turquoise with heightened awareness. Green with envy. Black… with fear." She hesitated. "There are rarer hues I haven't mapped yet, but each one so far seems to tie to an emotional state. Resonance doesn't create feelings…it manifests them."

The turquoise leaped in her skin. The wave came on like vertigo, like standing on the edge of a roof and feeling the city lean toward you. She sat suspended between worlds: the ordinary shapes of furniture, the unnatural tide of turquoise snaking through her veins. It was as if her skin were a map the city kept redrawing.

Out in the hallway, the radio's half-song was a strange comfort, familiar and warped, slipping from melody to static and back again. The world outside vibrated with color and possibility, but inside, Elena was simply waiting: collecting data, marking the shifts, riding emotion as if it were weather. Each breath fanned out into the unknown, and every gentle flare in her wrist was a reminder that change had arrived, not with violence, but with invitation. In this moment, she was both observer and participant, her story threaded through the pulsing light, her silence holding space for whatever came next.

A sharp knock at the door broke the spell. Elena set the scanner down carefully, her hands unsteady. She checked the peephole—a gray shoulder too close to the frame—then opened the door on the chain. Water flashed in the hallway light; the man beyond was a shape built from steadiness and command.

"Doctor Markov," he said. "It's Darren Briggs."

She slid the chain. His coat was wet, his eyes were not. The veins at his throat burned cobalt, clean as a blade. The car behind him idled with its lights off, its engine a soft animal clearing its throat.

"The phenomenon has affected you as well," she said, her voice steadier than she felt.

Briggs's expression didn't change. The light at his throat flickered once, then held. "This isn't isolated, Doctor. The whole world is turning colors."

She stared past him to the car, its windows breathing faint light, the city shimmering beyond. He continued, "We need you in the lab. The world as we know it is about to change."

She raised an eyebrow, the hint of a smile pulling at her lips. "Containment? That's the plan? You really think anyone could bottle a cosmic storm?"

Briggs's eyes narrowed, letting the silence draw out between them. "It's not about control anymore.

Containment is irrelevant. Adaptation is all that's left. Change is coming, whether we're ready or not. Now get your coat."

She thought of saying no. The turquoise brightened at the thought, pleasure and anticipation rising, a feeling like stepping into warm light. Not hers, not entirely. She shut the recorder off and grabbed the old olive jacket from the chair. The fabric held the memory of winter.

Out on the street, rain wrote the city into soft focus. The neon of a closed coney island smeared across puddles, red becoming pink becoming silver as if the stormlight couldn't make up its mind. Something thumped beneath the People Mover track and kept thumping, a machine trying to remember how to be itself.

Briggs opened the back door of the unmarked sedan for her, a habit that wasn't chivalry so much as choreography. Inside smelled like clean mechanics and river air. The partition was lowered. A driver sat very still, hands on the wheel, veins at his temples a dull, flickering gray.

"Hey," Elena said gently to the back of his head. "You okay?"

He nodded, too much.

Briggs slid in beside her. The door thumped closed, the rest of the city went away a little. He rapped the seatback with two knuckles. "Forty-five," he said. "Be quiet about it."

The sedan slid into the rain. Headlights made tunnels out of water. The tires signed their names across Woodward, down past a theater whose marquee tried to spell SALVATION and got as far as SALV. A group of kids in garbage bags for coats walked shoulder to shoulder through the crosswalk, laughing too hard, their laughter had a color. Elena watched it fog the air like breath on a cold day, pale gold that steamed and was gone.

On the corner, a man in a business suit sat on the curb and sang, not well, not terribly, voice bent into the key the storm had chosen. Two street medics wheeled a woman past them on a squealing gurney; the woman's eyes were open and full of rain, the veins at her throat uselessly bright.

"It's when emotion comes untethered from memory that it destroys them," Briggs said gently. "Like a flood searching for a shoreline."

"You've had time to practice that line too," Elena said. "How many have drowned already?"

He didn't pretend not to understand. "We're past counting; we're mapping."

"Oh." Her lips felt parched, and the turquoise against her skin chilled. "Mapping can mean survival."

"Sometimes," he replied. "Sometimes it just helps to name the bodies."

They took the ramp in a quiet hiss and joined I-75 as if merging into a river that remembered being a road. The skyline shouldered to their right, all those square windows blinking the same wrong blink. The storm's aurora hung low and indecent, a curtain that didn't understand the stage was everywhere. On the bridge to Canada, trucks idled with their lights like patient ships, casting shifting halos through the storm's shimmer. Elena's gaze swept past a line of vehicles, each cab glowing with its own private story, silent and sealed against the weather. The sight pressed at her, odd and solemn, and for a moment she wondered what else the city might surrender to the night and rain, what stories drifted between the headlights, waiting to be noticed or quietly dissolving before anyone could.

Elena turned her wrist so the car's console screen could reflect in her turquoise. It made a false green, then corrected. Her stomach climbed a rung and stayed there.

A flash across the overpass, paint scrawled in quick, terrified letters so large the writer must have felt briefly immortal. DO NOT FEEL, it said, and the rain did its best to erase the imperative and failed. A block later another wall offered the counter-command, clumsy and tender: FEEL OR DIE.

Briggs touched the partition switch with one knuckle; it rose and sealed them in the softer noise. He looked to her. "You're not afraid."

"It's not that I'm unafraid," she confessed softly. "It's just that my fear is misplaced, I worry about losing where I end and everything else begins."

His composure shifted just for a moment. Behind it she saw it, felt it, a private fear shaped like a map with too many pins. The cobalt climbing his arms stepped up its burn as if offended at being seen. He didn't flinch, and she didn't look away.

"Lines can be drawn," he said after a moment. "That's what the lab is for."

"And the city?" she shot back.

"The city will decide what it wants to be," he said, looking back out at it. "The best thing we can do now is figure this event out."

Rain blurred the city's edges, turning roads into shifting streams and headlights into restless searching. Police cars clustered around a stalled taxi, their lights reflecting off the wet pavement in fractured patterns. Officers spoke quietly to the driver, their voices calm amid the storm, a moment of reassurance in a world that seemed less certain every day. Nearby, a boy cycled past, eyes upturned toward the strange glow in the sky. His wonder cut through the anxiety that clung to the night, reminding Elena how young people find hope even when everything feels unfamiliar. She watched, thinking how quickly ordinary routines can become something else when the world decides to change its shape.

"Who told you to come for me?" she asked.

His grin widened ever so slightly. "It was my decision."

She looked at him curiously. "And your reason?"

"You're the smartest scientist I know, and the only one who's kept her head since this started."

Elena's mouth quirked. "I want to understand it and fix it."

Briggs offered a rare nod. "That's exactly the kind of mind I need on the front line."

They came off the freeway into a district that was all new glass pretending not to be, scaffolds with the nerves showing, rain-vexed cranes holding their breath. Reservoir hum turned into transformer hum. The lab sat where a grocery had threatened to open for three years and hadn't, the sign still insisting it was COMING 2022, a calendar that didn't get the memo.

Security lights found the car and held it without hurry. Briggs flashed a card through the window slot; the gates swallowed them like a decision already made. The building did not boast; it laid itself out low and square and sure, the kind of architecture that had never practiced applause.

As they rolled into the bay, the driver breathed out for the first time since the river ramp. The partition dropped. "Sir," he said, his voice a shade too bright. "Do you want me—?"

"Park," Briggs said, gentle as a command can be. "Then take a lap and tell me if you feel something you can't explain. If you do, come inside and we'll name it."

The driver nodded too many times. Elena filed the sentence in the drawer labeled Darren Briggs, Contradictions.

Inside, the air was colder without being cold. The vibrations reorganized themselves into layers, patterns nested in patterns until the part of her that loved equations forgot to be afraid. People moved fast without running. A woman in a lab coat crossed their path with a tray of syringes that glowed like caught lightning, her eyes red from crying or from not blinking. A man with a buzz cut and a wedding band stood very still under a sensor arch while his veins argued about whether to announce themselves.

Briggs's color brightened as they walked, an answer thrown to a question the room hadn't yet asked. He wore his calm like a uniform. Elena felt the room relax into it by reflex, then reminded herself that reflex wasn't consent.

A woman hurried over as Elena entered the lab, relief and surprise on her face.
"We've been trying to reach you, Doctor Markov."

Elena set down her bag. "I was at home."

The woman's eyes widened. "Is it safe for you to be there?"

Elena glanced at the faint turquoise glow in her veins, a reminder of the storm's changes. "It's not about safety," she said quietly. "Sometimes it's just what I need to do."

The woman nodded, understanding more than she said. "Well, we're glad you're here now. The team's been waiting for your input." She handed Elena a badge and a tablet. "You'll need these to access the new systems. We've set up a station for you in the main lab."

Elena sat at a station with three screens and a view into a room that looked like a chapel until she realized it was a negative-pressure chamber. On the far wall, three colors pulsed in slow discourse—amber, slate, lavender—each mapped to a heartbeat that was not yet a person she could save.

Briggs stood near but not over her shoulder. "You'll like the new array," he said. "It listens."

"Does it learn?" she asked.

"It pretends to," he replied. "That's some of learning."

Elena set her palms on either side of the keyboard and let the turquoise in her veins speak to the sensors. The room obliged. The hum leaned closer. The screens did what she always wanted screens to do; they stopped being glass and became translation.

Data rose, not numbers, not as such, curves like gestures, frequencies that wore faces when she didn't blink. She isolated a single, steady signal from the chaos, a frequency that seemed to quiet the noise in the lab, letting everyone breathe a little easier. Elena paired it with the data she'd collected at home, weaving the two together until the pattern stabilized. The result was a gentle, resonant hum, soft and familiar, like the distant sound of a train passing at night and making the dishes on the table tremble. For a moment, the lab felt almost safe.

"Darren," she said.

He did the half-turn. "Yes."

"It's not the storm that's spreading."

He waited. He was good at that.

"It's what we carried into it," she said. "All of it, all at once."

The blue glow at his throat faded slightly, tension leaving his posture. He gave a small nod. "Then let's figure out how to bring it back."

The room shuddered with a subsonic that might have been the building settling or the city changing its mind.

On Screen Two, one of the slate heartbeats hiccupped into teal, then corrected to blue, then steadied in a pale green Elena had seen only twice today, and both times on children who didn't know enough to doubt. She marked it, she didn't name it yet. Names stuck too hard.

Briggs leaned in, not to her, to the work. "We'll have to decide what to anchor," he said, "and what to let go."

"You say that like you haven't already decided," she laughed.

"I'm good at rehearsals," he replied, returning her smile. "Final decisions are for rooms we haven't built."

She thought of the house she hadn't locked, the kettle on the burner, the chair with the coat no longer on it. For a second she wanted her own small life so fiercely it bruised. The wave came on and wanted for her, wanted other things, louder. She caught its sleeve like a friend about to run into traffic.

"Teach me where to draw the lines," she said without looking away from the screen.

Briggs's reflection in the glass offered a slow, reassuring nod. It was a gesture that carried both warning and hope. "We begin by setting boundaries," he said. "Then we figure out how to open ourselves to what matters."

The tremors intensified. The turquoise hue settled into a consistent glow, as if her veins had struck a bargain with the unfamiliar climate the world was testing. Overhead, the silver clouds grew brighter. In another hour, morning would attempt to arrive, only to discover the day had already begun.

"Elena," Briggs said.

"Mm."

"When we leave this room, don't let it decide who you are."

She almost laughed. "What if that's the only way it works?"

"Then let it decide the part of you that can't be bought," he said quietly, "and build from there."

She didn't look back. Instead, she gave a silent nod, with intent on catching every word the screens offered. The data was gathering, forming into something almost tangible. Beyond the glass, the rain found a fresh cadence and kept time with it.

The lab doors behind them slid open for a team carrying a case that hummed from the inside, a note that had learned to walk. Cold air from the corridor poured over Elena's hands. It smelled like the world just before you name a thing.

The hum thinned to a line, pure, high, ordinary.
It pressed through the glass; it pressed through the room.
It pressed like evening through blinds, like water through glass.

Chapter 2

Evening pressed through the blinds like water through glass.
The kitchen smelled of garlic, soap, and something faintly electric.

Emily stacked Lily's drawings on the table; stars, rooftops, a crooked sun that leaned toward both. As she reached for another sheet, a faint, pale-yellow shimmer flickered along the veins at her wrist, restless and unsteady. Kalen noticed it, the way her hands never quite stilled.

He tugged his own sleeve down, heartbeat rising as the blue-gold shimmer in his veins refused to fade.

Emily noticed. "It's spreading, isn't it?" She glanced at her wrist, then met his eyes. "Mine too. The more it spreads, the more restless I feel."

He didn't tell her the truth, that what terrified him wasn't the color spreading, but what the storm might turn him into. He hesitated. "It's… inside now."

Her hand tightened on the edge of the table, the yellow at her wrist brightening. "We stay in tonight."

"Please?" Lily's voice piped from the floor, where crayons rolled in slow circles. "Can we see the lights? Just one more time?"

Lily was sprawled on the floor, giggling as she studied the shifting colors on her skin. Where her wrist caught the light, a soft, pearly-blue shimmer glowed. It was brighter than Kalen's but gentle, almost joyful. She turned her hand this way and that, watching the glow dance, her eyes wide with amazement.

"It's like magic," she whispered, tracing the light with a fingertip. "I love it."

Kalen crouched, meeting her gaze and rubbing her head. For a moment he let himself see it through her eyes, the beauty, not the fear.
"Only to the corner store," he said softly. "We stick together. No wandering, no games."

She nodded, solemn as only a child could be before breaking the rule a minute later.

A low hum threaded through the apartment walls—the same faint vibration he'd started hearing whenever the sky brightened. The news said it was the grid reacting to the storm, but the tone carried something more human, almost thoughtful, as if the city itself were listening.

The stairwell buzzed as they went down.
On the landing below, a neighbor stopped under the

flicker of a dying bulb. For a heartbeat his pupils flashed red before settling back to normal.

"Evening," Kalen offered.

The man muttered something and hurried past, eyes fixed on the floor.

Through the cracked stairwell window, a small drone drifted by, its lens glinting blue. City-wide surveys they called them—tracking atmospheric charge, measuring compliance. It hovered for a moment too long before sliding on, leaving a faint electronic buzz in its wake.

Outside, the aurora wasn't a ribbon tonight; it was a curtain, green fading to violet, low enough to stain the street signs. Windows reflected it in soft waves, the city breathing it back.

Lily tilted her face upward. "It's closer."

Emily took her hand. "Just milk and back home, that's all the adventure tonight."

They stepped through puddles that reflected the swirling sky above, each footfall sending waves of color skittering across the water. At the bus stop, a woman clutched a photograph that pulsed softly with light in rhythm with her breathing. The glow faded as she lowered it, disappearing completely.

Two kids argued near a drain; each shout sent rings across the water that only calmed when they fell silent.

Kalen felt the pulse under his sleeve again, gold answering the sky's rhythm.
He tried to ignore it, but the colors in the air pressed against thought itself.

The sensation wasn't just under his skin anymore. It brushed the edges of memory—half-formed pictures, a whisper that wasn't language at all. The more he tried to push it away, the clearer it became, like someone breathing through his own mind.

Inside the store, the fluorescents buzzed too loudly.

Emily steered Lily toward the aisles.
Kalen nodded absently, the words echoing his own unease.

He opened a cooler door, its glass trembling as if resisting his touch. His reflection looked back at him, eyes ordinary, almost, the faint gold at his wrist said otherwise.

"Daddy," Lily whispered, "the bottles are singing."

He listened—and heard it too, a thin tone, harmonic, just above hearing.

He forced a smile. "Just the power surge, sweetheart." But the word didn't feel real in his mouth.

Somewhere beyond the aisles, a speaker crackled—an emergency broadcast test repeating code strings he didn't recognize. The announcer's calm voice mentioned "containment-readiness drills" before cutting to static. Emily pretended not to hear; Kalen couldn't.

Down the next aisle, a man stood shaking, a cereal box crushed in his hands. A red shimmer crawled up his arms, bright as a wound.

"Sir?" the clerk called. "You okay?"

The man didn't move. "Too loud," he whispered. "Too much… feeling."

The air shifted. Cans rattled on the shelves. The red beneath his skin brightened like wire burning through insulation. His breath fogged in the warm air.

Emily's voice trembled. "Kalen…"

He squeezed her hand, steadying himself. "I see him. Stay with Lily."

He took a step forward, palms open. "Breathe with me, guy. Look here."

The man's eyes flared. He began to yell. "I can't stop—feeling it!"

He let out an ear-piercing scream. Light burst from him, a shockwave of anger turned physical.

The man fell to his knees, sobbing, smoke rising faintly from his clothes.

Kalen stared, heart pounding, his own hands shaking. He hadn't meant to do anything, he hadn't even known he could.

He knelt beside the man, voice unsteady. "Are you... are you hurt?"

The man's voice broke. "It was like all my anger just... exploded. I couldn't stop it. I thought it would burn me alive."

Kalen swallowed, glancing at the glow fading from his own skin. He didn't know what he'd done, or if it would happen again. He just knew the fear wasn't gone, it had only gone deeper.

At the end of the aisle, Emily held Lily close. The girl's small face pressed into her mother's coat, silent.

They left quickly after that.

Outside, the air had a new taste, like metal and sweetness, something about to break.
Far east, beyond the skyline's blur, lightning flickered in the heart of Detroit, a pulse that seemed to echo his own.

The streets felt thinner on the walk home.
Storefront glass trembled as they passed, reflecting colors that didn't belong to neon. A man stumbled out of a café, eyes blank, hand over his chest. A woman reached to help him, then recoiled, gasping like she'd touched a live wire.

Emily whispered, "Kal, everyone is changing."

"They look just like us," Kalen said, "but the others— like the store."

From beneath her coat, Lily murmured, "They're scared, Daddy. I can feel it."

He swallowed hard. "That's why we're going home."

Far behind them, glass shattered. No scream, just the sound of breath and static.
The buzzing followed them, steady and patient, as if counting their steps.

Their street was quiet, too quiet.
Every window glowed the same faint green, as if the aurora had seeped through the walls.

They were halfway to the apartment when Mr. Dalca fell by the hydrant.
Oil-stained hands clutched his head. His voice came ragged. "Run, Kalen. I can feel it. I can't hold it."

Kalen moved between him and the others. "Dalca, everything is fine. You have to just—"

The words died.
Dalca's veins lit violently, red crawling up his neck like a fuse finding its end. He gasped, clawing at nothing.
"Everything… burns."

Then came the scream. It wasn't sound, not exactly; it was feeling turned inside out. The world pulled taut around him, like the storm itself was holding its breath.

His body lit from within—rage and pain made every nerve a visible fiber. The ground cracked beneath his knees. Steam rose. His face was terror caught mid-change.

Kalen stepped forward. "Dalca! Listen to me, you have to stay calm."

For a heartbeat, the eyes behind the light flickered—recognition, pleading.
Then they glazed over.

"Emily," he said, "run now. Take Lily and go."

"I'm not leaving—"

"You have to." His voice shook. "I can feel it again too. If I lose control, you can't be near me."

"Kalen—" She tried to argue.

"Go!"

She pulled Lily close and ran, sobbing as she turned the corner.

Dalca—or what he'd become—lurched forward. Kalen planted his feet. Something inside him answered, not choice, not control, just instinct sharpened by fear. The hum inside him rose, filling the world.

He felt it this time; he called, and it answered. The light in his veins burst, meeting the creature's red in a collision that tore color from the air. Sound vanished. Glass shattered. Rain turned to steam.

Dalca's hand shot out, faster than Kalen could react. With a guttural snarl, he struck Kalen across the head. The blow landed with a force beyond possibility, sending a sharp crack through the night. Kalen's vision burst with stars; the world spun, and it was clear this strength came from something changed, something unnatural. Then the world became white.

When it cleared, he was on the ground, chest heaving, the street still glowing at the seams. He saw Emily, far down the block, Lily in her arms. She turned back, her mouth forming his name before the light swallowed it.

Then everything fell into silence.

For a moment before darkness claimed him, he thought
he heard drawers sliding shut in his head, quiet,
deliberate, locking the noise away one heartbeat at a
time.

Chapter 3

Sound returned wrong, more pressure than noise.
A low undertone hung in the air, as if the city was
relearning how to breathe.

Kalen opened his eyes to fractured light trembling
across the street. Cold pavement pressed against his
back. A burn ran from wrist to shoulder where the
glow had touched. Blood clung to his temple, his mind
groggy.

He rolled to his side, glass grinding beneath his palms.
The street lay in pieces, windows collapsed inward,
asphalt split as if struck from below. Heat shimmered
across the ruins; more echo than flame.

"Emily." The name rasped out, dry and small.
He remembered seeing her turn, light blooming
beneath her skin, hand reaching. Now only the thrum
remained.

He pushed upright. Smoke drifted from a collapsed
awning. Car alarms blinked silently, red lights pulsing
without sound.

"Emily." The cry tore loose, raw, useless.
The echo bent midair, unable to find home.

He staggered toward the alley; the last place he'd seen them. The ground flexed under his boots, soft as breath. Puddles quivered when he passed.

It didn't take long to find her.

At first, Kalen almost didn't recognize her. She was half-veiled in ash and strange, shifting light. Then the shape of her hand, the fall of her hair, the curve of her cheek beneath the soot—every detail was achingly familiar.

He stumbled forward, knees hitting the ground. "Em." The name broke out of him, raw and useless.

He reached for her, hands trembling, afraid to touch and desperate too. Her hair was matted, her skin still warm beneath the grime. One hand was outstretched, as if she'd been reaching for Lily in her last moment. The locket he'd given her years ago, on a day full of laughter, hung open at her throat, the picture inside smeared with ash.

He pressed his forehead to hers, breath shuddering. For a moment, the world narrowed to the scent of her hair, the weight of her in his arms, the impossible stillness. He wanted to call her back, to bargain, to wake up, but there was only silence and the ache of everything he hadn't said.

Her skin was cool, too still.

He tried to remember her laugh, the way she said his name, but the memory slipped away, drowned by the ache in his chest.

The gold-white glow that had burned in him during the blast flickered to life, warm for a heartbeat—the color of her smile. It rose from somewhere deep, a last echo of hope refusing to die.

Then grief crashed in, heavy and unstoppable, and the light inside him changed.

He felt it physically, like a cold tide swallowing warmth—the gold fading, blue flooding his veins. Sorrow wasn't just emotion; it was weight, pressure, a chill crawling through his blood. His hands shook harder. The world blurred, color draining to blue. He clung to her until all that remained was the glow, quiet, endless, and unbearably real.

The city's resonance swelled. Glass vibrated. Puddles dimpled. Somewhere, metal sighed as if it had been holding its breath too long.

He held her until the light beneath his skin dimmed to a faint tremor.

He sat for a long moment, just holding her. The world seemed to shrink to the space between his arms and her stillness. He didn't speak. He didn't move. He simply let the silence settle, the ache in his chest echoing in the hush.

Then a shift, a whisper of movement. The world exhaled after holding its breath.
He wanted to stay, to stop existing. The air itself seemed to wait, afraid to move without him.

Then he saw it, a small handprint glowing faintly on the scorched concrete, fading even as he stared. Lily. The ache in his chest sharpened to panic. He gently set Emily down before the thought had time to form.
"Lily."
The sound tore something in his throat.

He was already moving, grief and hope colliding with every step. Behind him Emily was still, her name on his tongue but lost to the wind.

The world pulsed in colors that didn't belong, windows flickering, glass trembling with his breath. He saw only shadows that might be small and moving.
He darted through the alley and across the street, calling again. The bakery's front was blown inward; sugar and flour spilled across the floor like snow. He kicked through it, coughing, scanning under the counter, behind the oven—nothing.
"Lily." His voice cracked.

The back hallway opened to air. Wind pushed through, carrying the scent of scorched rain. He laid both hands against the walls, cold radiating from his skin. He pivoted away before the rest of the thoughts could take shape.

He ran up the stairs. The air hung heavy with dust and ozone. He climbed. The stairwell narrowed to a hatch. He ran to it, one shove and it shot open. Cold air knifed his lungs. The roof opened the city like a wound.

Aurora light drifted between towers, green and violet with a faint thread of gold breathing through. Streets below ran in crooked veins of dim color. Here and there, patches pulsed brighter, movement or memory, he couldn't tell which.

For a moment, he simply stared, chest heaving. The world spread beneath him, unrecognizable. He spun in place, scanning every direction—down streets, across rooftops, into courtyards.

Bodies lay strewn like broken silhouettes. Some twisted beyond shape, others still and numbly glowing. He saw no motion, no small figure in a blue coat. No Lily.

Realization hit, and the absence struck harder than any wound. He gripped the rusted edge, wind tearing the breath from his lungs. Smoke hung low over the river. The city's pulse seemed to flow through the buildings themselves, a rhythm older than machines.

His mind fractured in a million pieces. He took off running. The stairs blurred; his breath stayed behind somewhere near the roof. When he reached the alley, his knees nearly gave. The air felt heavier, as if the city drank his grief.

He dropped beside Emily once more, voice small. "I have to," he whisperd, swallowing hard. "I'll find her." He lifted her carefully. She was light now. Ash clung to his sleeves and fell from her hair as he moved.

He crossed the street, one step, then another. It was the same path he'd walked a thousand times with groceries or Lily's scooter rattling beside him, Emily laughing at the elevator that never worked. Now the elevator doors hung open, melted into the frame.

He climbed the stairs. Each landing held something, or someone, half-changed, half-gone. A neighbor slumped against the wall, face softened and still. Another body lay twisted, veins of glass-light running through it, as if fear itself had shaped the man and let go. Kalen kept his eyes forward, one step at a time.

The apartment door hung crooked but opened. Inside, the smell of detergent, smoke, and garlic from a meal that never finished cooking made the grief sharpen. He carried Emily to their room. He laid her on the bed, smoothing her hair as he tucked the sheet at her shoulder. Some part of him refused to believe everything that was happening.

"Hey," he whispered, taking her ring from her finger. He brushed her cheek once, letting one final tear fall, then turned away before the glow under her skin could take control completely.

On the dresser sat the framed photo, three faces pressed close at the pumpkin patch, Lily's grin too wide for her face. He picked it up, thumbed the corner, then slid the backing free. He folded the picture carefully, once, then again, until it fit inside his pocket.

The ring in his palm pressed against it, two promises, the only ones left.

At the door, he hesitated, he looked back. "I'll bring her home," he said quietly. "I swear it."

He closed the door gently. The latch clicked, small and final. The sound lingered in the air like it didn't know where else to go.

He stayed until the silence was too much, the sirens changed pitch, becoming orders.
He walked out the door, the blue inside him settling into something deliberate.
He would carry her and the silence both.
When the screams cut through the haze, he didn't run.
He had already decided what to carry.

Chapter 4

The conference room glowed sterile and white, the last clean color left in a world repainted by living light. Overhead, harsh fluorescents flickered, forcing back the darkness that pressed against the thick concrete walls of the bunker.

Outside, the storm raged unseen, its presence felt only through distant rumble and the subtle vibration underfoot—violent, electric, threading through the shelter's silence like a pulse.

General Darren Briggs stood at the far end of the table, hands clasped behind his back, posture unyielding. At the console, Doctor Elena Markov adjusted the projector feed until static cleared to a shaky field recording.

The screen filled with the image of a man kneeling in an alley, rain and ash mixing around him. His veins shimmered gold-white, pulsing in rhythm with a heartbeat.

"This is Kalen Rourke," Elena said evenly. "Footage from Sector Twelve, approximately twenty-one minutes ago. Three days since the storm hit."
She pointed to the slow, steady light under his skin.

"This frequency corresponds to protective love, what we classify as a stable gold resonance. It's one of the few that remains coherent under stress. That's his baseline."

On-screen, the color shifted. Blue spread from his fingertips, swallowing the gold until nothing but deep azure remained.

"Then it changes," she said. "Dominant emotion from hope to grief. Full transition in under three seconds."

Briggs's reflection in the glass barely moved. "He's losing control."

"Not yet." The blue flared once, then steadied. The monitors leveled out.

Elena's voice dropped. "He regulates it. Two dominant emotional states back-to-back, and he holds equilibrium. That shouldn't be possible."

Briggs's jaw flexed. "Then explain what we're looking at, Doctor."

"The color," she said, "isn't a side effect. It's the emotion itself—given form. Every person we've observed shows the same link. Emotion and perceived color are one."

Briggs folded his arms. "You're certain?"

"I've run the data six times. It's consistent. The resonance defines us now."

He glanced at her hands, faint turquoise light glowing beneath her skin.

"And that?" he asked.

Elena met his eyes. "Empathy, curiosity, call it balance. It keeps me steady."

She gestured toward him. "Your glow, that cobalt, domineering control, it's a form of anxiety. You hold yourself together through order."

Briggs grunted. "You just say that because you know me."

Elena turned to the rows of technicians behind the glass. "Not at all. Look—Doctor Harrow is pale gray. That's despair, suppression. His body mass has dropped twelve percent since exposure. Cognitive drift is increasing. Our emotions are changing us on a cellular level."

Harrow lowered his gaze, embarrassed by the evidence shining through his skin.

Elena faced Briggs again. "Every emotion manifests differently. Each carries its own frequency, its own shape. Over time, those shapes define us."

Briggs nodded once. "And those that have become feral beasts?"

She hesitated. "A result of emotional collapse. One emotion consumes the rest—rage, fear, despair, it doesn't matter which. Once it overtakes the others, consciousness breaks. We call them Echoferals."

"And the rest of us?"

She turned back to the screen, where Kalen still knelt in the rain, the glow beneath his skin dimming to a calm pulse.

"Echoform," she said quietly. "What I think is the next level of our evolution. We have changed but are still in control, so long as we don't allow emotion to consume us."

Briggs stared at the image. "I need you to contain him. We can talk about your philosophy later."

"It's not philosophy, sir. It's biology."

For a long moment neither spoke. Only the low buzz of the lights filled the silence.

"He's not resisting it," she said. "He's living with it."

Briggs turned toward the door. "Then we'll see how long that lasts." He paused before leaving. "Begin cognitive-isolation trials on the others," he added, voice flat. "No restraints. I want to know how long equilibrium lasts without pain—only the mind."

Elena hesitated, recognizing what that meant: psychological testing, sensory manipulation, emotional induction. Briggs called it science. She called it torture.

Hours later, Elena stood in the lower labs, separated from the testing floor by reinforced glass. Condensation crawled down the inside of the barrier. The hum in the walls climbed with her pulse.

Inside, a soldier sat strapped to a chair, heart monitor spiking in sharp peaks. His veins glimmered dull red, light crawling under his skin.

"Sergeant Avery," Elena said into the intercom, calm and clinical. "Focus on what angers you most. Let it rise."

He gritted his teeth. Slowly the glow spread, deepening to crimson. His muscles began to bulge the brighter the color became. The chair anchors strained. Then a guttural growl rolled through the speakers.

Elena raised her hand. "Stop. Sedate him."

Technicians cut the resonance field. The soldier sagged, gasping, red fading to threads. His eyes flickered open, dazed.

"He came back," Elena said quietly. "Emotion fuels it. The stronger the emotion, the quicker it consumes you."

One of the junior researchers, a young woman, pressed a hand to her chest, startled.

Elena noticed. "You felt that, didn't you?"

The woman nodded. "Like it hit me. Right here."

Elena looked at the rest of the team. "That's what links us. Our resonance feeds between us now. One person's emotion can amplify another's. If it's too strong, or you're too close to the threshold, it can be enough to lose yourself to the feeling."

Uneasy silence. Beyond the glass, the soldier whispered something they couldn't hear.

Elena's eyes softened. "Until that line is crossed, we can come back."

Her gaze lifted to the upper monitor—to Kalen's frozen image, blue still glowing faintly beneath his skin.

"He walks that line without help."

Briggs's voice cut in, cold. "Then build something that lets him cross it on command. A controlled discharge."

Elena frowned. "You mean weaponize it."

"Refine it," Briggs corrected. "If emotion can level a city, we can't afford it in the wrong hands. Prototype a stabilizer. Something portable."

Without another word, he turned and left the lab.

Elena turned slowly toward her bench, where an unfinished device lay. It was a metal cuff threaded with crystal conduits and insulated wiring. She stared at it a long time before reaching for her tools.

"The first gauntlet," she whispered, almost to herself. "You want control. I'll give you truth."

Later that evening, Elena stood at the whiteboard, the last of the day's notes bleeding through in gray smudges. Lines and symbols sprawled in restless clusters, a map of guesses more than answers. She circled a jagged diagram showing the storm center, arrows branching, and feedback loops curling back into themselves.

Briggs stood behind her, arms crossed, eyes on the shifting colors beyond the glass.

"You really believe it, Doctor?" His voice was low, tired. "That we're not looking at fallout or infection?"

Elena turned, marker still in hand. "I don't think it's fallout, sir. I think it's something else."

She tapped the diagram with the marker's end. "Every time we record an emotional spike, the field intensity rises. The colors in the sky get denser. It's not random. It reacts to us."

Briggs frowned. "Reacts how?"

"The storm amplifies whatever we feel," she said. "Rage, grief, hope, it doesn't matter. The more we feel, the stronger it gets. It's a loop. People lose control, they burn out, and the storm grows."

He studied her, eyes unreadable in the dim light. "You're saying it's alive?"

Elena hesitated. "Maybe not alive, but aware. It learns, adapts. And if I'm right, we're not just surviving it, General. We're feeding it."

The silence between them thickened. The buzz of the floodlamps grew louder, pressing against the glass.

Briggs finally spoke. "And if you're wrong?"

She shrugged, exhaustion softening her tone. "Then we're still changing. But I'd rather understand what's changing us than wait for it to finish the job."

Briggs's reflection turned in the glass, half shadow, half color. "Keep your theories quiet, Doctor. And keep me updated."

Elena stood there a moment longer, marker still in her hand, staring at the storm's reflection. The turquoise under her skin pulsed once, soft, uncertain.

If it was learning, she thought, then so was she.

Chapter 5

By dawn, the city had stopped pretending to sleep.
The hum was deeper now, a low vibration living under
everything, like the world thinking through itself.

Kalen stepped into the street.
Ash drifted in thin veils through the light. Every
surface shimmered faintly with trapped color, as
though night had forgotten to end.
The blue beneath his skin pulsed slow and steady, dull
as mourning light.

It wasn't pain anymore, just weight, a hollow ache
filling the space where everything else had been.
He felt emptied out, scraped clean, grief settling into
his bones until even breathing seemed borrowed.
Every thought moved through water.
Only Lily's name still reached him.

He walked because he couldn't allow himself to stop.
He had stopped thinking each echo he heard might be
her voice, that each flicker in the distance was her
small shape turning a corner.
Hope had thinned to a thread, but it was still there, and
it kept him moving.
Sometimes the resonance beneath his boots climbed
higher when he whispered her name, like the world
was trying, in its broken way, to answer.

He whispered again. "Lily."
The echo came back warped, but softer this time, almost like memory. For a moment he stood in the hush, listening to the city breathe around him, the silence stretching, uncertain.

A loud scrape of metal drew his attention to the left. He saw prints glowing faintly in the dust. There, a dog waited at the end of the alley, ribs showing beneath its hide.
He recognized it, a stray from the market. Now one eye glowed blue, filaments of light webbing down its muzzle.

"Easy," Kalen murmured, crouching, slowly moving his hand out.

The dog's body trembled. A sound began to build low in its throat. Not a growl exactly, something deeper, almost normal in its confusion.
Its light pulsed red through the blue, colors flickering like a warning.
Kalen took one step closer, trying to calm the animal.

The dog lunged.
It hit him mid-chest, its weight far heavier than it should have been. Kalen fell backward, his shoulder cracking against pavement. The dog bit down, jaws snapping inches from his throat.

He caught its neck out of reflex, one hand gripping fur that burned beneath his fingers. The glow crawled up his arm, biting at his skin.
He shoved, but the creature didn't budge. It was impossibly strong; muscles tense and glowing with threads of light. Its teeth scraped across his collarbone, sharp and cold. Pain flashed through him, white and blinding.

Something inside him surged. It wasn't panic or anger, but something beyond.
A memory flickered—Emily's laugh, Lily's hand tugging his sleeve.
His vision narrowed. The hum in his blood spiked, flaring bright beneath his skin. For a heartbeat, the blue deepened, streaked with gold—the color that once reminded him of love.

He twisted and slammed the dog sideways into the wall. The impact cracked brick and air.
The animal yelped but charged again. Kalen was faster. He met it mid-jump with a punch, strength not his own. He pulled back and struck again. This time he felt bones give. The light in the dog's body dimmed, fading to a weak pulse that guttered out.

Kalen staggered back, panting. The world rushed in around him, the hum, the smell of iron, the faint steam rising from his arms. He felt it for a second time now, the draining ache that lingered after summoning that unnatural strength. It was as if each surge left something hollow in its wake, a cost paid in pain and exhaustion that echoed deep inside his chest.

The glow beneath his skin pulsed wildly. It was brighter now, unstable.
He stared at his hands, slick with blood and light that wasn't his.
The air seemed to pull away, and every sound bent with his heartbeat.

He wiped his palms on the cracked pavement, breath trembling. The dog lay still, its light cooling to pale gray.
Kalen's pulse wouldn't slow. He pressed a hand to his chest, trying to steady it.

"What am I becoming?" he whispered.

The sky didn't answer, it never did, but somewhere beyond the alley another sound rose to meet it: screams.

At first, they came as silhouettes through the smoke, a handful of figures moving wrong, limbs jerking too sharply, light leaking from their skin in fractured bursts.
He thought he recognized one, but the body was too distorted to tell. Her skin glimmered gray-violet, eyes wide, unfocused.

Their movements were all edge and noise, like music
played on broken strings.
Colors flared through them; red, violet, and green
shifting too fast to belong to a single feeling.

Kalen ducked behind a burned-out car, every muscle
wired tight.
He didn't have words for what he was seeing, only the
sick certainty that they had felt too much for too long.
Their footsteps dragged, but when they lifted their
heads, he saw the light rippling beneath their skin—
bright, unstable, burning itself out.

He took one step back.
Glass cracked beneath his boot.

The nearest one turned. Its mouth opened, light spilling
out where a voice should have been. The others,
alerted as well, all stared in his direction, then they
charged.

Kalen turned and ran.
Screams followed, jagged, layered.

He sprinted between overturned buses and hanging
wires, each footfall sparking color from the street.
Fear turned the air alive.

He cut through a narrow alley, vaulted a fence at the
end, and dropped into a courtyard littered with

overturned tables.
For one breath, silence returned.

Then came the mechanical hiss.
A clean white beam swept the courtyard, a surgical
light cutting through haze.

Kalen froze. He looked up to see a drone drifting
between the towers, metal smooth and gray, a single
white lens burning steady.
He recognized it—the same one he'd seen leaving the
apartment. It moved with deliberate patience, scanning
the grid in perfect lines.

The sound of its rotors merged with the pulse in his
veins. The light passed over him once, then stopped.
For a breath, nothing happened.

Kalen stood perfectly still, hands half-raised, heart
pounding.
The drone hovered above him, silent, its lens
narrowing and widening as if adjusting focus.

It wasn't attacking. It was looking. Studying.
Then the beam shifted color—from white to a steady
red.

"Please," Kalen said, his voice hoarse. Then, when the
light flared hotter: "Wait, don't."

The first pulse hit.
It came without sound, just pressure, the air collapsing

around him. His body arched, every muscle seizing as the red light carved across the courtyard.

He hit the ground, the smell of ozone flooding his lungs. Sparks of blue and gold flared beneath his skin. The drone descended a few meters, hovering close enough for him to see faint ripples of heat along its frame. Its lens dilated, the red flickering faster, as if reacting to him.

He tried to crawl backward, hand scraping broken glass. The red swallowed his reflection.
The light pulsed again, sharp and consuming. Pain overtook him. The world shrank to light, pressure, and soundless impact.

Through the haze, he thought he saw his own reflection in the drone's metallic surface—blue fire crawling through his veins, the street around him bleached of color.
Then there was only silence.

His last clear thought was of Lily's hand in his, her laugh erasing the pain.
Then the world folded in on itself, and everything fell still.

Chapter 6

The fluorescents hummed, steady and sterile. Their
white glare flattened everything it touched.
Elena Markov stood inside the testing chamber,
turquoise shimmer pulsing low and calm beneath her
skin. It was her own private metronome against the
stillness.

The walls around her vibrated faintly with the deep
buzzing of the bunker's resonance grid, the sensors
overloaded by the emotional surges above. The Veil
Division insignia flickered across one screen:
SECTOR CONTROL: DETROIT.

Kalen Rourke sat shackled to the restraint chair, wrists
cuffed, ankles bolted, head tipped forward. The
morphine drip whispered beside him, slow and steady.
Through the pale of his skin ran a muted blue light,
soft as moonlight underwater, grief so deep it had gone
quiet.

Elena glanced toward the observation glass. Behind it,
General Briggs stood with hands clasped behind his
back, a statue carved from control. Beside her, Johnson
arranged syringes by color, his face half-hidden by the
sterile mask of procedure.

"Vitals stable," he said. "We can begin."

Elena hesitated. "He's still sedated."

"Enough to keep him from tearing loose," Johnson replied. "Not enough to keep him from answering."

She exhaled slowly. "Let me try to reason with him first."

Briggs's voice carried through the speaker, measured, cold. "You get five minutes, Doctor."

Nodding, Elena stepped forward until her reflection overlapped Kalen's in the mirrored wall.
"Mr. Rourke?" No answer. "Kalen?" There was still no response, only the hiss of oxygen and the slow drip of morphine.

She softened her voice. "My name is Elena Markov. I'm sorry for the restraints, for all of this. It's not punishment. We're trying to understand what's happening to you, to all of us."

Her turquoise light flickered faintly with the words, a pulse of empathy reaching for him.
For a long moment the room stood in silence, then his lips moved. A whisper scraped out, rough and small.

"Where… is Lily?"

Elena's chest tightened, recognizing the name from his file. "We're still searching," she said, keeping her tone steady. "We're trying to gather those not completely turned."

His head lifted slightly, the blue in his veins stirring.
"Where is Lily."
No pleading now, just repetition, a heartbeat turned
into language.

When she didn't answer, he said it again but quieter,
almost mechanically. His light dimmed until it was
barely there.

Johnson's sigh broke the silence. "He's
nonresponsive."

"He's grieving, Johnson," Elena replied softly.

"Same thing," Johnson muttered. "Clip the drip."

The soldier hesitated, then obeyed. Clamping the line,
the morphine slowed, bead by bead.
Kalen's breathing began to change after a few minutes,
less sedated but no less empty.

Elena crouched beside him, voice near a whisper.
"Kalen, please. When the emotion inside you changes,
when its dominance turns from blue to something
else," she paused, "do you feel it coming, or does it
take you?"

Kalen didn't respond. He sat, head bowed to the floor.

Elena pressed on. "Do you remember how you stopped
it before, how you kept yourself from losing control?"

Johnson's pen clicked once. "Time's up. Give him the stimulus."

"Don't," Elena said, rising sharply. "He's not refusing, he's just lost."

Johnson's patience cracked. "You think compassion will get us data?" He leaned close to Kalen, words precise and venomous. "Your daughter is dead, Mr. Rourke. Accept it."

The sound in the room vanished.
Kalen's eyes opened, empty, unfocused. The blue inside them deepened suddenly, painfully bright. A pulse spread from him, invisible at first, then felt. The air thickened, the walls hummed like struck glass.

Elena gasped as her turquoise light flared wild across her hands. Johnson stumbled back, a red flicker searing through his neck. The soldiers froze, eyes glassy, tears sliding down without knowing why.

Grief filled the chamber, raw and suffocating. It pressed into every heartbeat, surging through Elena. It lasted only a second, maybe two, but that was enough for her to understand this man.
As quickly as it came, it was gone, the room fading back into silence.

Kalen slumped forward, the blue fading out completely. The monitors steadied into dull, mechanical rhythm. Not peace. Not sleep. Just emptiness.

Elena stood trembling, every nerve aching from what she'd felt. "How?" she whispered. "He wasn't holding back information. He was holding that."

Johnson straightened, his own glow receding, eyes wide behind his glasses. "Record the surge," he muttered, already retreating into data. "Duration two seconds. Amplitude—"

"Enough," Elena said. Her voice broke, small and furious. "You felt it too. You had to."

Behind the glass, Briggs's reflection didn't move. "End the session."

The soldiers unlatched the cuffs. Kalen didn't look up. Elena's light gradually dimmed beneath her skin until only a faint shimmer remained.

Through the side window she saw the prototype bench where the gauntlet lay half-assembled, metal casing open, its crystal core pulsing faint red. She knew Briggs wanted it finished soon, but the sight of it now made her sick.
Something had ended here. It was not just the session, but the last illusion that this was science.

The conference room smelled of burnt coffee and printer toner. Screens around the table froze on still images from the session. It was the interrogation earlier, Kalen slumped forward, light extinguished, graphs locked mid-spike as if mocking her.

Elena hadn't sat down before she spoke.
"You broke protocol. You antagonized the subject with unverified information. You poisoned the line."

Johnson leaned back, adjusting his glasses with deliberate calm. "He was unresponsive. We don't have time for sentiment. Shock is a treatment variable."

"Treatment?" Elena barked. "You severed the only thread keeping him coherent. He was showing volitional control. You destroyed it."

Johnson didn't flinch. "Control that doesn't scale is irrelevant. One Echoform shutting himself down won't save the rest. We need replicable curves, decay rates, thresholds, something I can put in a manual."

Elena slammed her folder on the table. "You'll drive him feral. Then all you'll have left is an Echoferal we can't learn from."

Briggs, silent until now, spoke with the weight of judgment. "Or one we can aim. Either way, he has value."

Elena turned on him, heat rising. "You can't mean that. You'd risk turning him into the very thing we're trying to contain?"

Briggs's eyes were steady, the calm of someone who had already decided the ending. "Control is a story we tell ourselves, Doctor. The resonance decides what survives. Direction, however, is real. In a storm, Elena, would you rather hold the lightning rod or be the lightning?"

She stared at him, caught off guard by the simplicity. "That isn't research. That's conquest."

Briggs's mouth ticked, not a smile, not quite. "You call it conquest. I call it adaptation. The world hasn't even found its footing yet. Cities are fracturing, command centers blind, every new flare rewriting the rules. I don't have the luxury of patience or optimism. We need to fix this before it's taken too much."

Elena leaned forward, voice tight. "At what cost, Darren? His mind? Ours?"

Briggs didn't blink. "Conscience is a comfort, Doctor. Comfort doesn't survive emotional resonance. What matters is who adjusts first. Rourke is adjusting. That makes him dangerous. That also makes him useful."

Johnson shifted uneasily at the edge of the table, but Briggs didn't glance his way. His gaze stayed on Elena, weighing her, measuring her.

"You think compassion will hold this line," Briggs said. His tone wasn't mocking; worse, it was patient, instructional. "It won't. Discipline will. Sacrifice will. We are standing on the knife's edge. Decide which side you intend to fall on."

Elena's pulse hammered. She wanted to argue, to shout that he was wrong, but the conviction in his voice chilled her. He believed every word, and that terrified her more than his cruelty.

Briggs finally stood. "We're finished here."
He gave her a single nod, dismissive, and walked out.

The door hissed shut behind him, leaving the echo of his boots and the faint static hum of the frozen monitors, each pulse on the screen still spiking where Kalen's grief had broken the room.

Elena's lab was quiet but for the sound of servers. She sat at her desk, eyes fixed on the frozen feed of Kalen slumped in his chair, the light gone from his veins.

She pressed her wrist against the desk, hiding the faint shimmer that pulsed beneath her skin when her emotions slipped. She would usually clench her fist until it dimmed, but it lingered this time, longer than before, a faint trace crawling up her veins toward the elbow before it finally faded.

Her reflection in the monitor stared back at her. She looked tired and pale, her eyes rimmed with sleeplessness. For the first time, she wondered not just how close Kalen was to breaking, but how close she was.

Her mind drifted, unbidden, to a memory from before the storm. Briggs had found her at a conference in Vienna two years ago. He'd been different then. He was still just as sharp, still ambitious, but his eyes were alive with possibility. He'd spoken about building something that could change the world for the better. She'd challenged him, and he'd laughed, a sound she hadn't heard since.

"We need people who aren't afraid to ask the impossible," he'd said, offering her a place on the project. "People who still believe in more than just control."

She believed. She wanted to believe in him too.

Now, in the sterile hush, she wondered where that man had gone. The Briggs she knew now was carved from discipline and necessity, every word measured, every gesture calculated. She could still see the shadow of who he'd been, but it flickered only in memory.

Briggs's words echoed like a verdict: "Do whatever it takes to get me answers."

Her gaze drifted again to the gauntlet prototype. Its crystal core pulsed faintly, half machine, half heartbeat. For the first time, she wondered not what it could do for Briggs, but what it might do for Kalen, for everyone still holding on.

She opened her notebook and wrote a title she could live with.
Protocol: Drawer Method — Iteration One.

She underlined it once, hard. It stood as a promise to him, and to herself.
And when the faint turquoise glow sparked again beneath her skin, she didn't stop it.
She simply pulled her sleeve down and kept writing.

Chapter 7

The door slid open, earlier than it should have. Kalen knew the rhythm of locks, their precise choreography of click, pause, hiss, and silence. This time, he noted how it had faltered, skipping beats in the measured quiet. Something had changed.

He kept his head down. The cot pressed into his back, chilled through the thin blanket.

Someone moved inside, soft shoes, not boots. The air shifted, warm and uneasy, carrying a trace of perfume through the disinfectant.

"Rourke."

Her whisper barely reached him.

He didn't answer. He'd stopped answering days ago.

She waited. Her heartbeat filled the small silence between the vents.

When she spoke again, her voice was low, deliberate, the cadence of someone explaining survival, not comfort.

"I understand your pain," she said. "But you don't know what's coming. Tomorrow, they start full conditioning, field exposure, deprivation, fracture. It breaks the mind from the inside out. You can't fight it by being strong. You'll lose."

He studied the seam where wall met floor. The words slid past him.

Undeterred, she pressed on. "If you want to survive, you have to learn to disappear without dying."

For a moment, the silence stretched between them, heavy with the weight of unspoken fears. Her words lingered, each one deliberate, preparing him for what lay ahead.

"Seal it."

Her tone sharpened, precise and absolute.

"Pain is a key, Kalen. It opens everything if you let it. You must give it nowhere to turn. When the current starts, it'll crawl through every thought you have. You can't stop it, but you can misdirect it. Give it an empty room. Hide yourself somewhere else. That's how you survive."

She moved closer, her sleeve brushed the IV stand. Metal clicked. A sharper hiss followed as the drip deepened its rhythm.

Morphine softened the edges of his awareness.

"You'll need the rest," she murmured. "They won't let you have it later."

He turned his head slightly. Her outline wavered against the fluorescent light. Her shoulders were tight, hair drawn back, eyes hollowed by sleeplessness.

"I've watched this too many times," she whispered. "Build the drawer. Shut the door. Promise me you'll try."

Footsteps echoed down the corridor. She froze, glanced toward the door.

She hesitated, one heartbeat, two, then whispered,

"I'm sorry."

The door eased open and closed again.
The drone of the vents returned, steady and indifferent.

He watched the ceiling blur, lights doubling in his vision.
Morphine pulled at him, soft and heavy. Somewhere deep inside, where thought thinned into instinct, he began to picture what she'd described, something solid, something that closed.

A drawer.

He didn't know what to place inside yet, only that it was waiting.

Time meant nothing, hours or minutes marked only by a louder pulse in the vents.
The lock released. Two soldiers entered and unbuckled

him, changed the IV, and chained his wrists to the transport bar.

He didn't fight. He had nothing left to fight for.

They moved him down the corridor. Solid white walls with mirrored panels, the air smelled like bleach. He simply put one foot in front of the other.

The testing room waited. The same chair. The same glare.
They strapped him down, his shoulders first, then his chest, his knees last, each buckle stiff from being new.

Johnson's voice drifted from the monitors.
"Start low, this one is an anomaly."

The first current came in a measured wave, light behind his eyes, the world tightening at its edges.
He clenched his teeth and counted, one to ten, ten back to one.
He imagined the feel of a rifle bolt, the click of certainty.
He thought about nothing.

Another wave hit, this one stronger.
His jaw locked; muscles trembled.
He refused sound.

"Level two," Johnson said.

Again he counted. Endurance was arithmetic now.

The third surge tore through him, white heat from chest to fingers. Every muscle screamed, then fell silent.
He kept his eyes open until vision smeared.

Elena's voice echoed in his mind, protesting, but the ringing drowned her out.

Finally, there was stillness.
They left him strapped down, metal warm beneath his skin.

Through static he caught fragments of voices:
"He's stable." — Johnson
"He's resisting." — Elena
"He's stalling." — Briggs

The door sealed. He was alone with the machinery's thrum. The tremors never stopped.
Light shimmered faintly in time with his pulse, warmth trapped under skin, restless, alive.

He ignored it. He was still strong enough. He didn't need the drawer. Not yet.

The straps bit harder this time. Metal cuffs at his ankles, chain across his chest. Water lapped his jaw, cold enough to sting his teeth.

"Begin," Johnson said.

The harness jerked, lowering him down. Sound vanished as the cold reached bone, then his memory. He clenched his fists until the cuffs cut.

Up again. Air scalded his throat as he took large breaths. He was becoming used to this now. He'd lost count of days, weeks, everything just blurred.

The world went white behind his eyelids. They were back at the beach. Lily was calf-deep in the surf, laughter bright as glass; Emily on a towel, her hair across her face, waving him over. He felt the weight of sunlight on his back.

He tried to hold onto that memory, but the pump roared, his concentration broke.
The warmth didn't fade though. Something stirred beneath the gray. It felt like a low current moving through his ribs, crawling the lines of his veins.

Not pain. Not memory.
Something alive.

Up again. He coughed salt and blood. Air hit like fire. His vision was blurred.

"Duration?" Briggs asked.
"Ninety seconds," Johnson replied. "No loss of consciousness."

Briggs scowled. "Increase it."

"Wait," Elena said, too fast. "Look at him. Just stop."

Kalen looked down. Skin slick, trembling. The surface shimmered; he felt something burning beneath.
For the first time since the chamber, he felt warm.

"Do you see that?" Elena cried. "His light, it's shifting again."

"Finally," Briggs said. "Record it."

"That's not progress," she snapped. "That's ignition!"

The harness jerked again.
Down.

Cold struck like a fist. Water filled his mouth; his lungs locked.
He held the last breath without meaning to, the body's refusal to die.
Fire clawed through him, panic, instinct, the scream for air.
He kicked once against the chain; it gave nothing back.
Pressure climbed his chest until he thought his ribs would split.

Every cell demanded life, but somewhere beneath the frenzy a decision formed: no more fighting.
He let go.

The world narrowed to red behind his eyes, the burn of collapsing lungs, and then nothing.

No sound, no light, just the slow slide of himself disappearing.

When he returned, heat pressed against his skin and a mechanical whine filled his ears. His eyes stayed closed. The room tilted, his heartbeat stumbled against the monitors.

Voices cut through the fog.
"You pushed too far," Elena said. "He lost consciousness. His body's still reacting, look at his vitals!"
"That's data," Johnson replied. "It's the response we wanted."
"It's a death spiral!" she shot back.

Hands worked near his face, mask removed, water wiped from his mouth. The sting of antiseptic burned his nose.

"I didn't agree to this," Elena said. "You promised containment, not torture."
"Containment needs thresholds," Briggs answered, voice level. "We find them by crossing them."
"You crossed them hours ago!"

Metal slammed against the table.
"He's burning up," she said. "You're watching it happen. He's dying."

He tried to move but couldn't. Heat rolled beneath his ribs like a second pulse, steady, aware.

"Pull me from the project if you want," Elena argued. "I'm not doing this again."
"You'll do what's necessary." Briggs's tone ended the matter.

Silence followed, only the steady hiss of the IV. Something cold brushed his wrist. Her hand. A heartbeat of contact. Then it was gone.
He listened to her footsteps fading.

The warmth inside him shifted, deliberate, as if it had been waiting to hear every word.

When he woke up the third time, the IV whispering beside him was the only sound he heard. The drain beneath the cot still glistened from where they'd washed the floor. The air smelled of salt and steel.

He stared upward, letting the vibration of the walls fill the silence left by voices.
Elena's words came back soft and relentless: build a space in your head that pain can't find.

He took a deep breath and turned inward.
It wasn't imagination; it was architecture. He pictured a drawer, dark wood, smooth edges, hinges that groaned when they closed. He filled it, piece by piece.

A pressure gathered behind his ribs as he did it, not pain, just something shifting, as if a part of him were being moved somewhere deeper.

Lily's laughter went first.
Then Emily's face. The beach. The warmth that had followed him into the dark.
The taste of salt. The pulse under his ribs.

Each memory sank like a stone into deep water.
Noise faded. The ache behind his heart eased.
He almost felt normal again.

When he pushed the drawer shut, it was like stitching a wound. Pain folded in on itself, tidy, clean, contained.

Relief never came. Only quiet, heavy, rising, filling him until he could hardly feel where his body ended.
Air thickened. The thrum of the building deepened.
His heartbeat sounded distant, borrowed.

He understood too late: the drawer hadn't just taken what he'd hidden.
It had taken him.

Breath slowed. The ceiling wavered into a blur of light.
The edges of the room drew inward, doors closing without a hand.
Stillness pressed from every side, sealing him off from the world.

It wasn't locked from outside.
It was locked from within.

A thought surfaced, slow and cold:
He hadn't built a drawer. He'd dug a grave.

He tried to speak. The breath failed halfway.
Only the low vibration of the walls remained. It was
steady, patient, listening.

He thought he heard her voice once, faint as memory,
saying his name.
He closed his eyes, and in the dark behind them, the
latch clicked.

Chapter 8

At first there was nothing.
Not darkness, darkness had weight, and this had none.
It was stillness stripped of meaning, the breath before
sound.

Kalen felt the pulse in his veins, the ache in his chest,
even here. Every sound he made was absorbed before
it reached his ears.
He turned. The world turned with him.

Endless space. No ceiling. No walls. Just reflections of
what might have been walls, shifting and folding over
one another.
The drawer.
He'd built it to hold everything, and now it also held
him.

Shapes flickered in the distance, faint and colorless.
Slowly, they began to form.
A table.
Chipped wood. A vase with one white flower,
trembling in a wind that wasn't there.

He took a step, and the space rippled around him, soft
light blooming where his feet touched the ground. His
heartbeat echoed, distant but real.

The first image rose out of the air, Emily beneath a
veil, eyes glinting with nerves and laughter. She stood

in a place half real, half memory. The sunlight had turned the world pale gold. He remembered the smell of her perfume, the tremor in his hands when he touched her cheek.

She vanished too quickly, and just as quick, another appeared.
Hospital light. A cry that was small, new, real. Lily's first breath cutting through the noise. He saw her tiny fist curl around his finger, skin to skin, perfect and impossible.

More followed one after another, pieces of his life unspooling like film underwater.
A porch at dusk.
Rain against glass.
Lily's first steps, her arms open wide, Emily's delighted gasp.

Each moment glowed faintly, hovered near him, then drifted away as if ashamed to stay too long.
He reached out—when his hand brushed one, it broke apart like mist.

The drawer wasn't giving them back. It was showing him what he'd traded for silence.

As he continued walking, the ground pulsed faintly with each step, resonating with a sound that wasn't quite a heartbeat anymore. The world around him adjusted to more memories rearranging into a long corridor that bent in on itself, smooth and endless.

He didn't know how long he walked before something changed.
The light began to ripple. The air tasted different, it was dry, burnt, and electrical. He felt it before he saw it, a flicker at the edge of his vision. Color seeped slowly into the emptiness, blooming outward like a spreading bruise.

Then they were there, Emily and Lily.
Not the soft versions from before; these were sharper, too bright, every detail wrong.

Emily's dress fluttered in a wind that didn't exist.
Lily's hair hung damp across her face, eyes wide and unblinking.

Emily's voice, low and fractured:
"You're holding ghosts in a box that won't stay shut."

Kalen's breath hitched. He shook his head. "No."

Lily's words, sharp:
"We're gone. You're trying to keep us alive in here, but it's only hurting you."

He staggered back. The floor rippled beneath his feet, the world bending with the sound of his pulse. The visions wavered—too bright, too close—and he felt something inside him fracture, the drawer cracking open from the pressure of what he'd tried to bury.

Emily's eyes softened just enough to hurt more.
"Let us go," she said. "Or you'll hollow yourself until there's nothing left to love."

The pain didn't fade this time. It sharpened. It gathered.
For a moment he saw them not as ghosts, but as the spark of everything he'd lost, everything stolen. Love twisted itself into purpose. Grief became movement.

The hum beneath the world swelled, rising with his heartbeat. The air trembled.
Lily's face blurred as she stepped forward, eyes infinite. Her voice was quiet, final.
"Daddy's gone."

Their shapes stretched, dissolving into light that seared his vision.
When they vanished, heat remained under his ribs, it was steady, alive, waiting to be named.

The silence that followed was heavy, watchful. It wasn't absence anymore. It was presence.
The light bent inward, folding into the shape of a pulse. The floor rippled. A low vibration crept up through his spine, growing louder with each breath.

Then came a deep sound, split-toned laughter that rolled like thunder through an empty valley.
Not haunting. Not cruel. Just vast.

The air fractured. Reflections shattered outward like glass thrown against stone.
He stumbled back, throwing an arm over his face. The light changed. Red started bleeding through the white, flickering like molten veins beneath skin.

The laughter faded into a voice that seemed to come from everywhere inside him at once.
You built a cage, it said, rich and layered. *You locked every scream, every thought, every piece of yourself behind these walls. You really thought I'd stay quiet in the dark.*

The sound hit his bones; he almost swore he could taste the heat.

Kalen's throat was dry. "Who—?"

Quiet. The word rumbled through him, low and amused. *You can feel me now, can't you? The thing you buried. The part that kept breathing when the rest of you gave up.*

The world around him shifted, walls stretching, heat rising. The air shimmered as something began to take form ahead of him—tall, humanoid, its edges smoldering, its shape flickering like fire trying to become flesh.

Two eyes opened, bright as iron pulled from the forge. *I'm what's left when grief stops whispering and starts to scream. I'm what's born when endurance curdles into rage. I am the animal that nobody can break.*

Flames climbed its shoulders, unfurling like wings that never finished forming. The corridor trembled; fragments of memory—his wedding, the beach, Lily's laugh—all ignited around them and turned to ash.

I've been here the whole time, Kalen, it said. *Every test, every cut, every second you clenched your teeth and called it strength. You were never the cage—you were my fuel.*

It took another step, heat rippling through the corridor. *You think you survived because of discipline? Because of control?*
No. Its grin spread wider, voice dropping to a growl. *You survived because I held back the storm for you. I kept the tidal waves from ripping through your skull while you built your precious walls.*

Flame crawled down its arms, wrapping its hands like claws. The ground hissed where the heat touched.
Do you know what happens to a caged animal, Kalen? It waits. It studies its prison. It learns the scent of its captor. And when the door cracks open... The

creature's grin widened, sharp and bright. *It doesn't run. It kills its way out.*

Kalen's pulse hammered. "What are you?"

The figure straightened, voice deepening until it felt more like an earthquake than sound.
You may have given up and tried to die out there, the voice thundered, *but I am very much alive... and hungry.*

The figure leaned closer, grin widening into something almost human, eyes burning like coals in a furnace.
Call me Cinder.

Flame rippled outward. The heat hit like breath from a living thing, and for the first time, Kalen felt what it was to burn without breaking, to embrace the rage.

And for the first time, he didn't flinch from it.

He felt it pour through him, raw and wild, uncontainable.
A single thought echoed through the blaze, not in words but in feeling:
We fight back.

The sound of his own heartbeat dragged him upward, fast, heavy, real.

Chapter 9

Kalen jolted into consciousness, his eyes locking onto the ceiling. The cold metal and glaring lights came first, followed by the soft hiss of the IV cutting through the quiet.
He was back in the lab, in the chains. The smell of antiseptic and iron returned once more.

But everything was different.

His body hummed louder now, in ways it never had. Every breath vibrated beneath his skin. The faint mechanical beeps around him sounded slower, smaller. The air in his lungs was hot.

He stared at his arms. The veins that had once flickered blue now burned with faint red light, pulsing like molten threads beneath the surface. The glow followed his heartbeat—steady, patient, alive.

He flexed his fingers, feeling the cuffs bite into his wrists as a low groan of strained steel filled the room. He lifted his arms, and the chains trembled—not violently, but with a subtle shudder, whispering that something impossible was happening. He hadn't meant to pull; the motion had come from somewhere deeper, beyond conscious intent.

He exhaled slowly, and the metal sighed with him.

For a moment, he just stared at his hands, at faint trails of smoke curling from his skin.
The exhaustion was gone, and so was the emptiness. In their place burned heat, focus, and the pulse of something immense pacing beneath his ribs.

In the corner, the observation light flicked on.
"His readings are spiking," someone muttered behind the glass, voices overlapping in rising urgency.
"Power surge in the stabilizers."
"That's not possible, he was sedated."
"Look at his vitals. He's... he's conscious."

The words blurred together, a chorus of disbelief and fear.
Kalen didn't move. He let the red light in his veins pulse once, twice, syncing with the rhythm in his chest. The glow answered the machines like a taunt.

He raised his arms again, slowly this time, feeling the chains tighten as links stretched taut. The metal groaned, louder now—a single creak away from breaking.
He stopped, letting the tension fall slack. The sound of the steel settling was almost a groan.

He closed his eyes, steadying his breath.
Not yet, Cinder murmured. *Let's see how this plays out.*

Kalen's lips curled into a small, quiet smile.
The reflection in the one-way glass stared back at him—pale skin, hollowed face, and veins that lit red beneath the surface like live embers in ash.

The man they thought they'd broken was gone. Kalen reveled in anger, the rage making him feel alive once more. What the reflection showed was something else entirely.

Time blurred, marked only by the hiss of the door lock breaking the stillness. Two guards entered in unison, but their rhythm faltered when they saw his eyes open. Uncertainty began rippling through their practiced movements.

He didn't look at them. He watched the floor, the faint pulse of red chasing the vein lines up his arms like molten mercury.

"Prep him," one said. The other hesitated before stepping closer.

Cuffs clanked. Monitors beeped. The same ritual.
Only this time, he wasn't drifting through it.
He was present.

The restraint bands cinched across his chest. Cold metal touched his skin. He waited for pain to follow—but when it came, it didn't burn.
He could feel it feeding him.

The voltage hit like a hammer, the glow beneath his skin flaring bright crimson. He didn't jerk against the straps; instead, he inhaled. The air tasted of salt and blood, and when he exhaled, the light pulsed brighter.

"Again," Johnson said.

Another shock. The veins in his neck lit like fuse wire. He gritted his teeth, not in defiance, but in focus.

The guards exchanged nervous glances. One muttered, "Sir, he's not reacting."
"Oh, he's reacting," Briggs said. "Look at his vitals. He's stabilizing under it."

"Stabilizing?" Johnson's voice sharpened. "He should be flatlining."

Kalen tilted his head, eyes half-lidded, breath slow. The next current rolled through him like a tide, and a smile ghosted across his mouth.
The room seemed to tilt. The lights flickered once, then twice, before holding steady. Each jolt now echoed through the air itself, a low vibration that made the walls buzz.

The soldiers tensed, staring at the faint shimmer of heat rising from his shoulders.
Elena stepped forward, eyes wide. "Stop the current," she said. "Now."

Briggs didn't move. "Explain."

She pointed to the monitor—to the bright red waveform no one had seen before. "He's not absorbing pain anymore. He's resonating with it. The red bursts along his veins, they're not bleeding, they're cycling. He's converting the stimulus into energy."

Silence fell except for the steady beeping of the monitor and the faint, rhythmic groan of the restraints.

"You mean he's... feeding on it?" Johnson whispered.

Elena didn't answer. Her gaze stayed on Kalen.

He looked up, meeting her eyes. For an instant, his smile widened, and the lights dimmed across the entire wing.
The vibration in the walls grew louder, steadier.

Briggs exhaled slowly. "Keep it running. Let's see how far he goes."

Kalen's eyes flicked to the ceiling, to the trembling light overhead. He flexed his wrists once; the sound of metal stretching carried through the room.
He could feel it now, the rhythm beneath everything, the storm inside his veins answering every surge they gave him.

It wasn't pain anymore.
It was a heartbeat.

He leaned back against the chair, his eyes half-shut, and waited for the next jolt.

Now you see it, Cinder murmured inside him. *They're the ones chained here, not us. Let me show you the echoes of my rage.*

Kalen's lips curved into a slow grin.
"Why not," he whispered. "But I remain in control. You just act. If you never take full control, I'll let you get us out."

Agreed, Cinder said, almost gleeful.

Kalen flexed, muscles coiling as red light flared down his arms.
A roar ripped out of him—it was raw, primal, unstoppable. The restraints shrieked, metal tearing apart under the force.

His whole body glowed red, the air around him trembling with heat.
The room went deathly quiet.

He lifted his head toward the observation booth, eyes burning like fire made flesh.
For one long heartbeat, no one breathed.

Then he spoke—his voice layered, two tones entwined, soft yet thunderous. Kalen and Cinder spoke as one, final and absolute, their words echoing together for all to hear.

"You picked a fight with the wrong man."

Kalen stood alone in the battered chamber; the world reduced to smoke and silence. Power surged within him, a pressure coiling tight and immovable deep in his core. It was strong enough to drown thought, to burn away fear. It grew with every breath, every heartbeat, every flicker of red beneath his skin until it was all he could feel.

There was no warning. No chance to resist. The pressure snapped. Energy erupted outward, raw and physical, tearing from the center of him in every direction. The blast slammed through the chamber, shattering steel, scattering restraints, sending a shockwave that swallowed every sound and every trace of control.

When it was done, Kalen remained at the heart of the storm, lying on the ground, changed and trembling in the aftermath.

Chapter 10

Smoke curled through the ruined chamber, sinking into the cracks of scorched steel and shattered restraints. Alarms began to howl somewhere beyond the room, but inside, the silence had weight. It pressed down, thick and metallic, as if the air itself were holding its breath.

Kalen pushed himself upright. Every muscle trembled. The red light running beneath his skin pulsed to its own heartbeat, alien and alive.
He stared at his hands. The skin looked solid, but the light beneath it said otherwise.

Elena's voice bled through the intercom, thin with static.
"Kalen, stop. You're at the threshold. Pull back before it's too late!"

He shook his head. Her voice felt a mile away.
"This isn't me... this isn't."

The word broke into a scream, raw and animal, tearing through the ruined room.

Cinder rose through it—slow, delighted.
This is your potential, boy. The door's already open.

The air shivered. Heat rolled through him. Muscles spasmed and tightened until his spine arched against the weight of it.

Guards burst through the smoke.
Kalen didn't think. He moved.
The first one dropped before a shout could form. The second managed half a step before red light tore the space between them, leaving only motion, too fast, too violent, too quiet.
When it ended, he stood in the ruin of what used to be control.

Cinder's voice flew through the heat.
See how simple it is when you stop pretending?

Through the haze, he saw movement, Elena stumbling from the observation booth, coughing. He reached for her on instinct, pulling her behind the column of his body as gunfire cracked somewhere distant.

No, Cinder growled, furious. *You waste it on her.*

Kalen's vision burned white. His veins blazed. Skin shifted like liquid glass. For a heartbeat his reflection in the warped steel was something half-feral, half-echoform—a shape of light and teeth, eyes deep red.

"This is too much," he rasped. "You're done."

You think you can control me?

Silence settled, uncanny and misplaced, slowing the rhythm of the world. With a faint, defiant smile, Kalen thought of Cinder—then decided that would never shape his fate. His voice was calm, unwavering. "I do."

He slammed his palm to the floor. The surge burned down his arm and into the metal, his veins dimming visibly. The floor shuddered and alarms shorted out mid-scream. Sparks rained from the ceiling like falling stars.
The shimmer faded from his skin, almost completely.

Cinder hissed. *you can't cage me forever. You need me.*
"Maybe, but on my terms," Kalen replied.

He turned to Elena. She looked at him as if seeing man and beast at once.
"Can you move?" he asked.
She nodded, breathless. "Let's go."

In the next room, he kicked one of the fallen guards over with his boot and ripped the telescoping baton from the man's belt. It felt light, and he didn't know if it was from adrenaline or the faint tremor now living in his fingers. The veins in his wrist began to pulse brighter, as if Cinder were laughing under his skin.

They entered a corridor that smelled of disinfectant and burnt plastic. The vibration of the building was alive again, low and dangerous.

Elena swiped a stolen badge. The first lock clicked open, and they ran through.

A door across the hall hissed open. A guard stepped halfway through but fell before sound caught up. Kalen eased the body down so the helmet didn't hit tile.

Mine, Cinder whispered, smug.

Dizziness chased the power from Kalen's limbs. His pulse staggered, and the world swam for half a second. He caught the wall and kept going.
"Move," he said, and they moved.

At the next door, Elena swiped again. Nothing. She swore under her breath, yanked the handle, slapped the reader.
"Come on!"

Kalen brushed her aside gently. "Let me."
He faced the lock, the glow along his veins gathering like breath before a shout. Red bled across his forearm, crawling to his fist.
He hit the lock once.
The metal erupted inward with a scream of sheared bolts. Smoke curled from the dented frame.

Elena blinked at him. "That works."
"Go," he said, already moving.

They slipped through as the facility woke fully.
A low tone slid into the air, setting his teeth singing.

Red strips along the baseboards began to blink in patient rhythm.

"Code Black," the intercom droned. "Containment sweep commencing. Dampeners cycling."

Elena's face drained of color. "Containment sweep. The pulses catch any resonance spike, blocking and lowering emotional output."

The lights stuttered. Pressure vanished.
Steel tore free down the corridor. A containment door blew outward.

What came through had once been a man—broad, red-lit, wrong. Its veins glowed silver. It saw Kalen and charged.

He felt the pressure in his chest, his veins flaring red again. "Not yet," he muttered to Cinder.
He slipped aside, caught the thing's weight, and turned it. Impact cracked the wall, sending grit across his cheek. The creature staggered, roared, gathered for another rush.

Let me just finish this and be done with it.

It lunged. Kalen stepped into its path, heel snapping into the inside of the knee. A wet pop, then the body folded. He was already moving past it.

Elena was at the next panel. "Door!"
Another lock hissed open. Something green and
narrow darted out with eyes bright, hands too long. It
swiped the badge from her grip.

Mine, Cinder said. The world sharpened to a blade.

Kalen only had time to respond, "Do it."
The baton cracked open in his hand. One swing and the
thing staggered sideways: the second caved in its ribs.

Pain hit him back. The light under his skin faltered,
then steadied weaker. His pulse thundered in his ears.
Using Cinder's rage felt like breathing molten glass; it
gave him power but scraped him hollow every time.

*Too weak. My cost is too much for your body to
handle.*
"What does that even mean?" Kalen said between
breaths.

Without an answer, the world slowed to normal speed
again. His nose bled.
"We need to go," Elena said, and the two ran.

They reached the stairwell. The reader blinked red.
"Field's back," she gasped. "Ten seconds—I can drop
it."

Kalen planted his hand on the bar, testing the weight.
Sparks crawled across his fingers. "Make it five."

She bridged the contacts, blue light climbing her wrist. "Now."

He drove his shoulder into the door. Metal screamed, bolts popped, and the lock gave. Heat raced up his arm, leaving it numb.

Boots thundered above. A drone's hum tightened the air.
"If I say drop," Elena said, "hit the floor."
He nodded.

They burst onto a landing—MAINT. ACCESS. AUTHORIZED PERSONNEL ONLY.
Elena slammed her palm to the reader. Nothing.
She ripped the cover off, electricity jumping from her fingertips. The lock chirped and died.

The tunnel beyond smelled of mildew and dust. Water dripped in slow, even beats. The sound steadied him.

Overhead, Briggs's voice came through the speakers, calm as ever.
"Rourke. Doctor Markov. Stop at the next checkpoint and this ends with you alive."

"He lies," Elena said without looking back. "We keep moving."

They followed the tunnel to a low-lit bay. Crates stacked to the rafters. A rolling gate holding the rain at the seam. Two soldiers. A drone charging toward white.

If he failed here, he went back to the table.
Briggs would turn his bones into a manual, Elena into a case file.

Elena lifted the badge like a prayer.
"Stay back," Kalen said.

He breathed, letting out a slow breath, and ran.
The first guard raised his rifle too slowly, and Kalen shattered it—and the man behind it.

"Down!" Elena shouted. On instinct, he hit the floor right as the drone fired. The second soldier took the blast and folded.

"Again," said a voice from the shadows—close, confident.
Briggs stepped into the light.

He wasn't a monster. He was precision in a lab coat.
Steel-blue veins pulsed under calm skin.
"Stand down, Rourke," he said, already sure of the outcome.

Kalen rose instead.
Elena's whisper: "Don't."
Briggs glanced her way. "Doctor."

Kalen struck first.
Three strides. The baton met Briggs's hand and stopped. The General turned Kalen's wrist, took the weapon. Pain flared bright.

Stop fighting me, Cinder urged.

Kalen let it in. Power flared heat through muscle. He ripped free, slammed a shoulder into Briggs's ribs. The man moved one step back, eyes sharpening. The steel-blue in his veins brightened.

"Better," Briggs said, breathing harder. "You do adapt fast."

Elena threw a switch. The bay lights died and flared again, a deeper red. The gate started to climb, teeth grinding.
"On the floor," Briggs ordered.

Kalen ignored him.
He stepped inside the General's guard and drove a kick at the knee. Briggs blocked it and countered with an elbow to the side of his head. Stars burst behind his eyes, but he didn't fall. Blood from his nose hit the floor in small, red drops.

I have nothing left.
You're too weak, Cinder said.

"Move!" Elena yelled, hitting a second switch. The gate climbed faster.
Briggs turned toward her.

"Cinder," Kalen said.
Last time.

The world tilted. Heat exploded along his arm. He caught the baton against bone, forced Briggs's wrist back inch by inch. The drone's pitch climbed, the air whitening with light.

"Stop," Briggs commanded.
Kalen leaned close enough to see his own reflection in the other man's eyes. "No."

He slammed his forehead forward. Cartilage broke. Briggs reeled, blood streaking his face. For the first time, the calm broke.

Cinder's laughter rolled through the smoke. Kalen felt his hand go numb, his lungs clawing for air. Every time he drew from Cinder, it left something behind—strength, breath, color.

The gate was nearly high enough.
"Go!" Elena shouted.

He grabbed her sleeve and dragged her low. They slid beneath the half-open gate, concrete scraping their backs. Kalen turned, hitting the control panel with one fist. The panel sparked once, then went dead, the gate slamming shut.

Night air hit like a flood—wet, cold, alive.
Rain washed the lab from their skin.
They ran.

Chapter 11

The world beyond the gate felt wider than it should, the air too open, sound too sharp.

Kalen slowed at the edge of the cracked concrete, chest heaving, the red glow along his veins dimming to a dull ember. For the first time since the lab, he could smell real rain, dust, and something clean beneath it. He looked around at the skeletal skyline breaking through the storm.

"This bunker is in Detroit?" he asked, voice hoarse. Elena wiped rain from her eyes, scanning the shadowed outline of towers that leaned like broken teeth against the clouds. "What's left of it." She caught his shoulder, made him face her. "Focus, we still have to get clear."

He nodded once, eyes narrowing as thunder rolled over the yard. The light behind his ribs flickered, weaker now—spent fuel running on fumes.

Ahead, a squat patrol shed hunched beside the chain-link, its windows fogged and its door sagging on battered hinges. Elena pointed. "There, the shelter. We need a minute."

They hurried across the broken pavement, boots splashing through puddles. Elena skidded to the lock, pressed her palm flat, and let a thin ribbon of blue climb into the steel. The shackle spat a spark and fell. She wiped blood from her nose and shouldered the door open.

The place smelled of rubber and cold fuel. Two battered dual-sport bikes waited nose-to-nose, mudguards scarred, racks bent, tanks stenciled with faded unit codes. No computers. Simple chokes and kick-starters. The kind of machines that stayed loyal when the world didn't.

Kalen leaned against the wall, catching his breath. Elena peeled off her soaked jacket and let it drop onto a crate. For a moment, the only sound was the rain drumming overhead and their ragged breathing.

Elena broke the silence, her voice low but urgent. "Kalen, in the six months we observed you, not once did you go feral. Not once. But in there, you stopped it, mid-transformation. You used that power to fight, and then you just… came back. Like it was nothing. How is that even possible? What are you?"

Kalen didn't look up. His jaw tightened, hands steady on the helmet. "Why is that all you care about?" He shook his head, voice low. "You know as much as I do, Elena. I embraced how I felt, and I made sure I was in control. That's all I know."

She studied him, searching for something in his face. "No one else has ever done that."

He shrugged, the motion tired. "Maybe no one else tried."

Elena let out a breath she hadn't realized she'd been holding. "That's not nothing, Kalen."
He met her gaze, rain streaking the glass behind her. "Nothing is all I've got."

For a moment, the storm outside seemed to quiet, as if listening.

Kalen screwed the cap back on the tank. "Can you ride?" he asked, neither knowing what came next.
"I can ride," Elena said, already swinging a leg over one.

Kalen nodded, no questions. He checked the petcock, cracked the choke, and rolled the engine through once to feel compression. The lever bit his arch. He kicked again, harder. The motor coughed like a smoker and caught. The shed shivered to the pulse.

He winced. Every muscle screamed from the inside out. Each breath scraped his ribs raw. The glow beneath his skin stuttered, fading to a faint pulse. Using Cinder's rage had left his nerves frayed—like something vital had been burned out and not yet replaced.

Still think you can hold the leash? Cinder murmured. "Long enough," Kalen said under his breath, and swung onto the seat.

Somewhere behind them, the bay gate slammed open, and an engine much heavier than theirs came awake with a patient growl.

Elena's first kick bounced. Her second found it. The bike barked, then settled into a lean idle. She glanced across the seats at him, rain beading on her lashes. Her face was set, focused and alive with purpose rather than panic.

They rolled out into the wet, tires hissing on painted lines. Kalen cracked the throttle and the rear stepped sideways, slick as a fish. He didn't reach for the thing in his head. He rode the slide with his hips and breath, eyes quiet, weight light on the bars until the tire found grip again.

They cut across the yard as the armored SUV shouldered into the rain, a roof bar humming with that disciplined blue. The first pulse from it passed over them like a pressure wave. Both engines stuttered, coughed, then caught again when they slipped behind a stack of pallets and out of line.

Elena pointed with two fingers and took the lead toward a gap in the fence where the links had been peeled back like foil. He fell in on her shoulder.

The drone's coil cried. He heard the shot before he felt it, a clean white sound that sliced the air behind his rear tire and turned puddles to steaming lace. He put the bike where the ground was dirtiest, gravel, and the tires answered.

The SUV angled to cut them off. Briggs didn't lay on the horn or shout. He didn't need to. The roof bar's pitch climbed. The rain around it seemed to flatten.

"Left," Elena called, and they took it, a sloping access road that tunneled under the city. Water sheeted down the concrete walls; a rusted sign lay broken across the mouth. Kalen lifted the front wheel just enough. Elena skimmed it clean.

Another pulse washed the tunnel. Both engines hiccupped hard. He rolled off the throttle, let the wheels free-spin a heartbeat, and when the spark came back, he steadied the bike with his knees.

They burst out the far side into the industrial fringe full of stacked containers and dead forklifts and followed the long black line of river beyond the fence. Behind them, the SUV fishtailed into the underpass, roof bar dragging a dirty comet-tail of light.

Kalen looked once over his shoulder. **Briggs remained composed behind the windshield, as unruffled as someone quietly reviewing paperwork.**

"Keep moving," Elena said, as if she could feel his glance without seeing it.

The sound rolled across the empty flats like thunder that wouldn't die. In the distance, scattered survivors were piecing walls together from scrap and memory. Their glow flared faintly through the rain, hands reaching, rebuilding, refusing to fade. The roar of the chase drew them from their work; some turned, startled, unsure whether to hide or help. Others simply watched the storm run past.

Further out, the noise woke the ferals. They came from the ruins beyond the freeway, thin silhouettes lit with unstable color, drawn by motion and heat. Their cries wove into the wind, a chorus that chased the engines down the long stretch of flooded asphalt.

They slipped under the wake of a half-toppled bus and took the feeder angling up from the Delray flats toward the westbound artery. Behind them, ferals chased the heat of what had just passed, and echoforms hauled barricades back into place.

At the next intersection, a grief-hollow lurched across their line, wailing. Kalen leaned and missed it by a hand's width. Briggs didn't. The SUV clipped it; the thing folded under wheels with a wet sound and was gone. Kalen didn't flinch. He didn't put feeling anywhere it couldn't buy him forward.

Now? Cinder stirred under his ribs, amused. Let me take the bars, she'll see how small your courage is beside mine.

"Save it," Kalen said. "Later."

They rode onto the ramp two wide. The right edge had slumped into a chewed cliff; he kept left, skimming the barrier, letting the mirror kiss wet reflectors. The freeway rose like a dead river into stormlight, the curtains above bending with a wind no one felt.

Then the road was gone.

The bridge ahead had been damaged. Rebar dangled, rust bleeding from the cut. The far span hung there, reachable only by people who didn't count cost. Rain drove through the gap in hard sheets; the edges shone slick and jagged.

Kalen rolled the throttle open. The front brake lever wobbled, maybe from rain seeping into the housing, maybe from his grip, but he didn't bother to test it again.

"Kalen!" Her voice cut through the rain.

He lifted a hand without looking back. Not a signal to slow but an answer to commit.

He picked his launch. The broken shoulder on the left had buckled into a small, mean ramp where the guardrail flared. He set the front exactly where the concrete would give him the least lift it could spare and still be enough. Measuring is for people who plan to stop.

Spend? Cinder asked, ready.

"On landing," Kalen said. "Only if I call it."

He stood on the pegs, knees soft, chest low, eyes on the far side. Throttle full. The edge came fast.

They hit the lip.

For a heartbeat the rain went quiet. Air took the weight out of his joints. The gap opened beneath—just long enough for rug fibers and a stuffed hedgehog's cheap fur to claw their way in. He shoved the memory aside and kept his hands light.

The far side rose.

"Now," he said.

Now, Cinder agreed, and nudged the angles, front a breath higher, rear squared.

The front wheel touched down and tried to snake. He let his knees swallow it and pushed his hips into the slide without fighting the bars. The rear landed with a slap up his spine. The bike skittered on the paint; he fed it throttle and it straightened.

Elena landed a heartbeat after. Her back tire hydroplaned, caught, and the whole machine made a swallowed-scream sound. She didn't yank the bars; she rode it with her body and the bike obeyed. For a second they ran parallel, both slewing, both saved by the same refusal to fall. She didn't speak, but her eyes asked if he'd do it again. His were already answering.

Across the gap, the SUV's brakes barked. It seesawed at the edge and stopped with its nose over nothing. For once, discipline cracked. Through the rain came a ragged, tinny shout—one word, thrown like a leash: "Asset!" The roof bar sang higher and threw a blue sheet into empty air. Lightning clawed after them and died in the rain.

Kalen didn't look back. He gave Briggs nothing.

Chapter 12

They kept riding, pushing through the sheets of rain while the world blurred at the edges. The engines sputtered only when the tanks were finally dry, coughing them to a halt beneath a low overpass tangled with wild grapevines. Elena swung off first, scanning the road before guiding her bike down an embankment and into a tangle of sumac. Kalen followed, hands steady but legs aching, and together they tucked the bikes out of sight beneath a drift of wet leaves and branches.

Elena's voice came low and certain: "We should be getting close." She shouldered her pack and nodded west along the rail bed, her silhouette sharp against the bruised sky. Kalen fell in beside her, boots crunching on gravel, and they started out on foot into the hush between thunder.

Hours stretched as they walked the rail bed west. Gravel shifted under their boots; wet sumac dragged across their sleeves. The storm didn't just hang above, it pressed down, its shifting colors turning puddles into panes of moving glass. Sometimes the light ran green along the steel, other times violet, as if the rails themselves were remembering old fire.

Elena set the pace, eyes flicking from the tracks to the black line of cottonwoods that meant water wasn't far.

She only spoke when the ground changed. Kalen kept a half-step behind and saved his breath.

You need to grow stronger, Cinder said dryly.

"That's obvious," he thought back. "But I won't let you take control of me. I won't be like them."

You already are, Cinder whispered. *Learn where your edges are, or the world will find them for you.*

"Stronger for what?" His eyes stayed on the ties. "Why not disappear? Hut, stove, no one to find me."

You make jokes of graves, Cinder hissed. *This storm feeds on feeling. It strips and hollows until only echo remains. When this place is husk, only one world will be left.*

Kalen gave a humorless breath. "Good. I'm already a husk, so get on with it then."

Don't ration me. We die smaller that way. Yield and we live larger, longer, on terms that belong to us.

"Useful to who?" he asked. "Me or you?"

To me, Cinder said plainly. *And if you breathe another year, it will be because I carried you through the teeth. You are only the hinge. I am the door that opens.*

"Shut up already and leave me alone," Kalen muttered.

We are bound now, Cinder replied, voice like steel dragged across stone. *You are weak; allow me to show you strength.*

Elena lifted her hand ahead, signaling at the point where the tracks vanished into the water. Kalen acknowledged her with a single nod, his gaze fixed straight ahead.

You will surrender, Cinder murmured. *Better to choose it before the storm takes it.*

"The storm can have it," Kalen said quietly.

"I've been here before," Elena called back. "We're close."

She offered him a small, tired smile. Kalen just stared blankly as he continued walking. She stepped into his path, not allowing him through.

He looked at her curiously. "What's wrong with you?"

Her voice was tight, not loud. "Help me find answers. We could be a team. I did save you."

He looked past her shoulder. "Team?" His voice went flat. "Saved me? You stood behind glass. You let them strap me in."

He moved to pass her, and anger rose like heat. Stormlight ran red beneath his skin, thin threads sparking across his forearms. His shoulders bunched. The jacket seams creaked. The air went sharp.

Yes, Cinder purred. *Show her who you truly are.*

"Shut up," Kalen thought, and pushed past her.

Elena turned, wide-eyed, not at the words, but at the light under his skin. She fell in beside him without speaking. For a while there was only the click of rails and the river's voice drawing closer.

"Kalen... I am sorry," she said at last. A pale blue brightened along the veins at her wrist. "I thought if we knew why you stayed in control, we could learn to help others prevent turning. I had to try."

She dipped her head, looking younger for a moment, less like the woman who wrote protocols and more like someone fumbling for grace. "It took too long to accept that ethics don't go on hold just because the world is burning."

He pressed two fingers to the lump in his jacket. He felt the photo; the corners had gone soft from months of handling. The red light faded from his arms.

"I wasn't joking," he said quietly. "I miss them with every step I take." He hesitated. "I refuse to build a future that's paid for with someone else's suffering."

He walked on. "You pulled me out. That matters. But I'm not safe to stand beside, and I don't have room for anyone to lean on me. Once we reach Traverse City, we split."

Elena gave a small nod, her gaze fixed on the rails. She offered no protest. "Got it."

Alone? We can feed off others; we can fill that hole, Cinder hissed.

"Enough," Kalen commanded, and together, man, storm, and the creature coiled within him, all continued west.

As the river's voice faded behind them, the world seemed to hold its breath. Even their footsteps, which were sharp on the fractured rails, grew cautious as the scenery changed. The horizon took on a different texture, the sky bruising with distant thunder, and the wind carried a warning, heavy with the scent of rain and rust.

Elena and Kalen walked in silence, each step drawing them further from what they'd left behind and deeper into the uncertain edges of civilization.

The countryside gave way to broken towns by slow degrees. Fallow fields turned to cracked parking lots; hedgerows to bent fences and hollow storefronts. Echoferals moved in twos and threes now, slipping down alleys, circling doorways. Kalen and Elena slowed. The road didn't always let them choose peace.

On a stretch of highway, a collapsed storefront sagged across the lanes. Rain tapped bent tin. Kalen caught a glimpse of something shifting inside. Then the gravel hissed.

The red burst out, low, claws already a wide swing for his spine. Elena reacted first. She stepped forward, hands pressed outward as the turquoise seemed to all follow the same patch, building up brighter at her palms.

Kalen heard a small cry, as color shot forward. Elena fell to one knee. The creature's jump veered off course, crashing into a slanted cooler and breaking its momentum.

Kalen moved forward through the gap. He placed his heel outside the feral's knee, applied a palm to the jaw, and positioned the elbow across the collarbone. A distinct crack was heard as the creature staggered backward.

Let me, Cinder whispered. *You are not strong enough.*

"Fine, you get one use," Kalen answered.

Amber stitched his forearm as time seemed to slow. He watched himself catch its wrist mid-swipe. He twisted the limb back, bending it sharply until his knuckles pressed against the crook of the elbow. A sharp crack sounded.

The creature's other claw lashed out in panic toward his throat, but another surge of energy passed him, forcing the attack off course. Kalen kept moving. He chopped at its ankle, stamped down, and drove his shoulder hard into its ribs, forcing it backward into the tangled rubble threaded with jutting rebar.

The creature responded with raw, wild strength, tossing him aside. He landed on the gritty tile, rolled instinctively, and sprang up with his hands at the ready.

It lunged again, head down. Kalen lingered an instant longer than fear would permit. He pressed his forearm against the creature's throat, gripped the skull, and drove forward. Bone struck metal with a muffled, underwater clang.

Light flickered wildly beneath its skin. It clawed for his eyes. Another pulse shot past him, just enough. Kalen leaned in, pinned it against rebar, and held through the screams until the glow went out.

The impact left a white haze clouding his vision and a tremble running through his fingers. Elena stretched her numb hands, the blue draining from her skin—and blood from her nose.

See? Cinder said, almost gentle. *No tools. No machines. Just us.*

"I'll give you one more chance," Kalen decided. "But that's it."

Elena interrupted his moment when she met his eye. "I need a minute."

After a few moments of silence, Kalen began to speak. "That was a good fight," he said. "You had my back." Something else began to rise in his throat, but he pushed it down. "Anyway, we're close," he added. "What part is this settlement in? We should be there in just a few miles."

Elena steadied her breathing. She looked toward the pale sheet of water, the line where shoreline blurred into storm. "If the rumors are right, on a peninsula. Walled landward side. Water on the others. Hard to take. Harder to leave."

Nodding, Kalen sat down and leaned backward, trying to recover from the fatigue brought on from accessing the emotional energy. The world around him receded, leaving only the steady rhythm of water against shattered glass and steel.

His clothes clung damply to his body, the chill settling deep in his bones. For a while, he just sat there.

Elena pressed her back against a twisted barricade, letting the rain soak into her hair, eyes drifting closed as she tried to steady her heartbeat.

Kalen traced the ragged edge of a broken tile with his boot, watching the rain pool in the cracks, reflecting fractured lantern light from somewhere beyond the ruins.

Time passed in uneven waves. The noise of their recent struggle melted into the restless hush, leaving only the sound of rain and the fragile peace holding them together.

At last, Elena pushed herself upright, voice barely above a whisper. "Ready?" she asked.

He met her eyes, nodded once more, and together they gathered themselves and continued to walk.

They followed the waterfront north, past rusted slips, half-sunk boats, the skeleton of a pier leaning into waves. The storm reflected itself in oily puddles, green and violet sliding like restless ghosts.

The shoreline narrowed into a finger of land, and there he saw it, a wall of steel, plates stitched together with angled braces like ribs. Watchtowers punched the sky, lanterns burning steadily along the parapet. Shapes moved above, measured and deliberate.

Kalen and Elena slowed as the gate came into view. The storm mirrored itself in the black water on both sides of the peninsula, scarlet flickering without sound.

"Travelers, halt at the marker," a voice called, flat and amplified. "Hands where we can see."

A rusted post jutted from the broken curb ahead, paint banded faint blue. Kalen stopped on it. Elena stopped with him.

"State your intent," the man yelled across the distance.

"Sanctuary," Elena called back. "We need a place to stay for a little while. We are in control, neither in danger of a feral swing."

There was a pause, filled only by rain on steel. Then the reply: "Where from?"

"Detroit," she said. "East side."

"Is it still standing?" the guard asked.

"Pieces are," she answered. "Held together by echoforms and barricades. No organized recovery effort."

A murmur ran along the parapet. Another guard called down. "How bad?"

Kalen's voice came flat, final. "Bad enough."

Silence stretched. Rain tapped glass somewhere far off. Finally, the first voice spoke again.

"Not ours to judge. The mayor decides who passes. We'll take you to him."

Kalen tilted his head. "So, are you going to let us in, or what?"

Bold, Cinder laughed in his ribs. *I like it when you sound like me.*

One guard bristled. "Watch your tone."

The words came fast, sharp, the green in his veins glowing brighter. He caught himself, forcing calm back into his posture.

An older voice cut in. "Gate."

Chains stirred. The seam in the wall split wider, lantern light bleeding out across wet pavement. The opening widened into a mouth just large enough for two.

Two guards waited inside, rifles slung low. One raised a hand in something between a warning and a welcome. "Walk clean. Straight to the mayor's house. He'll decide if you stay."

The other guard added, firm but not unkind: "Welcome to Veil Harbor."

Kalen smirked. "Oh, so I guess Traverse is too old world."

Can you feel my influence? Cinder purred. *You and I are the same.*

The guard's jaw tightened at the quip, but he kept his temper. He only gestured them forward.

Elena gave Kalen a single, tight look warning not to push further.

Sighing, he fell into step beside the man. Together they crossed under the steel, into lantern light and the waiting streets of Veil Harbor.

Chapter 13

The gates clanged shut, chains rattling into place. Two guards fell in beside them, rifles low, fingers easy on the triggers. Rain beaded on their coats and on the storm-metal plates welded over the seams. Their sleeves bore colored bands of red, blue, and green. Each was rain-darkened and scuffed.

The pattern meant something here, a code Kalen didn't yet understand. Elena followed his stare, and her gaze lingered on the markings, her mind already sorting possibilities. The bands echoed the hues that glowed beneath their skin, but here it seemed color was more than biology, it was law.

"Mayor's expecting you," the guard on Kalen's right said, startling him out of his thoughts, the man's chin flicking toward the heart of town. His voice carried the flat confidence of a man who'd survived by saying what he pleased. "Keep pace. Don't stray from your hue."

The peninsula opened slowly as they pressed forward. An old city's bones patched to stubborn life. Cracked pavement buckled in long ribs. Power poles leaned like drunks, wires braided and scavenged, insulators cut from bottles and melted plastic.

Storefronts were stitched with tin, storm-metal, and signage scavenged from older lives. Between them, canvas stalls huddled against wet stones. A makeshift market breathed a tired rhythm.

People traded with sharpened politeness: a jar of gray grain held to the light; a coil of copper weighed in a callused palm; a tin of peaches dented flat; a cart stacked with filter canisters, "most of them good," swore a man with storm scars veined along his neck. A child counted nails into a cup with solemn precision.

Somewhere, a burner hissed, and the sweet-metal scent of anti-freeze drifted through the rain.

Above the stalls, lanterns burned in the same four colors of red, blue, green, and white. Each set up in a section of the town, seemingly marking a district's heart. The rain turned the dirt to mirror, reflecting those shifting hues across puddled stone.

"Don't let the chatter fool you," the guard said, not bothering to lower his voice. "Half that grain's mold. You boil twice or you say goodbye to your guts. Filters are worth more than pride. We keep score by survival, not by fairness."

They passed a woman haggling over bent spoons and bottle caps. The guard jerked his chin toward her. "She was a banker before the storm. Now she's queen of scrap. Veil Harbor'll make a farmer out of a priest if it has to."

Kalen kept his eyes forward. He felt the looks, some measuring, some wary. Not superstition. Survival math. Another mouth. Another risk.

Elena walked at his shoulder, chin tucked against the drizzle, eyes moving over everything with the alert calculation of a scientist dissecting a living organism. Her gaze lingered on a row of grain jars, fuzzy pale at the seams with moisture trapped behind glass. She was already running the numbers: contamination rates, calorie yields, how long a town could last on half-rotten food. She didn't say a word. Not yet.

At the next checkpoint, a scanner pulsed a soft blue light across their faces. The guard watched the readout, expression unreadable.

"Just protocol," he said. "Color keeps the peace."

Kalen's brow creased. "What color?"

The man simply pointed to the red band on his sleeve and offered a faint, knowing smile. "You'll figure it out soon enough."

A line of graffiti glowed faintly where moisture darkened the wall:

KEEP YOUR HUE STEADY. UNDER GLASS, WE
ENDURE.

Kalen shot Elena a sideways glance, suspicion and
confusion flickering in his eyes. Elena met his look,
brows drawn, but after a brief pause, they both
shrugged. It appeared answers weren't coming yet.

They fell in step behind the guard, boots splashing
through rain-soaked stone as the lantern colors shifted
above them.

Sound reached them first. Kalen heard voices braided
in rhythm, low and sticky, seeping through broken
glass. A church. Stormlight leaked through shattered
panes and pooled across the floor inside.

The congregation swayed in tight rows, faces upturned.
Glows moved beneath their skin, blue sorrow
blooming along cheekbones, green flickers at the eyes,
red threads pulsing faintly beneath clenched fists.
Hands lifted toward the fractures as if the light itself
could be caught and cradled.

The chant rose and fell, steady as surf:

"The storm breaks, the storm takes,
The storm remakes, the storm remakes…"

Another verse swelled, cracked with devotion:

"Glow in the rain, glow in the flood,
Storm in the sky, storm in the blood.
Walk through the fire, walk through the pain,
Born of the storm, we rise again…"

Under it all, a whisper, relentless. The smallest children were mouthing it, the oldest keeping time with their fingers on the pews.

We are the storm. We are the storm. We are the storm.

The first guard spat into the gutter. "Storm-lovers," he muttered. "Think the glow's a blessing. Think the beasts are chosen. They'd kneel to a knife if it shone."

Elena's voice came tight, uneasy. "Do they cause trouble?"

"They sing," the guard said. "It's annoying, but better than how others are dealing with it."

Kalen didn't look in. The rhythm caught on something raw and half-buried. A memory split through, bright and cruel: a feral's roar, his wife's voice cut short, his own hands pulsing, the gray afterlight when he came to, Emily already lying there. Tiny canvas shoes by her.

The chant rolled on: *Born of the storm, we rise again…*

Pressure gathered in his chest, tight and mean. Before he could cage it, the thing inside slipped.

The air changed, low, heavy, not sound but weight. Rage spilled into the street like heat from an opened furnace. For one stuttering heartbeat, the world tinted red.

A woman at a stall hissed, a boy's jaw locked, one of the guards lifted his rifle, eyes flashing crimson at the edges. Elena's breath hitched, anger that wasn't hers clawing at her ribs.

Kalen's veins lit faintly and faded. His face didn't move.

Inside, the chant faltered. Heads turned toward the door.

"What was that?" the second guard muttered.

In Kalen's skull, Cinder uncoiled, pleased as fire catching dry wood.

Yes. Let it out. Stop pretending to be small. Make them feel it.

He flexed his hands once. The pressure bled away, leaving the street colder for its passing.

For a few long moments, confusion lingered in the air. People were shifting uneasily, glancing at one another as if searching for an explanation. Gradually, the tension ebbed; voices resumed, the rhythm of the street stumbling before righting itself.

The first guard cleared his throat, uncertainty knitted across his brow. "Whatever that was," he muttered, "it's over now. Let's keep moving."

His partner nodded, eyes wary. They exchanged a glance, unwilling to guess at the cause, and waved Elena and Kalen on.

He kept walking. Silence was the only shape that fit.

Elena studied him sidelong as they walked, concern in her eyes. It was not fear, but recognition. The look of someone who'd seen men break before and knew how much it cost to stay unbroken.

No one spoke again until the church was well behind them.

The mayor's office smelled of woodsmoke and oiled leather. The man sat behind a broad desk, silver threading through black hair. His hands were the kind that had built as much as they had broken.

Another man stood half a step behind him, broad and still, coat dark as night. The lamplight bent toward him as if the air itself deferred. A faint hum clung to his presence, too low to hear, too steady to be weather.

"You want in my city," the mayor said, not as a question. "If you want to stay, you must work. No work means no food. And if you cause trouble, you're out, simple as that. That's how things are here."

Elena inclined her head. "We have no problem working sir. I excel in science, engineering, and medicine when needed. My strength is keeping things running before they break you."

The mayor studied her for a long moment. "And you think we've got problems worth solving."

"If I haven't figured out the storm, you haven't figured out the storm," she said quietly. "The question is how long this place lasts without someone who can see ahead."

That drew a flicker from the man. Not approval, not irritation, just interest. "Alright, I'm sold, miss."

His gaze shifted to Kalen. "And you, Mr. Red?"

Kalen met the look. "Whatever you need."

The mayor's brow arched faintly. "Fight, is it?" He leaned back in his chair, tapping the ledger with a calloused thumb. "Just know everyone who fights goes through the same door first. We don't hand weapons to ghosts and wish for luck."

Kalen didn't answer, just a confused look.

"Before you see a scavenging team," the mayor continued, "you prove yourself in the arena. It's not for sport, it's for calibration. We measure if you can hold your resonance without cracking the floor."

He gestured toward the man beside him. "Thane here will explain the rules in the Arena waiting room tonight. Be sure to register before nightfall."

At the name, the silent figure finally moved. His eyes, calm as banked fire, lifted to Kalen. The air between them tightened, a low buzz of recognition neither could name.

"Understood," Kalen said, eyeing the man beside him.

The mayor stood, ending the conversation. "Captain Mercer will find you quarters. Survive the pit and we'll see if you're worth feeding. Dismissed."

Kalen turned for the door.

Thane stopped him, voice low, even, and edged with experience that didn't need to boast. "The pit's not about winning. It's about not losing yourself when the crowd starts to glow. If you can walk out of it with your eyes still your own, you'll do fine."

Kalen held his gaze. "I'll be fine."

For the first time, Thane's mouth twitched, something like a smile, worn thin with years. "Then we'll see if you stay that way."

"Captain Mercer," the mayor said, "see them settled."

A man stepped from the hallway's edge, tall and square-shouldered, a faded green band around his sleeve. His expression carried the calm of someone who had long stopped mistaking courtesy for weakness.

"This way," Mercer said simply.

He led them through the administrative corridors and back into the wet glow of the evening. The settlement's inner district opened around them, narrow streets, stacked housing, workshops cut from the skeletons of pre-storm buildings. The air smelled of iron and damp grain. Guards moved in quiet pairs. Lanterns hummed behind fogged glass.

"You'll get quarters," Mercer said as they walked. "But first, introductions. The mayor likes to know what kind of tools he's working with before he puts them on the shelf."

The laboratory had the first stop. It was an old library with shelves that sagged under glass jars and scavenged parts. A woman in her forties looked up from a table, goggles pushed to her brow, hands black with grease.

"Doctor Halvik," Mercer said. "This is Elena. She says she can help."

Halvik's mouth pulled thin. "Everyone says that. Most can't tell rust from steel. If you want to prove yourself miss, start with the bins."

Elena set her pack down, calm and deliberate. "If I may, I was chief scientist for the Directorate of Applied Biogenetics. My work was systems, designing, repairing, optimizing. I can triage if I must, but if you want my worth, it's not sorting scrap."

Halvik studied her, eyes narrowing as they ran a quick calculus. Something shifted in that face, not softened, but recalculated.

"…We'll see," she said at last. "Don't waste my time."

Elena nodded once. "I don't waste anything."

Mercer gave a single approving nod. "Good. You'll report here after sunrise unless told otherwise."

He turned to Kalen. "You sir, follow me. You'll want rest before the pit."

They followed him down narrow lanes where laundry sagged between walls and lantern smoke hung low.

"You earn tomorrow," Mercer said. "You eat after."

He glanced back long enough to make sure Kalen had heard.

Kalen gave a small nod. Mercer turned away, satisfied.

Their quarters were a door with a ratchet latch. Inside were two cots, a crate for a table, a lantern with a patient wick. The room smelled of damp wood and old soap.

"Bell at dawn," Mercer said. "Don't be late."

The door shut. Footsteps faded.

Elena set her pack on the crate, hands lingering on the straps. "You okay?" she asked, knowing the answer would be simple.

Kalen sat on the cot, boots dripping. "I'll do what I have to."

She nodded. That was enough.

She lit the lantern, checked seams, and tested the window. She was practical, methodical.

Kalen lay back. Rain painted constellations across the ceiling stains. Outside, the city murmured: laughter from a tavern, the clink of a bottle, the whisper of trade. And faintly, from the church, he could still hear the chant.

We are the storm. We are the storm. We are the storm.

Cinder's voice followed, quiet as cooling iron.

Tonight, you either let me bleed them dry or you will. Either way, I'll give them a show.

Across the room the lantern burned low. On the table lay a scrap of paper with the mayor's seal and a blue-stamped time:

Register by eight. Arena at nightfall. Thane will explain the rules.

The ink had bled where rain kissed it. The order felt like a blade.

Kalen sat up, his veins dimming softly. He pushed his boots off and set them by the cot, fingers brushing the photo tucked inside his jacket as if closing a loop on something that hurt.

Elena watched him, her blue glowing faint and steady.

"Later," she said, meaning the arena. "You want a minute?"

He shook his head. "It doesn't matter. This needs to happen."

Outside, the rain sharpened. Veil Harbor folded itself into night, lanterns swinging, doors latched, and somewhere the low hum of guards taking shifts. The city waited.

Later that night, when the bell calls the tired and the dangerous, Kalen will stand in the pit and prove whether he's ready to be fed into the world they're trying to build.

Chapter 14

The hangar reeked of fuel and damp steel. Floodlights hummed against stormlight bleeding through the patched roof, throwing long shadows across the gutted helicopter. Darren Briggs moved in slow circles around the machine, boots echoing on concrete, hands clasped behind his back like a man pacing the edge of an old wound.

"Report," he said.

Sergeant Monroe straightened, envy green faint beneath his skin. "Rotor assembly's reinforced, sir. We stripped storm metal from the rail bridge wreck. It appears stronger than steel, lighter too."

"And the dampeners?"

"Almost ready. Field coils should cut interference from the storm for a few seconds at a time, long enough to lift if we time it right."

Briggs let the silence stretch until the men shifted. Sweat pooled despite the cold. Then, a single nod.

"Make it fly. I don't care if it eats you alive when it does. We're not scavengers, we're the blade. And I want it sharp."

"Yes, sir."

The men scattered, boots ringing hollow. They moved with obedience, not pride. Briggs preferred it that way. Pride breaks faster than bone.

Outside, thunder rolled like a long breath drawn through metal lungs. The storm never really slept, it only listened.

He followed the hum of patched wires into what had once been an office. Cables coiled like veins across the floor, monitors flickering pale against an engineer's gaunt face.

"Well?" Briggs asked.

The man's fingers twitched against the console. "We... found something, sir. We rode the aurora bands, unstable, but it held. For a moment, we had clear signal across thirty miles."

Briggs leaned closer. "And?"

"Interference," the man said, voice shaking. "Not static. A voice almost, layered, both pitches at once. It responded when we called the coordinates. It... knew us."

Briggs's voice went soft. "I see. Figure it out. What about the target?"

"Confirmed, sir. A resonance unlike anything we've mapped. Two signatures, folded together."

He hesitated, pulse visible in his throat. "When we pushed the coils last time, the feedback flash boiled the housing. One of the techs caught the surge through his glove. Skin fused to the conduit before the system shut down."

The engineer's hand trembled over the dials. The smell of fear was sharp and metallic.

Briggs didn't blink. "Amplify the signal. Lock it to the aurora pattern. I want a trace, not a ghost."

"Sir, if we push it again…"

Briggs turned, already leaving. "Then burn for it. Some things are worth the fire."

The man's breath came ragged as Briggs disappeared through the doorway. Behind him, the screens stuttered, their flicker timed to the slow heartbeat of the storm.

Outside, hunting teams crouched beneath a sagging tarp, rifles across their knees. The storm pressed close around them.

Lieutenant Christian Vale rose first as Briggs approached. He was older than the rest, storm scars webbed faint gray along his throat. His rifle leaned against one shoulder like it belonged there. The others quieted when he stood.

"You found nothing," Briggs said flatly.

Vale met his gaze. "Trail ends southwest of the city."

"The target doesn't vanish," Briggs said. "It waits. And you, Vale," his finger cut through the rain, "you'll bring it back. Recovery is priority alpha. Fail again, and the river will drink you."

Vale's jaw worked. "Understood, sir."

"You sound almost uncertain, soldier," Briggs snapped.

"Just cautious," Vale said. "Things that wait usually mean to be found on their own terms."

A pause stretched after that. Thunder in the distance murmured like a living thing.

Briggs smiled thinly. "Then find it before it chooses someone else."

Vale hesitated, eyes flicking toward the stormlight rolling across the sky. "Sir… if it's what you believe it is, using it could let something out that we can't put back."

Briggs's eyes hardened. "What I believe is irrelevant. It's power. And power belongs in the right hands."

Vale's silence said more than defiance would have. Briggs filed it away.

He'll find it, Briggs thought. And if he hesitates, I'll find what he's loyal to.

His quarters were bare, cot, table, cracked mirror. A single medal lay beside a folded scrap of paper, its edges worn soft by years of touch. He picked it up. The paper smelled faintly of oil and rain, like the hangar where he'd once promised he'd always come back.

He hadn't.

A flash of memory flickered, a small hand gripping his sleeve, a voice calling after him through turbine noise. Then the surge, the first flare, and the sound stopped forever.

He closed the paper carefully, breath steadying through clenched teeth.

Weakness, the voice had called it. And it had been right. It was weakness to remember what you couldn't rebuild.

He faced the mirror. Stormlight crawled over his reflection, cobalt lights racing the lines of his face like circuitry. Outside, lightning rippled across the clouds, no thunder yet, just light pulsing, waiting for a command.

The voice had returned, smooth and regal, not from the room but from the storm that lived inside his skull.

You think power answers duty, General. But what you're chasing isn't a weapon, it's a choice. One that still remembers you.

Briggs's jaw flexed. "I don't chase. I command."

Still, whenever the storm calls for you, you awaken. A moment stretched, delicate as spun silk.

The signal you uncovered, it recognizes you. It remembers the cadence of your commands, the authority in your voice when you demanded loyalty.

He pressed his palms to the table. "It's not memory, Sovereign, it's resonance."

Call it what you like. It's reaching for you.

Briggs's eyes narrowed. "Good. Let it."

You mean to control it. But the storm doesn't yield, it hungers. What if it chooses someone else?

Briggs's reflection smiled before he did. "Then I'll break it before it learns how to choose."

Yes, Sovereign purred. *Break it. Burn it. And when its light fades, Rourke will follow the dark straight to you.*

Briggs stood at the doorway for a long moment, watching lightning crawl across the hangar roof. The reflection in the glass smiled back at him, but the face wasn't his anymore.

"Perhaps," he said. "Let us find out together."

Chapter 15

Rain carried the city's breath down the gutter lines, thin rivers of silver that caught the light and vanished underfoot. Kalen and Elena walked in silence, boots splashing through shallow pools as they followed the sound of distant voices. Veil Harbor stretched around them like a patchwork lung still learning how to breathe. The markets flickering under tarps, food smoke curling through broken streets, laughter that didn't quite remember what it was for, all of it filled the air.

Elena kept close, hood drawn low, eyes tracing the fragile motion of survival.

"Look at this," she said quietly. "In six months they've built markets, guard posts, even trade routes. They've done everything they can to make the world still look like it's living."

Kalen didn't answer. He kept walking, hands in his jacket pockets, feeling the faint pulse in his wrists, the steady ember of what still burned beneath his skin. Her words washed over him, half-heard.

Life wasn't what this place had built; it was what it was holding off.

The street curved toward a wide square ringed with scaffolds and rusted lights. The arena sat at its center, carved out of an old industrial lot, steel walls pitted with corrosion, welded plates gleaming slick in the rain.

The crowd gathered beneath the awnings: guards off shift, scavengers in patchwork coats, faces tired and hungry for noise. Among them, mismatched jackets and worn scarves painted the dusk with flashes of amber, moss-green, faded crimson, and smoky blue colors mingling in the shallow light, bleeding together like rain through chalk. They leaned on railings, a restless tapestry, trading quiet wagers with the hush of gamblers who didn't want to sound like they cared.

Under the awning, the air thickened, smoke, wet metal, inhuman heat.

A man sat behind a desk made of repurposed shipping crates, sleeves rolled to the elbow, gluttony-brown light pulsing faintly beneath the skin of his throat. He looked up from his ledger with the lazy confidence of someone who'd seen too many men come and go.

"Evenin'. You must be Kalen." His grin showed a missing tooth. "Mayor said you're fighting tonight, yeah?"

Kalen nodded once. "That's what he said."

"Good. Means the schedule stays clean."

The clerk flipped a metal token between his fingers before sliding it across the table. "That's your pit mark. Gets you through the gate and the med line after. Waiting rooms to your right." He jerked his chin toward a corridor curtained with a tarp and lit by a single swinging bulb. "The Ghost is already waiting for you."

Elena frowned. "The Ghost?"

The man chuckled, leaning back until his chair creaked. "That's what they called him when the settlement was still fighting off the ferals. He'd go out alone with no light, no sound, just that white-gold glow moving through the dark." He tapped the side of his throat where his own resonance pulsed brown. "Fascinating story, that one. Maybe sometime I'll tell you, if you survive that is."

Kalen's expression didn't change. He pocketed the token, the faint light under his skin dimming to a patient throb. Without another word, he turned toward the corridor.

Elena touched his sleeve. "Kalen…"

He didn't look back. "Stay here."

Then he pushed through the hanging tarp and vanished into the symphony of lights.

Inside, the world shrank to concrete, low lights, and the muffled thrum of turbines. The smell of oil and dust hung thick. Benches lined the wall beside a rack of weapons stripped for cleaning.

Thane already sat there, eyes half in shadow. His glow was a muted gold, steady, disciplined, not a color that asked to be seen.

"You're early," Thane said.

Kalen closed the door behind him. "Didn't want to wait."

Thane's gaze weighed him, not unkindly. "Waiting's when most men start to think. Thinking's when they break."

He stood, motion precise. "You know what happens down there?"

"Fight," Kalen said.

"Not exactly." Thane moved closer. "The pit doesn't measure strength; it measures control. Lose your hue and the sensors trigger the floor. You stop glowing clean, you burn out, or worse. You hold, transform, and we take care of you."

Kalen's jaw tightened. "Wow, such a good motivational speech."

"Save your childish retorts for someone who cares what happens to you." Thane responded calmly.

For a moment neither spoke. The low hum under the floor pulsed once, steady as a heartbeat.

The door opened before either spoke. A man stepped through, helmet under one arm, rain still running from the edge of his coat. The light in him burned a brilliant amber, steady, but wild.

Thane gave him a short nod. "Right on time. Kalen, this is Silas, your partner in tonight's fight."

Silas straightened instinctively. "Oh, Mr. The Ghost—err, I mean, Mr. Thane. Thank you, sir. It's an honor."

Thane grunted, brushing past without slowing. The door creaked shut behind him.

Silas exhaled, half under his breath. "Still doesn't talk much."

He turned to Kalen, eyes sharp but calm, reading him the way a soldier reads weather. "You're the new one," he said. His voice carried the weight of a man who'd spent too long following orders and surviving by reading people. "Mayors got you listed for tonight."

Kalen said nothing.

Silas set his helmet on the bench. "Trial's simple. One round. You stay standing, you get your place. The crowd's here for blood, but the mayor's here for control. Lose that, and you're out."

Kalen met his gaze. "Control's never been my problem."

Something like approval flickered in Silas's eyes. "Good. Then maybe you'll last longer than most."

He turned for the hall, pausing at the threshold. "When they call your name, follow me. Don't let the noise get inside your head."

Kalen rose from the bench, the red light under his skin pulsing steady. He rolled his eyes. "I'd prefer noise over this thing."

Hey now!

"Just be quiet," Kalen muttered.

Silas blinked, uncertain, then shrugged and reached for his helmet.

The corridor pulsed with the crowd's distant roar, the air thick with anticipation and the metallic tang of rain. Silas walked beside Kalen, helmet tucked under his arm, amber light threading his veins in a steady rhythm.

Halfway down the hall, Silas glanced over. "You ever actually use your resonance on purpose?" he asked, voice low.

Kalen's jaw tightened. "It happens when it happens."

Silas gave a faint grin. "That's rookie talk. Resonance is power, it's emotional power. You want to hit harder, move faster, stay breathing? You pull from what you feel. Anger, fear, hope, it doesn't matter. Grab it, shape it, let it burn."

He spun his helmet once, amber light sparking along the rim. "Watch. I think about the crowd, pressure, nerves, the thrill of not dying. It runs through me, charges the batons. You do the same with whatever's burning inside."

Kalen frowned. "And if there's nothing left?"

Silas's grin sharpened. "There's always something left. Even emptiness has weight. Use it."

The gate alarm buzzed with a low, metallic sound. The next round was calling.

Silas rolled his shoulders, eyes flashing with orange. "Ready to make some noise, Captain Quiet?"

Kalen nodded, the red light in his veins answering, steady and patient.

They stepped into the arena, sand crunching underfoot, the crowd's hunger pressing down like weather. At the far end, a Grief Feral stood chained, aura a restless blue pulse straining against iron, the air thick with the promise of what might be unleashed if those bonds ever gave way.

The announcer's voice boomed through the static: "Two entrants this round. Rourke, our newest Rager, and Silas Vayne versus the Mourning Echo, also known as the undefeated Feral Grief Fighter!"

The Feral let out an ear-piercing roar, as if it knew it was announced. The air condensed, grief pressing down on everyone. Memories, regrets, the ache of everything lost, blasted through the arena.

Kalen staggered, breath catching as sorrow clawed at his ribs.

Silas moved first, batons spinning, orange light flaring. "Don't fight the feeling," he shouted over the roar. "Use it. Let it run through you. Whatever it is, anger, pain. Pull it up and push it out."

Kalen clenched his fists, the red in his veins flickering. He thought of Emily, of the chains, silence, and fire that refused to die. The heat crawled up his arms, resonance answering grief with defiance.

Silas darted in, batons striking the Grief Feral's aura. Each hit sent ripples of blue and amber colliding, bursts of color lighting the pit like a forge. The crowd gasped as Silas rebounded off the sand, landing beside Kalen, breathless but grinning.

"He absorbs kinetic force," Silas said through the noise. "But emotion hits different. You want to break him? Burn it."

The Feral swung, its emotions thickening into tar. Silas ducked, energy rebounding, slamming into the man's side. Sand exploded as the arena trembled.

Kalen stepped forward, heat blazing through his veins. He let the memories rise. His loss, his rage, hopelessness. He pulled them through his body, shaping them into fire.

Yes, Kalen. Use the rage! Let it consume you!

The creature roared, veering to Kalen's left, fast enough to blur. Kalen answered, unleashing a pulse of molten red that tore through the deep blue, scattering it in ribbons of light. The thing dropped to its knees and fell, grief dissolving into mist.

Kalen stood at the center, arms trembling, glass forming underfoot where sand had melted. Steam rose around him like breath in winter.

Silas steadied himself, awe flickering behind his grin. As the smoke cleared, he looked at Kalen in awe. "You dropped him in one strike. That's awesome, dude! You the man."

Kalen's eyes unfocused, exhaustion rising fast. The ache inside him deepened, pain folding into a hollow quiet.

Cinder's voice flared, sharp, tired. *That was too much, too fast. I need to recover.*

Kalen swayed, vision swimming. His chest felt light for the first time in months, the fire inside fading to a low ember.

Then the heat broke, rage, control, everything that held him steady slipping away. Emotion flooded in all at once, grief, fear, longing, the ache of what he'd buried. His veins flashed with color—red, green, yellow, silver, all before settling into a deep, quiet blue. The heaviness of loss sank into his bones, taking the last thrill of the fight with it.

The crowd roared above them, thunderous and alive. But Kalen only felt the silence that followed victory: the cold that came after the fire burned out.

For a moment, the world held still. The roar of the crowd dimmed beneath the hiss of cooling glass and the soft crackle of rain on steel. Steam rose from the pit, curling through the mist like breath after a scream.

The blue in Kalen's veins emerged. It felt cold, but not empty. Like an ache of memory, the echo of every loss he'd carried.

Silas's grin faded. He took one look at Kalen, veins pulsing in fractured color, shoulders trembling under invisible weight, and the humor drained out of him. Whatever that pulse was, it wasn't power. It was aftermath.

For a heartbeat, he wondered if grief could be strong enough to keep a man alive.

"Hey," Silas said, stepping forward. "You're done. Let's move before they realize what they saw."

Kalen didn't answer. His eyes had gone distant, caught somewhere between the heat that had burned through him and the cold that followed. He swayed, catching himself on the railing as the last of the light faded from his skin.

A memory flickered through him at that moment. Emily's laughter, bright and fragile as rain against a window. He tried to focus on that, but it was too much, he felt all his muscles give way.

Silas moved fast, looping an arm under his shoulder. "Easy man. You burn that hot, you crash hard."

The crowd kept shouting behind them, cheers, wagers, the hungry noise of survival, but the sound already felt far away, warped by the blue resonance chilling Kalen's skin.

They crossed back through the gate, boots grinding over scorched sand and shards of glass. The air grew heavier, thick with the smell of sweat and burnt air. The corridor's narrow light flickered against the wet steel walls, each pulse marking the slow drag of their steps.

By the time they reached the waiting room, Kalen's color had dimmed to a deep, exhausted blue. He sank onto the bench, elbows on his knees, chest heaving. Steam still rose from his clothes, the world seeming sharper and quieter in the aftermath.

Silas crouched beside him, watching the faint rhythm under his skin. "That thing you did back there, it wasn't just resonance. I've seen men light up, but never like that."

Kalen drew a ragged breath. "It wasn't a thing."

Silas's eyes narrowed. "No. Didn't think so."

Kalen inhaled unevenly, then let the words tumble out, quiet and soft, no traces of his former sharpness. "It was, as far as I know... just directed, I guess."

Silas watched him for a long moment, then nodded, his voice barely above a whisper. "Yeah. I see that now."

The silence between them grew thick, broken only by the hollow echo of the arena beyond. Fighters always burned red when they pushed too far, rage made visible, predictable, familiar. But now, under the dim light, Kalen's veins shimmered blue, alive with something colder and deeper than anger.

"I don't get it," Silas said, shaking his head. "How are you not red anymore? Our colors don't change. But you…" He gestured at the faint glow crawling beneath Kalen's skin. "From anger to sadness, that doesn't happen."

Kalen didn't look up. "This is what's left when everything else burns away. Anger, when it's there, it's like armor. It makes you feel strong, untouchable, like nothing else can reach you." He paused, the blue under his skin flickering softly. "But when the anger finally gives out, when it can't hold off other emotions anymore... the blue comes in. And it's quiet. Heavy. It isn't about fighting or surviving. It's just what's left, the weight of what you lost, and everything you still carry. It's colder than anger, but somehow… it feels more real."

Silas stared, the words sinking in. Grief, not fury. Stillness, not chaos. A color all too common, born not of survival, but of what survival cost.

Kalen's shoulders eased. "I don't know these new rules," he said quietly. "But what I do know is my family would want me to keep living."

The silence that followed was heavy and certain. Outside, the crowd still roared.

The door burst open as Thane quickly walked into the room. Locking eyes with Kalen, then Silas, he nodded sharply.

"You out," he said, voice calm but firm.

Silas stood up immediately, glancing at Kalen with a half-smile before slipping out of the room, the echo of his footsteps lingering in the corridor.

Thane shut the door behind him with quiet finality, then crossed the floor and settled onto the bench across from Kalen, his presence bringing a new, steady hush to the space.

"We need to talk."

Chapter 16

Thane didn't look at him at first. He just braced one hand against the frame, listening to make sure no one lingered close enough to overhear. Then he shut the door the rest of the way, quiet and controlled.

"The mayor is already circling," Thane said. "He doesn't know what he saw out there, but he knows he doesn't like it."

Kalen swallowed the heat in his throat. "I didn't do anything to him."

"That doesn't matter."

Thane's gaze held steady, sharp but not unkind.

"When someone like Calder can't understand or control something," Thane said, "he sees it as a danger. And you've just proven he can't figure you out."

Kalen looked away, jaw tightening. "I wasn't trying to make a scene."

"I know," Thane said. "But intent won't save you from suspicion."

A drip echoed from the pipe overhead. Outside the thin door, a cheer rose, then faded.

Thane stepped closer, not aggressively, but with the weight of someone who had seen this pattern before.

"Listen carefully," he said. "For the next few days, if you can manage it, you keep your head down. You take whatever tasks they assign without complaint. Stay unremarkable, and never draw attention to yourself, especially when Calder's nearby."

Kalen huffed a humorless breath. "You're telling me to hide."

"I'm telling you to survive," Thane said. "Calder is calm now. But calm men break sharper than the loud ones. You made the wall remember what resonance can do, and half the city saw it. If you push wrong, he'll box you in so tight you won't have a window to breathe through."

Kalen's shoulders tensed. "And what about you? What side are you on?"

Thane didn't flinch.

"I'm on the side that keeps the city standing," he said. "And right now that means making sure Calder doesn't decide you're a problem he needs to solve."

Silence pressed around them, thick and hot. Thane finally drew a slow breath.

"I'm telling you this because I watched the arena tonight," he said. "I saw you stop before the crowd asked for more. That matters. But it won't matter to a man already afraid of shadows."

He reached for the door latch.

"One last thing," he said, voice dropping. "Whatever power you touched out there? Don't let anyone see it again until you understand it."

He opened the door a crack, just enough for the hallway noise to rush in.

Then, quieter so only Kalen could hear:

"Watch your back."

The door clicked shut behind Thane, leaving only the hum of the generator and the smell of sweat on rust.

Kalen sat for a while after he was gone, eyes fixed on the floor, the light beneath his bandages dulling to a faint pulse, still there, still waiting. The air felt heavy, pressing in from all sides.

He walked out to the sleepless night in Veil Harbor. The rain had thinned to mist, but the streets glistened. Lamps buzzed above the walkways, their filaments pulsing with tired light. At the corner where the main dock met the market road, a battered sign flickered between BAR and REPAIR, caught between two lives, unable to settle.

Elena stood beneath it, one hand around a chipped glass, shoulders drawn tight against the damp. The shifting glow painted her face in pulses of red, then blue.

When she saw him, she raised a second glass.

"Thane said you might need this," she said. "Care for a drink?"

Kalen stopped beside her.

"What is it?"

"Something they call whiskey. I wouldn't trust the label."

He took the glass. The liquid smelled like engine fuel.

"Doesn't matter," he smirked, and drank. It burned straight through.

They leaned on the railing overlooking the docks. The tide rolled slowly between the hulls below, whispering against the steel supports. Laughter spilled from inside the bar, loud and desperate. Farther down the pier, a generator coughed sparks into the rain.

Elena glanced at his wrist.
"Somehow you're back to blue again, I see."

Kalen looked down. The faint shimmer beneath his sleeve pulsed once, then faded.

"I told you already, I just feel the way I feel."

"The blue from the lab was brighter. Now it's different. Quieter."

He said nothing.

She studied him, searching for a fault line before it opened.

"You ever wonder if the colors mean what we think they do?"

"I try not to."

"Of course you don't." She managed a small, tired smile. "Thinking hurts more than feeling for people like us."

He finished the drink and set the glass on the rail.

"You say that like you'd know."

Her gaze drifted toward the water.

"I used to."

A pause stretched, soft but heavy.

"The first patient I ever lost called out my name as he slipped away. An experiment gone wrong. I froze, and now, whenever I close my eyes, I still hear his voice, followed by that lingering hum. After that, I started quantifying everything, hoping I wouldn't have to feel that again."

Kalen's grip tightened on the rail, knuckles pale. He didn't speak. A memory flickered, Emily's hand, Lily's laugh, both gone before it could hurt.

"Did it work?" he asked.

"No."

The word was almost a breath.

Lightning flickered far off over the water. The reflections of the docks fractured across the waves.

"You could talk to me, you know," she said quietly. "About what happened in there."

He met her eyes. Whatever moved behind them wasn't warmth; it was the last flicker of something holding itself together.

"No point," he said. "Nothing's going to change."

She watched him, the turquoise glow under her skin brightening, then dimming as she breathed.

"Then maybe that's how it starts."

He exhaled, the edge of his breath shivering in the cool air. "I have to get some sleep," he said. "Early morning."

He nodded toward her glass. "Thanks for the drink."

He turned to go.

"Rourke?"

He stopped. "What is it?"

"Just walk with me for one more second. I want to show you something."

He hesitated. "Elena, I…"

"Come on. One minute. Then you can go back and brood all you want."

A faint sound escaped him, half sigh, half laugh.

"Fine. But then I'm going back to the room."

Her smile widened. It was a bright shine in the gray night. She led him down toward the marina.

The marina was quiet except for the slow slap of water against battered hulls. Most boats were half-sunken, their decks warped and their names faded to ghosts. A few, though they were scarred and patched, were stubbornly afloat, rocking gently in the mist.

Kalen walked beside Elena down the cracked boardwalk, boots echoing in the hush. He paused at the railing, fingers brushing a frayed rope. The cold air tasted like rain and engine oil.

He stared out at the ruined fleet, searching for something familiar. One boat, stitched together with mismatched metal. Its reflection broke and reformed in the ripples.

Elena leaned on the rail next to him, silent for a moment.

"This is Earth now, Kalen," she said quietly. "Look at it."

He nodded, jaw tight. The ache in his chest pressed deeper.

She gestured at the marina. "Most of us went under when the world changed. Our species has sunk." Her voice faltered, then steadied. "Those of us still floating," she pointed at the patched boats, "we're beat up and tired. But we're still here."

Kalen's grip tightened on the rail. He watched the boat rock, its mast splinted and crooked but refusing to go down.

Elena's hand found his, just for a heartbeat. "That doesn't mean we give up. We were never built for surrender."

He looked at her, searching her face for doubt. There was none.

"With enough work, enough stubborn hope, these boats can be patched," she said. "They can sail again.

Maybe not the way they used to, but they'll move. They'll matter."

Kalen let out a slow breath, the weight in his chest shifting.

"We're the same," Elena continued, voice fierce. "You, me, everyone left. We're not what we were. But we're not finished. Not yet."

He glanced at the water—at the boats that refused to sink, at the ones waiting to be raised. For the first time in days, something inside him loosened. Not hope— just the memory of it.

Elena squeezed his hand, then let go. "We fix what we can. We sail what's left. That's how we start again."

A laugh echoed from the bar behind them, too loud, too desperate. Lightning flickered over the lake, breaking the reflections into shards.

"I don't know if I remember how," he said quietly. "But maybe… maybe I could try."

Elena didn't push. She just stood beside him, shoulder to shoulder, watching the boats that refused to sink.

They stayed like that, listening to the water, the broken vessels, and the slow, stubborn heartbeat of a world still trying to matter.

Chapter 17

Dawn leaked through the fog like thin milk over steel. Veil Harbor's eastern gate loomed ahead. Kalen crossed the square, his coat damp with morning mist.

Thane stood with Mercer at the checkpoint, their voices low, trading plans. When Kalen approached, Thane said something that made Mercer grunt. Then Thane turned, eyes meeting Kalen's. No words were exchanged, just a nod heavy with understanding. Men who had both outlived something they shouldn't have. Thane walked back toward the city's heart, his steps slow, deliberate.

Mercer faced him. "Rourke. Team One patrol. East sector. Sweep the outer grid, mark drift shifts. Follow orders, stay tight, keep your color in check."

Kalen nodded. "Understood." Their objective was simple: sweep the outer grid and mark any drift shifts before they reached the residential blocks.

A voice called out behind them.
"Wait! I'm here. Don't start without me!"

Silas sprinted up, jacket half-zipped, batons swinging from a loop at his hip. He stopped beside Kalen, panting and grinning. "See? Not late, dramatically punctual."

Mercer gave him a dry look. "You redefine punctuality daily, Vayne."

"Perks of charm, Captain." Silas flashed a grin, eyes flicking to Kalen. "Let's go make sure the world's still ending shall we?"

Mercer shook his head and waved them forward. The gate groaned open, metal grinding against metal. Cold air pushed in like an exhale.

They moved through the ruined city in a staggered line. Mercer on point, two scouts ahead, Kalen and Silas were in the center. The streets were quiet but not dead. Wind hissed through hollow windows, and torn banners whispered against corroded steel. Somewhere far off, a lone bell clanged once, faint and irregular, possibly another settlement signaling the morning shift.

Silas filled the silence because someone had to. "Hard to believe this was Traverse," he said. "People used to complain about noise and traffic. Now we'd pay for a good traffic jam."

Kalen said nothing.

Silas smiled sideways. "Man of mystery. You ever gonna say more than five words in a row?"

"Maybe when they're worth saying."

Silas snorted. "Touché. I talk too much anyway, it's how I stay sane." He twirled his batons, amber glints threading along its edge.

They walked on, boots splashing in shallow puddles. Silas exhaled through his teeth.
"You're not easy to read. I've met ferals easier to talk to."

"You talk too much."

Silas grinned, but when he met Kalen's eyes, the humor thinned. There was something deep and controlled there, like a wound that had decided to heal on its own terms. For a moment, Silas stopped trying to fill the silence.

The patrol slowed near a collapsed block. A rusted sign still clung to a doorway: *Crescent Mart.* Mercer gestured. "Sweep it. Take anything sealed, anything sharp. Quick in, quick out."

Inside, the air was stale and thick with dust. Shelves leaned in slow collapse, cans and boxes scattered across the floor. A faded mural of children holding kites covered one wall, streaked now with mold and old handprints.

Kalen moved down an aisle, scanning labels through grime. Silas followed, kicking a can lightly. "Still sealed. Miracle."

"Not really," Kalen said. "Most people didn't die here. They left."

Silas hesitated, the grin slipping. "Guess that's worse."

Kalen didn't reply. He knelt beside a shattered cooler and brushed dust from a cracked watch face half-buried in debris. Its hands were frozen at 2:17. He pocketed it without a word.

The door creaked. A scout slipped in, breathing hard. "Two blocks north, two ragers, one griefer. Headed this way."

Mercer's eyes hardened. "Copy. Quiet and clean. We intercept before they hit open streets."

He motioned them out.

They spread along the old tram line, using broken vehicles for cover. Fog shimmered ahead, disturbed by motion. Mercer raised two fingers; the team sank low.

Three shapes emerged, twisted silhouettes, light flickering beneath skin in erratic pulses.

"Circle around the rear," Mercer whispered. The scouts slipped off to the sides, moving silently.

Silas crouched beside Kalen. "Just like the arena," he whispered. "Except no crowd."

The first feral staggered into range, red light crawling up its throat.

Kalen moved in fast, a clean strike, silent and final. The body hit the pavement hard. Silas rolled into the next, batons snapping against bone, each hit releasing a low hum. The last one turned on Mercer, who met it head-on, blade rising, motion precise. The sound it made didn't last long.

Kalen glanced between Silas and Mercer, a small smile forming. It was cut short when he heard a scream from up ahead, a high screech.

Voices cracked over the comm: "Multiple contacts! North block, coming fast!"

The fog turned black with motion.
Kalen stared wide-eyed as dozens of ferals surged through the mist, their presence almost palpable. The ground seemed to tremble beneath their determined march.

Mercer's shout cut through the chaos. "Pull back! Warn the city! I'll buy you time."

The team scattered, boots hammering broken concrete.

Kalen and Silas held their ground, neither flinching nor speaking. Their eyes met briefly in a wordless exchange. A slight nod, and in that instant, a silent pact was made. Together, they turned to confront the surge of ferals barreling toward them, bracing themselves for the storm ahead.

"Guess we're staying," Silas said.

"Guess so."

They charged. The street erupted in motion. Batons flashing, blue arcs flaring from Kalen's fists. The first wave fell hard, but the next came faster. Mercer cut through two more, voice raw: "Now! Fall back!"

Kalen slammed his shoulder into a feral, sending it spinning, and turned. "Go!"

They ran past the wreckage, past the store, breath burning in their chests. Behind them, the sound of pursuit blurred into the storm's low buzz.

Up ahead, the city's bell began to toll, deep hollow notes one after another.
A warning, a call to arms.

Veil Harbor was waking to war.

Chapter 18

Rain drummed softly against the windows, its rhythm unbroken. Veil Harbor drifted into shades of gray, the square barely stirring, lanterns sputtering, wisps of smoke winding through empty alleys. The generator inside the lab pulsed quietly, its sound weary and uneven.

Elena hunched over the resonance monitor, eyes gritty from a sleepless night. The graph pulsed too cleanly, each spike climbing a little higher, even when the city was still. No fights. No panic. No measurable stress response. Yet the numbers rose.

She underlined a line in her notebook: Predictive pattern confirmed. Then whispered, "It's learning."

Across the room, Halvik tightened a clamp on a coil without looking up. The rhythm of the wrench matched the hum of the machine.

Elena began a quiet voice log:
"Field analysis day two in Veil Harbor. Resonance levels climbing independent of external stimuli. The storm is no longer reactive. It's anticipating."

She paused, watching her reflection shimmer faintly in the glass. Turquoise light beneath her skin seemed to be answering the generator's pulse.

"If the storm predicts our emotions, then is it still feeding, or is it guiding?"

Halvik's wrench stilled mid-turn. She didn't interrupt, but her silence carried weight.

Elena saved the recording and straightened, exhaustion clouding her focus. The air in the lab felt charged, almost metallic, like static before lightning.

That's when the door opened.

Thane filled the doorway, coat dripping, gloves still damp from rain. His voice was low but clear. "Doctor Markov. The mayor requests your presence."

Halvik gave a dry, humorless chuckle. "Request. That's one word for it."

Elena wiped her hands on her coat, collected her notes, and followed Thane out.

The walk across the square felt longer than it should have. The city was quieter than usual. People moved like they were holding their breath, voices clipped, colors dimmed. The glow beneath her own wrist seemed out of place here.

At the gate to City Hall, guards stood stiff, eyes hollow from sleepless nights. No one stopped her. They all knew who she was now, the scientist who'd told the mayor the storm could be reasoned with.

Inside, the old council chamber smelled of wood polish and burnt wire. The mayor waited at his desk, posture straight, expression calm in the way of men who measured power by silence.

"Elena," he said, gesturing toward the chair opposite. "How are you finding Veil Harbor?"

She sat. "Functional. Which, these days, is saying something."

His mouth curved, not quite a smile. "That's all I ever promised. Function."

He studied her for a moment before continuing. "Your reports are impressive. This idea that the storm is anticipating us, it changes everything. But I think we can use it."

Her eyes narrowed. "Use it how?"

He clasped his hands, tone even. "If the storm amplifies emotion, then stability is our defense. The dampeners keep that balance, but they require too much power to maintain. I want them automated. I want a system that regulates resonance passively."

She frowned. "Regulates people, you mean."

"Prevents Transformation," he corrected. "A pill, or perhaps something simple and consistent. Something that keeps the population in equilibrium. Calm enough to think, too steady to break."

Elena stared at him. "You're asking me to sedate the city."

"I'm asking you to save it."
He leaned forward slightly. "You've seen what happens when control fails. If emotion feeds the storm, then real, manufactured peace, is our only weapon."

"Peace at the cost of free will," she said quietly.

"Free will is what started this," he snapped, then softened his voice again. "Doctor, this is mercy, not tyranny. People need someone to take the weight from them."

He turned a small case on his desk. Inside, faintly glowing pills shimmered a dull gray under the light. "Halvik's prototypes," he said. "Refine them. Perfect them. Report to Thane when you're ready."

Elena rose slowly. "And if I refuse?"

The mayor smiled thinly. "Then someone else will. But I'd prefer it be you."

Elena walked fast, coat drawn close. Thane matched her pace, silent as always, boots splashing through shallow puddles.

She broke first. "You don't say much, do you?"

"Not unless there's something worth saying."

She stopped short, turning on him. "You don't see it, do you? He's turning this city into a machine. He's making obedience a virtue."

Thane's expression didn't change. "It's order. It keeps people alive."

"At what cost?" she shot back. "You think survival's the same as living? You're guarding cages and calling them walls."

He looked away, jaw tight. "You don't understand the weight of peace. It's built on people who follow orders."

Elena stepped closer, voice low but sharp. "You've seen the way they look now, dim, tired, afraid to feel. That isn't peace, it's extinction, one heartbeat at a time."

They walked the rest of the way in silence.

At the lab steps, she turned to him. "You're a good man, Thane. But you're letting him turn you into a weapon."

His face twitched slightly, but he didn't reply. Rain ran off his coat, dripping between them like seconds.

Elena opened the door. "Maybe one day, you'll see what you're really protecting."

Then she went inside. The door shut on the echo of the storm and the sound of a city forgetting how to breathe.

The lights in the lab flickered once. Elena turned toward the window, the aurora's color shifted again. It was violet bleeding into red, bright as blood on glass. For the briefest instant, she thought she saw it pulse in rhythm with the city itself.

She was torn from her reverie as a bell rang across Veil Harbor, low and heavy.

Elena froze, her reflection flashing blue in the window.

The turquoise beneath her skin brightened once and steadied.

"Attack?" she whispered.

The bell tolled again. Elena's head snapped toward the window. People were moving in the streets outside, first walking fast, then running. A child's cry cut through the rain.

Her heart lurched.

Kalen.

She pushed into the crowd, forcing her way toward the ramparts. Guards shouted orders above her; the bell hammered again, shaking the air in her lungs. When she reached the gate square, half the scavenger team was already there, mud-streaked, blood-spattered, faces pale.

She grabbed the nearest one. "Where's Kalen? Where is he?"

The man's eyes flicked toward the wall, voice breaking. "He stayed back. With Mercer. Said he'd buy us time."

Before she knew it she was running. Up the narrow steps slick with rain, through the press of guards loading rifles and dragging crates into position. She reached the top and looked out.

Beyond the gate, three figures ran through the stormlight, Mercer, Silas, and Kalen. Behind them, the dark shimmer of ferals broke into motion. There were dozens, maybe more, all teeth, color and noise.

Her throat closed. "No…"

Beside her, the old watchman was shouting down to the gate crew. "Open the gate! Now! They won't make it!"

The gears below hesitated, grinding half-way.

Then the Mayor's voice carried over everything. It was calm, deliberate, the kind of quiet that ended arguments.

"Hold."

He stood on the platform above the square, rain dripping from his coat's collar, expression carved from stone.

"I fear we simply can't risk the city for three men."

Elena gripped the railing until her knuckles whitened.

Below, the runners closed the distance, shapes flickering bright against the gray, the ferals gaining with every heartbeat.

Her mind screamed *do something*, but her body wouldn't move. The guard beside her whispered a prayer.

The gate stayed shut.

Elena pressed a trembling hand to her mouth. Her whisper barely reached her own ears.

"Kalen, please."

The bell tolled once more, long and hollow. The city of Veil Harbor held its breath.

Chapter 19

The bell tolled again above Veil Harbor, each note a warning, each echo a countdown.

Kalen ran through the muddy streets, lungs burning, Silas and Mercer at his side.
Behind them came the ferals, red and gray lights twisting through the rain, claws scraping stone, shrieks carrying through the storm.

The gate loomed ahead, its blue lamps flickering like salvation.
Kalen's heart leapt as they approached, then fell. He stopped suddenly. The gears weren't moving, the doors sealed.

Guards crowded the ramparts, rifles raised, faces pale and wavering behind the curtain of color.
In the center, the mayor stood still as a carved idol.
Beside him, Thane's silhouette, watchful and silent.

Mercer shouted over the thunder.
"Keep moving! Almost there!"

Kalen looked back. The swarm was closing in, fifty, maybe more.
Each one burning through the storm like a broken star.
He could taste the metal, the emotional pressure palpable.

Then came the voice from above.
"Gate's sealed." The voice hesitated. "Mayor's orders.
No entry!"

The words hit harder than any blow.
Kalen looked the mayor in the eyes, confusion written
across his face.
The mayor didn't shout. He didn't need to.
His voice carried calm and final.
"We can't risk the city for three men."

A murmur rippled along the wall. One guard shouted.
"They won't make it."
Another hissed back, "Orders are orders."

Time slowed.
Rain seemed to hang in the air, each drop caught mid-
fall, suspended between sky and earth.

Kalen's breath came shallow.
He looked along the wall, at all those faces. Faces that
were fearful, ashamed, some were simply blank.
The world narrowed until all that was left was sound.
He focused on the pulse in his ears, the roar of the
storm, and the memory that had waited beneath both.

Emily.

She was standing just beyond the gate.
Hair caught by wind, eyes bright even in the gray.
Lily clung to her leg, small fingers curling around her

sleeve.

They were untouched by the storm, pure light and warmth in the rain.

They smiled, reaching for him.

He took a step forward.

Her lips moved, whispering his name. Lily's voice came after, faint but clear:

"Daddy, come home."

Something broke open inside him.

Every breath, every heartbeat since that day came rushing back all at once.

The color beneath his skin deepened further, shifting deeper into an endless blue of the sea before dawn.

The storm answered, its light bending inward, folding around him.

He reached for them, but the storm reached for him.

For a heartbeat, he saw Elena above him, her face streaked with rain, eyes wide, mouth open in a silent scream. She had her hand reaching for him, desperate to pull him back.

The world fractured.

Sound dropped away. The storm's colors thickened, swirling around him.

The ferals surged closer, their movements slowed to a crawl. They had claws raised and mouths open in silent primal roar.

Kalen's breath caught. He felt the storm inside him, grief rising like a tide. When he felt like he couldn't hold it any longer, he stopped resisting.

He slammed both hands into the street.

The moment stretched endlessly, suspended.
Ice erupted outward, freezing ferals, mid-motion.
Faces were locked in agony as bodies turned to crystal.
The rain paused, steam rising in slow spirals. Even the storm seemed to hold its breath.

Kalen dropped to one knee, power roaring through him. He fell to the ground as it faded, leaving only warmth and peace.
For a moment, he saw Emily and Lily running toward him, arms outstretched, laughter bright and whole.
He reached for them, tears burning his eyes.

Then their faces began to dissolve.
Their hands, their smiles, all gone, pulled back into the mist.

He called out, but no sound came.
The peace shattered as the cold turned to pain.

Kalen's eyes began to close, his body shaking, making the blue light flicker like a dying star.

Through the blur, a shadow moved. Heavy boots splashing through melting ice.

A hand closed around his shoulder, Thane's grip, iron and steady against the cold.

"Got you," Thane said, voice low and steady.

Kalen looked up, barely conscious.
The world swam, but still he saw it, the glint of metal on his wrist, the faint hum of containment.
A dampener.

The ice around them cracked, steam rising from the fractures.

"Easy, soldier," Thane murmured, tightening his grip. "That's enough."

Kalen's eyes closed.

Above, the ramparts were silent, guards unmoving, the mayor's face unreadable, the city silent.

The last thing Kalen felt before the dark was the weight of Thane's hand, and the quiet sound of a city waiting to decide what it would become.

Chapter 20

The storm had grown thicker, denser than he'd ever seen.

Briggs stood at the edge of the open bay, one hand resting on the cold, uneven surface of storm-metal. The aurora churned above the horizon, no longer a shimmer but a living muscle, yellow folding into blue, blue bleeding into violet. It didn't just light the sky anymore. It moved them. A pulse, restless and alive.

He didn't blink. He wanted it burned into memory. Proof that his work meant something. Proof that order could still shape chaos.

He remembered the first time he'd seen the aurora after the collapse. It had seemed beautiful, almost holy. Now it was a warning. A ledger of every decision he'd made.

He wondered, briefly, if the world would remember him as a savior or a butcher. The thought passed, but the ache lingered.

Footsteps echoed across the hangar.

Vale approached; gloves slick from rain. "Five settlements cleared," he reported. "Nothing left but wrecks and a few ferals scavenging the outskirts. All showing a struggle. We've consolidated what's useful."

Briggs's tone was calm, detached. "And the package?"

Vale hesitated, eyes flicking toward the far end of the hangar where the containment lights glowed faint blue. "Secured. Stable. Doesn't speak. Doesn't sleep much either."

Briggs turned his head slightly. "Possessing it is enough."

For a moment, he let himself feel the smallest flicker of guilt, not for what he was about to do, but for what he'd already done. "Load it onto the transport."

The order pressed on Vale's throat.
Finally, he nodded. "Yes, sir."

Briggs watched him go, wondering if Vale would ever understand the cost of obedience. Or if he himself still did.

"General?"
A comms tech stepped up, headset askew, voice thin but eager. "You asked for status on the signal project."

Briggs gestured for him to continue.

"We've got partial clarity across twenty kilometers. The aurora still scrambles anything past that, but we're piggybacking the carrier wave along the storm's resonance bands. It's like… talking through the storm instead of around it."

Briggs frowned. "That's supposed to be impossible."

The kid grinned nervously. "It was. Now it's just dangerous."

He offered the datapad. "If we can align the field frequencies during the next surge, we'll have long-distance comms for the first time since the Collapse. The storm amplifies the signal instead of breaking it."

Briggs studied the readings, thumb brushing the edge of the pad, feeling the static hum. "And if you're wrong?"

The tech swallowed. "Then it fries everything within ten meters."

Briggs handed the pad back. "Then stand ten meters away."

The boy nodded too fast and retreated.

Briggs began to wonder if the storm was truly listening, or simply waiting for them to make a mistake.

The air shifted, static crawling along the edge of perception.
The storm outside deepened, violet bleeding into black, too bright to exist.

Then came the voice.

In the west, Sovereign's voice shimmered, both mechanical and godlike. *I sense it. The force is unmistakable.*

Briggs's breath hitched. "Rourke."

Yes, Sovereign purred. *You've cleared five settlements, but I can feel another. That's where he is. The pulse came from there. You felt it too, didn't you? The grief that froze the sky?*

Briggs's hands clasped behind his back. "The readings spiked across our grid. The storm reacted like it was breathing for the first time."

Because it was.
The whisper slid through him like heat under skin.
He's the one, Darren. The pattern converges there. Trust me. This is him, I know a fellow Echo.

Briggs turned toward the storm, a small, sharp smile cutting through the dim light.
"Excellent."

For a moment, he wondered if Sovereign was guiding him or if he was simply walking the path it had built for him. Was he still in control, or just another instrument of the storm's will? He pushed the thought aside. Control was a story he had to believe.

Vale lingered at his shoulder. "You really think Rourke's still alive?"

"I don't think," Briggs said. "I know."

He gestured toward the far corner of the hangar, where
the helicopter waited, its surface plated in storm-metal,
coils humming faint green.
He ran his fingers along the armor, feeling the
unnatural chill. "Get the engine teams ready. We move
at first light."

Vale's eyes flicked toward it. "You tested it?"

Briggs didn't look away from the storm. "It'll hold.
Storm-metal bends but doesn't break. Like us."
He stepped closer to the open bay, wind tearing at his
coat. The cold bit deep, sharp as regret.
"Prepare the strike team. The moment Sovereign
confirms another pulse from the west, we move."

Vale hesitated. "And the package?"

Briggs's reflection glowed in the aurora, red, blue,
violet, all at once. "Leave it in the transport. I have a
feeling we will need it with us."

Lightning split the sky, turning the hangar white.
In that flash, Sovereign's whisper returned, soft and
coaxing,

You've done well, Darren. Soon, he'll see he isn't
unique.

Briggs tilted his head, a faint grin tracing his mouth.
"Soon, he'll see what I've become."

The storm answered with thunder. A sound too deep to
be natural, too rhythmic to be weather.
Briggs stared into it, unblinking, the light crawling
across his face.
For a moment, he wondered if order was worth the
cost.
If survival meant becoming something the old world
would have feared.

He pressed his palm to the storm-metal once more,
feeling its cold weight.
He smiled once, thin and certain.
"Then it begins."

Chapter 21

The dark wasn't sleep.
It was gravity.

Kalen fell through it, his mind unraveling, body dissolving, exhaustion stripping him past memory and pain. The storm inside him was quiet but not gone. It waited patiently, and when it opened, it took him with it.

He didn't fall downward. He fell inward.

For a moment, he was both Kalen and not-Kalen. Memories flickered, voices overlapped, and the boundaries of self blurred.

He felt the weight of a thousand lost names, the heat of a thousand broken vows. He was not alone in his own mind. Cinder's presence pressed close, not as a whisper but as a second heartbeat. It felt old, wounded, and agonizing.

When his eyes opened, he stood on a platform of black stone suspended in an endless void. The air shimmered like heated glass. Below him, drifted fragments of a world he didn't recognize. Jagged mountain lines, glimmering towers, and rivers of luminescence wound through darkness. Each fragment throbbed with feeling, every hue a drawn breath of longing. It was stunning. And it was fading away.

The sky burned violet and gold, alive and collapsing.

At the far edge of the platform, a figure sat on a throne carved from molten glass. Fire crowned his silhouette, flames bending like cloth in the wind. Beneath the blaze, Kalen saw a man's shape. It was broad-shouldered, weary, its hands clasped loosely around a sword whose edge flickered with light instead of steel.

Still, he recognized it. Cinder.

He was not the monster in Kalen's head now. The fire dulled, revealing the outline of a broken man. Kalen could feel the stillness of someone who had lost everything worth commanding.

Cinder didn't turn right away.
His voice carried like heat rising from stone.

"I was a ruler once."

Kalen stepped forward, the stone humming beneath his boots. He felt Cinder's memories crowding his own, the confusion sharp and dangerous. For a moment, he wasn't sure which thoughts were his.

"My city stretched from the river to the mountains," Cinder continued. "Every tower tuned to the colors of its people. I thought if I could hold their harmony, the storm would pass us by."

Visions began to unfurl, streets alive with laughter, glowing veins of green and blue pulsing through the crowd. Children painted light on the walls. Lovers glowed with hues that braided when they touched.

Kalen felt it: a civilization that had turned emotion into art.

Then the light changed.

The horizon split open, purple veins slashing through gold. The sky convulsed, folding inward like it was being pulled apart. The wind roared with voices, thousands screaming at once.

Cinder stood, fire licking his shoulders.

"We thought we were ready. We called it a storm. We were wrong. It was a monster."

Lightning like molten glass cracked across the skyline. Towers buckled. Rivers turned to vapor. The people's colors flared out of control, red screaming against blue, green devouring yellow. Hope became panic, panic became despair.

"I watched my world vanish," Cinder said, voice shaking, not from fear but from memory. "Not all at once, but piece by piece. First their joy, then their mercy, then their love. And when grief refused to die…"

He turned to Kalen, eyes burning white-hot.

"Rage was born."

The storm slammed into the city. A physical blast exploded in every direction. Emotions amplified beyond reason, burning the air itself. Cinder lifted his sword, but the blade fractured under the pressure of his own fury.

Kalen flinched as shards of light rained down. The memory cut him too. He could *feel* what Cinder had felt. He felt the desperation, the helplessness, the impossible urge to hold the world together with bare hands. The confusion of the merge sharpened: Kalen's grief and Cinder's loss tangled, indistinguishable, overwhelming.

Cinder's voice lowered, raw.

"Rage isn't just anger, Kalen. Its love denied. It's justice unmet. It's the refusal to let go. When grief refuses to surrender, it becomes fire."

The city was burning now, its streets bending, people collapsing into dust and light.

Kalen saw through Cinder's eyes: a woman running through the smoke, her glow bright gold, her laughter carried on the wind. In her arms, a child whose color flickered between blue and yellow.

They were almost to the palace steps when the sky split open.

A column of violet light struck the ground, swallowing the child's glow first, then the mother's scream. Primal cries that tore through both men. The storm wasn't listening anymore, it was answering.

Cinder staggered forward, reaching out.

"That was my daughter."
The words broke. "The storm took her. And the world didn't stop."

Silence swallowed the void.

Grief hit so heavy it cracked the island beneath their feet. Kalen dropped to one knee, choking on air that felt like ash. He had lost people, too. But not like this. Not everything. The pain was not just memory now, it was happening inside him, as if the storm was using his own heart to learn what loss meant.

"I begged for mercy," Cinder said quietly. "The storm gave me purpose instead."

The fire around him shifted, no longer wild, but deliberate. Controlled. Terrible. It wrapped him in armor, fused to his skin, burning and rebuilding all at once.

"Grief fed the storm. Rage fought it. And the storm learned."

The sky above twisted, clouds rolling in unnatural rhythm.

Kalen looked up and realized the storm wasn't just weather. It was watching. He felt its presence, vast and curious, absorbing every emotion, every lesson. Its hunger shifted, tasting the shape of rage and grief braided together. For the first time, Kalen sensed curiosity in its pulse. It was a question, not a command.

Cinder's fire dimmed, and the man beneath the flames was visible again. His face wet with tears that turned to steam before they fell.

"I became its memory of rage. I became what it couldn't destroy."

He turned to Kalen fully now, and the fire around him steadied, no longer consuming but illuminating. His eyes, no longer white but molten orange, met Kalen's with something almost familiar.

"You think I'm the monster in your heart. I'm not. I'm what's left when everything else dies."

Kalen stepped closer, trembling, the confusion of the merge fading into clarity. He was himself again, but different. Kalen carried Cinder's pain, his rage, his lesson.

"Then why arc you with me?"

"Because your pain, your loss, resonated with me."

The void trembled as the storm drew nearer, its color thickening, absorbing everything. The city's last tower cracked in half and fell into the black below.

Cinder spread his hands.

"Rage is not your enemy. It's your inheritance. It's every act of defiance carved into the dark. Rage is the shadow of love that refuses to die."

The words struck deep.

Kalen felt it then, the pull, the merge, the understanding. For a heartbeat, he was both men at once: father to father, grief to grief, rage to rage. The last song of Cinder's city folded into Kalen's chest. He was a memory not his, but now inseparable.

The island split, swallowed by light.

The storm's voice echoed through both men, vast and reverent, like a god trying to remember how to pray.

The world convulsed, memory collapsing into light. Cinder turned, flames rising again, and for the first time, Kalen saw him clearly: not as a demon or a ghost, but a father, a king, a man whose rage had outlived his world.

He reached out and touched Kalen's chest.

"Rage is the last defense of love. Spend it carefully."

The flames surged, not to consume but to pass on.

Kalen gasped. His world spun. The island fell away. The light became too bright to see.

And then, silence.

When Kalen opened his eyes, the world was still dark, but different. The storm outside had changed. It was less hungry, more watchful. Its color pulsed slow and heavy, as if listening.

He lay still, feeling the aftermath. His body felt scorched and remade. The rage inside him was no longer a scream, but a steady ember, warm and patient. Cinder's presence lingered, not as a voice, but as a shadow beneath every thought.

The blue glow beneath his skin had steadied, deep and calm, like the surface of an endless sea. The rage was still present, but it no longer screamed. It burned quiet.

He sat up slowly, rain tapping against the roof above. His muscles ached, his breath came ragged, but he felt whole. The confusion of the merge was gone, replaced by a sense of lineage. He was himself, but more.

Outside, the storm's color deepened, pulsing in time with distant alarms. The city was awake, holding its breath. The world would soon demand what Kalen had learned.

He flexed his fingers, feeling the quiet heat beneath his skin. The rage was a comfort now, not a threat, but a tool, a promise, a last defense.

Cinder's voice lingered in his chest, not as a whisper but as a promise.

Rage is the shape of love that refuses surrender.

Kalen closed his eyes.

"I understand now, Cinder," he murmured.

He lingered in the hush, letting the shape of Cinder's words settle into him like rain soaking deep into dry earth. Kalen drew a slow breath, aware that something fundamental had shifted in him. For a long moment, he sat with the ember's warmth nestled beneath his ribs. Fatigue crept up, heavy and irresistible, blurring the edge of his thoughts. He stretched out once more, letting his eyes drift closed, the storm's lull and Cinder's promise gentle in his chest. There, between one heartbeat and the next, he surrendered to sleep as the world waited outside his door.

Chapter 22

Kalen woke to the sound of voices.

Canvas walls breathed in the wind. The lanterns burned low, yellow and tired. He smelled damp cloth, antiseptic, and the faint ozone of resonance static still clinging to his skin.

When he tried to sit, pain flared down his ribs. A raw line circled his wrist, the mark from Thane's dampener. He stared at it until the memory came back in fragments: the blue surge, the gate refusing, the ferals breaking through the smoke, the mayor's voice on the loudspeaker, stand down, and Thane's hand shoving him clear just before the ice took everything.

"Careful," Elena's voice came from the next cot. She looked exhausted but alert, dark curls tied back, eyes sharp as glass. "You've been in and out of consciousness."

Kalen's throat was dry. "The wall," he managed. "Anyone hurt?"

She shook her head. "No. You froze the ferals clean through Kalen, every last one of them. The blast never touched the city. The gate held."

He let out a rough breath, relief mixing with something darker. "He cuffed me," he said, glancing at the mark again.

"Because you were halfway gone," she replied quietly. "Your pulse was spiking, eyes already showing color shift. If Thane hadn't clamped that band, you'd have become feral."

The tent flap lifted. Thane stepped in, shoulders filling the space, coat still damp from patrol. His presence changed the air—steady, heavy, deliberate.

"You're ok," he said.

Kalen met his eyes. "You left us on the wall."

Thane's jaw worked. "The mayor closed the gate."

"You didn't stop him."

Silence stretched for what seemed like eternity.

"I was following command," Thane said finally, the words thick. "We didn't know what would happen. Opening that gate could've allowed the city to be overrun."

Kalen's voice stayed low. "You saw them, Thane. You saw us, you know we had the time."

Thane remained firm. "I saw you glowing blue with ferals closing in," Thane said. "And I saw the wall still standing when it was over." The mask slipped a fraction; exhaustion edged his voice. "You both put the city in jeopardy as well as defended it."

Elena cut in before the air broke. "Enough Thane, he needs rest."

Kalen didn't look away from Thane. "I'm not blaming you," he said. "But don't ask me to forgive this city for leaving us to die."

Thane's silence was answer enough.

He turned to leave, stopping at the flap. "The mayor wants a report tomorrow. Get your strength back before then." He hesitated. "And for what it's worth… you stopped something that would've eaten this city alive."

The flap fell closed. The rain kept talking.

Kalen stared at the canvas, the faint pulse of blue still flickering under his skin. The city had survived, but it didn't feel like victory. It felt like something waiting to crack again.

By midday the rain had thinned to mist. The air outside the infirmary carried the sharp bite of iron and cold stone.

Kalen pulled his coat tighter as he stepped out beneath the overhang. Every muscle still felt heavy, as if the weight of the world hadn't truly left him.

Across the courtyard, soldiers were lowering the broken sections of the outer gate back into place. Steam curled where torches met frost, the metal hissing as it thawed. Beyond the wall, through the open slit of the viewport, the plain stretched white and still.

The ferals were statues now, frozen mid-snarl, claws buried in the ice. Their shapes glittered beneath the thin sunlight that broke through the sky. Some leaned against the wreckage of their own bodies, shiny and perfect like glass figures waiting to shatter.

Elena joined him, wrapping her arms around herself. "They're clearing them before nightfall," she said quietly. "Thane's leading it. The mayor wants the wall operational by dusk."

Kalen watched the workers haul one of the bodies away on a sled. The sound it made, crackling, faintly turned his stomach.

"Can't just leave them?" he asked.

"They're afraid the ice will thaw."

He didn't answer. The idea of those things melting, bleeding back into the mud, made the air feel thinner.

Thane's voice carried down, steadily giving orders. His silhouette moved between the workers, helping lift what two men couldn't. The guards obeyed him without question.

He noticed Kalen watching but didn't break stride. Only a brief nod across the courtyard, acknowledgment, nothing more. Then he turned back to the crew, motioning for the winch line to tighten.

Elena followed Kalen's gaze. "He hasn't stopped since he left you."

Kalen's mouth twitched. "Doesn't look like he plans to, either."

They stood there a while, the two of them quiet under the steady drip from the eaves. Inside the walls, the city was waking again, vendors calling out, generators starting, hammers ringing. It all sounded muted, like the world hadn't decided yet whether it should move on.

Elena touched his arm lightly. "When you can stand a little longer," she said, "I want you to see something I've been working on. A prototype."

Kalen glanced at her. "The one you kept locked in that case?"

She nodded once, eyes catching the light. "It's rough, but it channels resonance differently. It focuses it instead of letting it spill. I think it could help you control what happened out there."

Kalen's gaze drifted back toward the frozen field. "If it works," he said quietly, "it might keep it from happening again."

"That's the idea," she said. "Give me a few hours to calibrate it, then come find me in the lab."

He nodded, and she left him there beneath the overhang, her steps fading into the hum of the city.

Kalen looked back to the field where Thane was already shouting another order, ice splintering under the torches' heat. The man hadn't changed his loyalties, but the edge in his voice said he'd started to question the orders he was still giving.

The old library smelled of dust and leather. What used to be rows of shelves were now crowded with tables, cables, and humming coils. Light bled through the cracked skylight, scattering across broken glass and half-repaired circuitry. Between the columns, books were stacked waist-high, their spines warped from damp and age.

Kalen followed the faint thrum of power toward the back. A woman sat perched on a desk, legs swinging, a mug of something hot in her hands. Silas leaned against a collapsed bookshelf beside her, goggles pushed up into his hair.

"Look who's alive," Silas said when Kalen appeared. "You planning on freezing the rest of us next, or was that a one-time thing?"

The woman shot him a look. "You were out there, and I didn't see you doing anything to help."

Silas smirked, hands raised. "Seriously, Rissa? I was busy holding the line while the rest of you hid behind the city wall."

Kalen gave a faint, tired grin, the memory of the wall still burning cold behind his eyes.

Elena didn't turn. She was bent over her workbench near the old librarian's counter, where she'd carved out a nest of tools and parts scavenged from the storm-metal scrapyard. "Close the door," she said. "The light from the hall messes with the readings."

Kalen shut it and stepped closer. On the table lay a single metal glove extending up the forearm. The metal was sleek, patched together from alloy and crystal, its seams faintly glowing blue.

"This is what you wanted to show me," he said.

Elena nodded. "The prototype. A gauntlet designed to stabilize resonance frequency."

Silas raised a brow. "Or in common language?"

"Control," she said simply. "It channels the emotional output into a closed loop instead of letting it rip through you. Think of it as an outlet for what's inside."

Rissa leaned forward, eyes catching the glimmer off the alloy. "You built that from salvaged junk?"

"And whatever circuits I could salvage from the city," Elena said. "It's ugly, but it works."

Kalen studied it, the faint blue pulse reflected in his eyes. "You think it'll help control outbursts?"

"I think it'll give you a choice next time," she said. "The storm answers emotion. This might keep it from owning you when it does."

Silas gave a short, skeptical laugh. "And if it doesn't?"

"Then it explodes," Elena said dryly.

Rissa glanced at Kalen. "Does it hurt?"

"Not supposed to," Elena said. "But I won't ask him to wear it until I've run another calibration." She looked to Kalen. "Tomorrow, if you're ready."

Kalen gave a small nod, the faint blue reflection still dancing across his eyes.

Rissa shifted on the desk, setting her mug aside. "On the way here, I heard the mayor's planning a meeting at town hall," she said. "Wants to 'address the incident at the wall.' Do we go?"

Elena straightened slowly, the exhaustion in her face giving way to thought. "If he's talking, it must be to control the narrative. It might be worth hearing what kind of story he plans to tell."

Silas snorted. "Probably the same one he always does. 'Veil Harbor stands united,' while he takes credit for not freezing."

Kalen's jaw tightened. "Then we'll listen. See how much of the truth he decides to leave out."

The atrium had been cleaned for show. Floodlights hummed along the rafters, throwing a pale wash over cracked banners that read *VEIL HARBOR ENDURES*. Rows of folding chairs filled the floor, their metal legs screeching against the tile as citizens filed in.

Kalen stood near the back beside Elena, Silas, and Rissa. The smell of damp coats and rusted metal hung heavy in the air. Somewhere above, water dripped through a seam in the ceiling, each drop hitting the floor like a metronome.

Thane was already at the front with the rest of the guard detail, posture straight, expression unreadable. His presence alone kept the crowd quiet.

When the mayor stepped up to the podium, the hum of the lights seemed to fade. He wore his usual pressed coat and polished smile, every inch the man who'd built a city out of ruin. His voice carried with practiced confidence.

"Yesterday," he began, "Veil Harbor witnessed another reminder of the world beyond our walls. A swarm of ferals approached the front gate, drawn by the storm's lingering energy. Thanks to our wall division, the threat was stopped before reaching the perimeter. No lives were lost."

Whispers swept across the audience, a blend of relief, skepticism, and lingering anxiety that so often accompanied his declarations.

Kalen's jaw tightened. Stopped before the perimeter. He could still see the ferals frozen mid-charge, the gate sealed, and the mayor's voice echoing over the intercom: *stand down.*

The mayor let the noise settle before continuing. "I understand the fear many of you felt. You've given your trust to this city, to me, and yesterday that trust was tested. For that, I owe you an apology."

The crowd stilled.

He leaned slightly forward, hands resting on the podium. "But the dangers outside are growing bolder.

The storms are changing them, making them faster, hungrier, more unpredictable. To keep Veil Harbor secure, we must adapt."

A pause. Then his tone shifted to a still, heavy calm.

"Effective immediately, a nightly curfew will be enforced. All citizens are to be within their quarters by sundown."

Uneasy voices stirred, whispers darting between rows.

"To preserve our stores," he continued, "rations will be reduced for the next cycle. Supply teams will be reassigned to reinforce the wall and maintain order."

The murmurs grew louder.

"And finally," he said, raising his voice above the noise, "until the surrounding region is cleared and declared safe, all travel beyond the city limits will require authorization. These are temporary measures. Difficult ones. But they are necessary to protect what we've built."

Kalen could feel the mood shift like pressure before a storm. Relief curdled into resentment. The room had come expecting reassurance; instead, it was being caged.

Beside him, Rissa muttered, "There it is."

Silas folded his arms. "Always a catch."

Elena's voice was quiet. "He's turning fear into leverage."

At the podium, the mayor lifted a hand again, steadying the rising noise. "There is one more thing," he said. "In these uncertain times, Veil Harbor must not stand alone. We have been contacted by neighboring settlements, others who refuse to let the storm dictate their fate."

He gestured toward the side of the stage. "Today, I have the honor of introducing one such representative, a man who has led survivors in the southern sectors, a man whose courage and leadership have helped restore order where chaos once ruled. General Darren Briggs."

A few guards stepped aside as a tall figure approached the podium. Briggs moved with the easy confidence of someone who knew what command felt like.

The mayor stepped back, giving him the stage.

Briggs's voice was calm when he spoke, carrying easily through the room. "Your city stood through the storm. Not many can claim that. Out there, most walls fell, and the ones that didn't are still fighting to keep what's left."

The crowd listened, uneasy, curious.

"I came north," Briggs continued, "because the storm's changing faster than any one city can adapt.

Settlements fall, routes close, people scatter. We can't survive like that. What's left of the southern sectors is uniting under a single banner, one meant to bring structure back to what's left of this country."

He paused, scanning the crowd. "We're building a coordinated defense network. It will share supply routes, defensive measures."

A few heads nodded. Others looked wary.

Briggs's gaze swept across the hall, finding Kalen and Elena near the back. When his eyes met theirs, his expression shifted, a brief, knowing smile that didn't reach his eyes.

Then he looked back to the room. "Veil Harbor's strength could help turn that vision into reality. The question isn't whether you can endure. It's whether you're willing to stand for more than your own walls."

His words landed heavy, the kind that sounded like an invitation and an ultimatum at once.

The mayor returned to the podium, smiling thinly. "General Briggs will remain with us as a guest while we discuss cooperation between our cities. Let's show him the same trust and civility we show each other."

Polite applause followed, scattered and unsure.

Briggs stepped back from the podium, eyes flicking once more toward Kalen and Elena before he descended from the stage.

Silas looked at them both, brow furrowed. "What was that about?"

The rain outside hit the dome harder, echoing through the atrium like the slow ticking of a clock running out.

Chapter 23

Outside, Veil Harbor's streets hissed under the weight of it, steam rising where the storm-metal gutters met the heat vents. Inside the bar, the world felt smaller.

Kalen's group had taken the back corner, away from the main noise. The table was a clutter of half-drunk cups, damp coats, and ration wrappers pushed aside for a creased map. Rissa sat sideways on her chair, boots hooked on the rung, scanning the room through the rim of her mug. Silas leaned against the wall beside her, one arm crossed, the other tracing condensation down his glass.

Mercer occupied the end of the table, the old captain's bulk filling the space like another piece of worn furniture. His coat was still wet from patrol, and his badge lay on the table beside a small flask he hadn't touched. Across from him sat Elena, elbows braced on either side of the map, strands of hair escaping her tie.

Around them, two more of Kalen's quiet allies sat. Juno from the east gate and Marrek, one of the mechanics from the lower docks. Everyone listened without speaking.

"This is what his presence means," Elena said, voice low but steady. "Briggs isn't here to build peace. He's here to build control."

Silas gave a humorless laugh. "That's what the mayor already does."

"Not like this," Elena said. "Briggs operates through consolidation. He's uniting the southern settlements under a military banner. It may seem like protection, but it's really a takeover, subtle and courteous, right up until it turns forceful."

Mercer grunted. "And the mayor invited him in."

Elena nodded. "Because Briggs talks like a savior. He's offering structure, supplies, soldiers. Not to mention he's a general in the army. That's everything a city on edge wants to hear."

Rissa frowned. "Then why come here? We've got our own problems."

Elena's eyes flicked toward Kalen. "Because of him," she said quietly. "Briggs knows he is unique. Kalen is someone who survived his experiments and lived with more than one color. That kind of anomaly eats at him. He doesn't let go of things he can't control."

The table went still. Rissa's mug froze halfway to her mouth. Silas stopped tracing the glass. Mercer's shoulders shifted, the motion heavy.

Kalen said nothing, his gaze fixed on the grain of the table. "She's right. This man is a wolf in sheep's clothing. He'll find a reason to take me back in."

No one argued.

Silas exhaled through his nose. "The mayor has no idea what he's invited inside."

"Oh, he knows," Elena said. "He just thinks he can use Briggs before Briggs uses him."

A long silence followed. The sound of rain on the roof deepened, slow and constant. Rissa looked toward Mercer, and he met her gaze, both of them reading the same thought without saying it. She gave a small nod.

Mercer leaned forward, forearms braced on the table. "The town's split," he said quietly. "Half of 'em still believe in the mayor. The other half's tired of being treated like prisoners inside their own walls. If Briggs starts throwing his weight around, it'll push people to choose sides."

Elena's eyes narrowed. "What are you implying, Mercer?"

He held her gaze for a long moment, lowering his voice before he spoke.

"A rebellion."

The word hung in the air like static before a storm, and no one dared breathe until the thunder outside broke it apart, making the night pass by in uneasy silence.

Morning came gray and reluctant, seeping through the cracks of the old administration hall's windows. Kalen sat in a hard chair outside the mayor's office, hands clasped loosely, eyes fixed on the cracks in the floor tile. A guard stood at the end of the corridor, still as a shadow. The sound of typewriters and distant voices drifted from deeper in the building.

The latch turned. Kalen straightened. Thane stepped out, coat buttoned high, the red-and-black band on his arm newly scrubbed. His expression carried that same iron control, but his eyes were tired.

"Kalen," he said.

Kalen rose. "He's ready for me?"

Thane nodded once. "He's got questions about the wall. You'll answer what's asked, nothing more."

Kalen's brow furrowed. "You sound like I'm walking into a tribunal."

"Not yet," Thane said. "But the wrong tone could make it one."

He started down the hall, motioning for Kalen to follow. Their boots echoed softly against the tile.

"Keep your temper in check," Thane said quietly. "No challenges, no lectures. The mayor doesn't like reminders that the wall almost fell, or that you were the one who kept it standing."

Kalen's jaw flexed. "You mean the one he locked outside."

Thane slowed just enough to glance over his shoulder. "I mean don't give him a reason to see you as a threat. He already does, whether he says it or not."

They reached the double doors of the mayor's office. The brass handles gleamed, polished bright under the harsh overhead light. Two guards stood motionless to either side, red lines pulsing slowly.

Thane turned to him, voice low and deliberate. "Let him lead the conversation. Be respectful. Whatever he says, you don't react. Understood?"

Kalen met his gaze. "I'll try."

"Don't try," Thane said. "Do it."

He opened the door.

The mayor's office smelled of paper, oil, and faint tobacco. It was an indulgence in a city living on rations. Sunlight cut through tall windows, washing across stacks of files and a detailed map of Veil Harbor pinned behind the desk.

The mayor looked up with a smile too polished to be real. "Ah," he said. "The blue man who froze the world."

Kalen stepped inside. Thane closed the door behind him but stayed near it as part guard, part witness.

"Sir," Kalen said evenly.

The mayor gestured to the chair opposite his desk. "Sit."

Kalen did, posture straight but cautious.

"I won't waste your time," the mayor began, folding his hands. "You've become something of a curiosity in my city, Mr. Rourke. Some are calling you a hero. Others... a liability. I need to know which you intend to be."

Kalen's voice stayed calm. "I didn't intend to be either."

"Intent rarely matters," the mayor said. "What matters is perception. You've seen what happens when people get ideas about someone. Rumors grow faster than food in this city."

Kalen met his gaze. "You think I'm encouraging them."

"I think," the mayor said slowly, "that a handful of people saw something they can't explain. And when people can't explain something, they start to believe in it. That belief can move mountains or burn them down."

Kalen's hands tightened against his knees, but his tone didn't change. "I was trying to protect the wall. Not to even mention saving my life and the lives of two fellow citizens."

"And you did," the mayor said, almost kindly. "But now I have to protect the city from the story that follows you." He leaned forward slightly. "I need you to stay quiet. Work, rest, keep to your section. No more heroics."

Kalen's eyes narrowed. "So, I'm under house arrest."

Thane's jaw tightened, but he didn't speak.

The mayor's smile never faltered. "Think of it as precaution. This city runs on stability. I won't have it unravel because one man made the storm blink."

Kalen stood. "If that's all—"

"That's all," the mayor said, then looked past him to Thane. "You'll be responsible for making sure Mr. Rourke understands the importance of restraint. I always want eyes on him. If he sneezes near a power conduit, I expect to know about it."

Thane's expression didn't move. "Understood, sir."

Kalen looked between them. "So now I'm your assignment."

"No," the mayor said smoothly. "You're my responsibility. And I take those seriously."

Kalen's silence said more than words could.

"Dismissed," the mayor added.

Thane opened the door. The hallway beyond felt colder than when they'd entered.

As Kalen stepped out, the mayor's voice followed, calm and distant. "I trust I can count on your cooperation, Mr. Rourke."

Kalen paused, his hand on the doorframe. "You already did once," he said quietly. "You just closed the gate on it."

Then he walked out, and Thane shut the door behind them.

The hallways of the administration building were silent except for the echo of their boots. Thane walked ahead, posture rigid, eyes forward. Kalen followed a step behind, the air between them thick with everything neither had said in front of the mayor.

Outside, Veil Harbor moved under the sky like a tired machine, soft noises, lights flickering, the rhythm of survival stripped down to habit.

They crossed the main square in silence. Vendors were already setting up behind the checkpoint fences, their stalls half-stocked, faces drawn. A ration line stretched down the block, men and women hunched beneath hoods, holding out tin cards that no longer guaranteed enough.

Kalen slowed. "Look at this place, Thane."

Thane didn't stop walking. "Keep moving."

"I'm serious," Kalen said. "Look at what this city's becoming."

Thane finally turned, the rain sliding off his collar. "You think I don't see it?"

"Then tell me what you see," Kalen said quietly. "Because from where I'm standing, it looks like we're shrinking. Less food. Less light. More walls every day. People starving while he gives speeches about order."

Thane's jaw tightened. "He's keeping people alive."

"Alive isn't living." Kalen motioned toward the marketplace. "You lock them in. You shut down the arena, the one place they could still feel something. You segregate emotions like they're diseases, brand people for what they feel, and call it control."

Thane looked away, his shoulders stiff.

Kalen stepped closer, voice low. "Instead of helping us adapt and rebuild, you're aiding in our suppression. The city's not surviving, Thane, it's suffocating. And you're helping."

Thane's head snapped toward him then, the composure breaking for the first time. "Watch your tone."

Kalen didn't flinch. "You asked me to. You wanted me to stay calm, to show restraint. I'm doing that. I'm just asking you, what exactly do you stand for anymore?"

The words hit harder than any shout could have. Thane's eyes narrowed, not with anger, but with something deeper. Conflict was cutting through the soldier's armor, steel-blue light glowing brighter.

Rain pattered against the metal awnings around them. Somewhere down the block, a checkpoint alarm chirped as a gate cycled open and closed again.

Thane drew a slow breath, his voice quieter now. "I stand for keeping this city alive, Rourke. That's what I've always stood for."

Kalen's gaze stayed steady. "Then maybe it's time to ask what kind of city you're keeping alive."

Neither spoke after that. They walked the rest of the street in silence, the space between them wider than the road.

When they reached the final corner, Thane stopped. "You're still under my supervision," he said finally. "Don't make me regret fighting for that."

Kalen nodded once, then turned away into the thinning rain.

Thane watched him go, and for the first time in a long while, he didn't look certain which side of the line he was standing on.

The room carried the dim warmth of late afternoon, rain still whispering against the windows. Elena sat at the table, sleeves rolled, pages of notes spread beneath a half-dead lamp.

Kalen leaned against the cot, elbows on his knees, still running the last conversation with the mayor through his head. The vibration of the wall generators filled the quiet like a low heartbeat.

Then they heard Thane's voice. "No visitors."

Rissa's voice carried through the door, quick and fearless. "You can't stop a medical check-in. I'm his primary care lead, remember?"

For a moment there was nothing. Then the latch clicked. Rissa slipped in with a grin that said she'd already won. "See? All it takes is confidence." She shut the door, brushed the rain off her coat, and set her bag down on the table.

Elena didn't look up. "You're not his care lead."

Rissa smiled. "He doesn't know that."

Thane's shadow lingered outside for a breath before moving off down the hall, slow and steady, like a man trying to convince himself there was nothing worth listening to.

Rissa waited until his footsteps faded, then dropped the act. Her tone flattened. "Mercer and I have been asking around. Even without us, it's already happening. People are meeting in storage rooms, whispering through ration lines. It's not rumor anymore, momentum is building."

Kalen straightened slightly. "How many?"

"Enough," Rissa replied. "Mercer's taking lead now. He's already got the gate crews and half the dock workers on board. The city's split clean down the middle, and it's only getting worse."

She met Kalen's eyes. "And you need to come up with a plan. If that general is here for you, this is already half your fault."

Kalen's jaw flexed. "Half my fault?"

"You escaped," she said. "You showed people what he lost control of. The man wouldn't be here if he didn't want it back."

"That's a stretch," Elena said, finally glancing up from the table. Her voice was calm, almost detached. "Before we dive too deep, there's one very large problem."

She tipped her head toward the door. "Who's going to convince that guy?"

They all went quiet. Outside, the sound of Thane's boots traced a slow, deliberate line past the door, steady and protective.

Elena's gaze moved between Kalen and Rissa, eyes narrowing with a thought taking shape. "I think I know what we can do," she said softly, "but you might not like it."

Chapter 24

The harbor sat still beneath a kaleidoscope of colors swirling across the sky. Wind pushed off the water in slow, heavy gusts that carried the sting of salt and rust. The tide had pulled back, leaving the piers slick and empty, ropes hanging slack over the edge.

Elena walked ahead, coat drawn close, boots echoing against the soaked boards. Rissa, Silas, and Mercer followed a few paces behind. None of them spoke.

At the end of the dock stood a single warehouse, old and freestanding, its storm-metal doors chained shut. A lone man sat in front of them on an overturned crate, hands resting on his knees. He was burly, broad-shouldered, hair the color of iron dust with a thick red beard. His expression didn't change as they approached.

"I didn't think I'd see you so soon," he said.

Elena stopped a few feet away. "I didn't think I'd have to come back this soon," she replied.

The man's eyes flicked to the others behind her, then back. "You sure about this?"

"Never," she said softly. "But that's never stopped me before."

He grunted. "Still a scientist, then."

"Always," she said. "Before anything else."

He studied her a moment longer, then stood and moved aside. "They're still inside. Haven't made a sound since morning."

Elena nodded once. "Good. That means it's working."

She stepped to the doors and laid both hands on the cold metal. For a heartbeat she just breathed, slow and deliberate, then looked back over her shoulder.

"Okay," she said quietly. "Don't be mad. There's a reason."

The others exchanged uncertain glances.

Elena unlatched the crossbar. The chains rattled. When the doors swung open, the smell of antiseptic, metal, and filth assaulted their senses.

Light spilled across the floor, cutting through the dim interior of the warehouse.

Five figures stood within.

Red. Blue. Yellow. Green. Gray.

Ferals.

Each was chained to the floor by heavy restraints. Their veins pulsed faintly with color in the dim light.

Rissa's hand went to her mouth. "Elena…what did you do?"

Elena walked forward, the sound of her boots echoing through the hollow space. "I didn't bring them here," she said. "They came in from the water. The patrols were ready to attack. I stopped them."

"They were attacking?" Mercer asked.

"They were coming in," she said simply. "That's all I know. Threat or not, they were going to be destroyed."

Silas stepped beside her, his voice quiet. "And now they're experiments."

Elena's gaze stayed on the nearest one, a woman, or what was left of one, her veins pulsing faint green beneath gray skin. "Subjects," she said. "Alive. Stable. And maybe … the key to understanding what we're becoming."

Rissa shook her head slowly. "You're crossing a line."

"Crossing the line?" Elena repeated. The words hit hard enough that Rissa stopped breathing for a second. "What happens when we refuse to cross it? When we pretend that we understand what is happening to us?"

The light climbed her veins, brighter with each word.

"We were human, but not anymore. Echoform to Echoferal, that is our new evolution, whether we want it or not."

Rissa looked away. Silas shifted his stance. Mercer watched her with the kind of stillness that meant he was weighing every syllable.

Elena did not stop.

"People are losing control every day. They turn faster than we can track. We have only touched the surface of what we are becoming."

She stepped closer to the table, her fingers trembling over the scattered notes. The turquoise glow washed over the room and painted the walls with quiet urgency.

"What happens when the last of us turns?" she asked. Her voice cut the air clean. "Can we even reproduce anymore? Silas, do you know? Mercer, do you?"

Silas stared at the floor. Mercer's jaw moved, but no words came.

"Because I don't," Elena continued. "And that terrifies me more than anything outside these walls."

The glow pulsed once, then slowly faded as she forced her breathing to steady. The room seemed to settle with her, although no one spoke.

"This is not something I want to do, Rissa," Elena said. "It is something I have to do."

Silence held. No one dared move.

Elena looked at each of them, her voice calm again.

"You said we needed a plan. This is the best I can do."

The silence was overwhelming as everyone processed Elena's plan. Silas finally spoke, shattering the heavy stillness. "Let me make sure I've got this right," he said. "We're supposed to sneak this thing in after curfew, get it close to Kalen, and then I let it attack me? Is that really what you're suggesting?"

Elena didn't look up from the schematic she was tracing in the dust on the table. "Well, unless you have a better idea, yes."

Silas blinked. "That's your plan? To have me mauled for dramatic effect?"

"It's the best way to turn Thane to our cause," Elena calmly replied. "He needs to see what we're up against, what can happen within the walls. He needs to believe it's real, not staged."

Rissa crossed her arms. "Don't worry, Silas. I'll patch you up afterwards."

"That's comforting," he muttered.

Mercer cut in before the argument could stretch. "We're running out of time. I don't like it either, but she has a point."

Silas gestured toward him. "Easy to agree when you're not the bait."

Mercer ignored him and kept going, voice even. "We sneak it in through the drainage path after curfew. Elena overloads the sector's dampener grid. That should mask the resonance spike long enough to make it believable."

He nodded to Rissa. "You'll sell it. Scream, make noise, pull attention to your sector. When Thane heads over to investigate, Silas will inject it with the adrenaline needle. The thing wakes, thrashes, and attacks."

"Perfect," Silas said flatly. "Love it already."

Mercer didn't pause. "Then Rissa screams like she is turning. Thane will hopefully step in and use resonance to subdue it. He'll have no choice but to see the truth for himself. We sell the fright."

The room went quiet.

Mercer folded his arms. "Is there anything I missed, Elena?"

She finally looked up, eyes catching the low light. "Just one thing," she said. "Make sure Thane doesn't kill it before the point's made."

Rissa glanced between them. "And if he does?"

Elena's voice softened. "Then we improvise."

Silas groaned and dropped his head into his hands. "Fantastic. Nothing says confidence like that word."

Mercer smirked. "Then we're in agreement."

Elena drew a breath. "Tonight," she said, "that's when we take back control of our city."

The night had settled over Veil Harbor like a fog. The streets were empty, lamps dimmed, every sound too sharp. Above, a shimmering aurora stretched across the sky, more vivid than the northern lights, swirling with bands of brilliant hues that rippled over the city. The colors draped the skyline, reflecting in the wet pavement and casting shifting, prismatic shades over buildings and glassy water. Veil Harbor seemed at once otherworldly and electric beneath this living tapestry of light.

Elena moved with Mercer, Silas, and Rissa along the harbor's outer path, boots silent against the wet concrete. Mist from the water carried the taste of metal and oil.

They reached the drainage lane that cut through the lower district, narrow and forgotten.

Mercer scanned the corners. "No watchers, no sentries. It looks clear."

"Good," Elena said. "Then let's begin."

The tarp lay folded near the wall, wrapped around the feral they'd brought from the warehouse. Her breathing was shallow, skin pale, faint red light still ghosting beneath. Elena checked the pulse. "She's still under."

They staged the chaos fast. Rissa dragged a smear of blood, scattered a torn strap. Mercer tipped a bin, kicked debris into the puddles. When it looked convincingly violent, Elena nodded. "Positions. Silas takes it from here."

They melted into the dark behind a broken storefront.

Across the lane, Silas appeared, coat torn, flashlight out, looking every bit a patrolman off his route. He scanned the area, saw the mess, and stepped closer.

Elena's fingers hovered over the portable dampener control she'd rigged from old tech. "Now," she whispered, and flipped the surge.

The low hum beneath the street hiccupped. The air pressure shifted like the city itself had taken a breath and forgotten to let it out. Three blocks of sensors went deaf.

Rissa sucked in a breath, then let out the scream. It tore through the quiet night, sharp and terrifying.

She gave Silas a thumbs up and took off down the block, leaving the rest to him. He cursed under his breath, jogging toward the sound. He crouched beside the feral, pulled the injector, and drove it into its shoulder.

Instantly, its eyes shot open, locking onto Silas. He froze as he went to pull away, not from fear, but from the raw pain staring back at him, pain that didn't fit the twisted face. For a heartbeat, he couldn't look away.

Then the feral lunged. Pain slashed across Silas's chest, snapping him back to the present. He staggered, breath burning, and yanked both batons free. "Alright then," he muttered. "My turn."

Steel met bone as the batons cracked against its ribs, sparks scattering across the slick pavement. It rushed him again, claws scraping stone. Silas fought like a man who knew he couldn't win but was determined to make them remember the noise.

Elena watched from the shadows. Rissa bit her knuckle to keep from shouting.

Boots hammered pavement.

"A feral?" Thane's voice cut through the night.

The feral lunged again; Silas barely blocked, breath ragged. "Little help!" he yelled.

Thane rounded the corner, blue-gold flowing to his palms like a river. Both hands came up, veins glowing. "Get down!"

Silas hit the ground.

The air bent. Thane's glow intensified, and he shot forward, fists already in motion. The feral hit the wall hard, color flaring, limbs shaking. He pressed the force again, more control than brute strength, until the feral lay still, red quickly dulling to gray.

Silas stayed crouched, batons trembling in his hands. He couldn't get those eyes out of his head.

"Silas!" Thane shouted. "Explain."

Silas still stood there, staring at the crumbled form of the feral. He opened his mouth, words coming out numbly. "Heard a scream," he said. "When I got close, she was already too far gone."

Thane surveyed the scene, the bin, the blood, the chaos. His jaw set. "The dampeners... how?" The words came slowly. "I have to speak to the mayor."

Elena kept watching. Thane knelt, palm hovering above the feral's chest, resonance flickering faint and careful. Blood was pooling from his nose as he took deep breaths. Whatever he felt there changed his face for a heartbeat.

Wiping his nose with his sleeve, he keyed his comm. "Sector Five. Breach near the drainage lane. Containment team, move."

Static crackled back.

Elena exhaled.

Rissa whispered, "He saw it."

Elena nodded. "That's all we needed."

Thane stood, scanning the street once more. His gaze lingered on the dark where they hid, suspicion or instinct, but after another breath, he turned away.

They waited until his boots faded and the rain swallowed the sound.

Elena's voice was barely above the hum of the water. "We got him thinking," she said. "That's a start."

Rissa lingered in the hush that followed Thane's retreat, rain pulsing in the alley's veins. She searched for Silas, found him silhouetted in the flicker of neon, motionless, gaze locked on the body as if something vital might yet stir. Her urgency pressed against the quiet.

"Silas, we need to go," she called, voice threading through the wet gloom. "They'll be here any minute."

He didn't answer at first. The city's reflection ran amber down his cheeks as he stared, unblinking, as if the world might stop with him. For one suspended instant, he seemed lost to everything but the broken thing before him.

Then, with a slow shudder, reality reclaimed its grip. He turned, voice barely a whisper. "Rissa... its eyes. Did you see them? I swear I saw fear in its eyes."

Rissa's answer came soft. "Silas, we need to leave."

Chapter 25

Kalen woke to the sound of a latch clicking.

Light slanted through the blinds, pale and cold. The air in his quarters smelled like rain and metal again, the kind that settled into everything.

The door opened slowly. Mercer stepped in first, followed by Elena, Rissa, and Silas. None of them said a word.

They moved like people who hadn't slept. Elena set her notes on the table without looking at him. Rissa pulled a chair close and sank into it, eyes distant. Mercer leaned against the wall, arms folded. Silas dropped into the corner by the window and stayed there, elbows on his knees, head low.

The silence stretched until Kalen finally broke it. "What's going on?" His voice came rough, still half-asleep. "And why is Silas suddenly acting as depressed as me?"

Mercer's eyes lifted. "We may have done something necessary," he said, his tone steady but heavy. "Something that might've turned Thane to our side. But the methods left their marks on us."

Kalen sat up, blinking. "What did you do?"

Elena looked at Mercer, then at Rissa. No one jumped in, so she did what she always did, cut straight to the truth.

"We staged an attack," she said. "A controlled one. We needed Thane to see what the mayor's constant pressure is doing to the city, to the people living under it. We made it seem like a local lost control, that their emotions overflowed the dampener and turned them."

Kalen's jaw tightened. "You purposefully turned a living person?"

Elena shook her head slowly. "Not exactly. We had a feral available for use."

Kalen rubbed a hand over his face, breath catching. "You're not making any sense."

Rissa's voice came soft. "Supposedly some ferals came in through the water. That's a thing now, I guess. Elena had the guards bring them to a shed near the docks where she sedated them to study. We used one of those."

Elena picked up the thread. "We can talk about that later, Kalen. The point is, we cut the dampener grid, Rissa screamed, Silas played patrol, and the feral woke on cue."

Kalen looked toward Silas. The man didn't move.

"It attacked him," Mercer said. "He held his ground until Thane arrived. Did his part exactly as planned."

Kalen frowned. "That's it? So why is he suddenly quiet?"

Silas lifted his head, voice low. "You didn't see it." He sat up straighter. "Before it attacked, it looked at me. Right at me. There was pain in its eyes, fear. Not rage. Not hunger."

Kalen's breath stilled.

"He doesn't think she was all gone," Rissa finished quietly.

The room felt smaller. The pulse of the generator in the hall sounded too loud.

"So, what now?" Kalen asked.

Mercer's voice stayed firm. "Now we wait. Thane's questioning everything. He said he was going to the mayor. If he pulls on the wrong thread, it'll unravel fast."

Elena met Kalen's eyes. "We wanted him to see control. We just didn't expect what it'd cost to prove it."

Kalen leaned back, staring past them at the pale stripes of morning bleeding through the blinds. "So, you wanted him to see what can happen inside the city," he said quietly. "That it's not as protected as everyone thinks?"

No one spoke for a while. The silence didn't feel like guilt, it felt heavy.

Mercer let out a long breath, slow and deliberate, then stood. His voice came low, steady, somewhere between conviction and fatigue.
"So now we have two wars," he said. "One with the city, and one with morality."

The group stared, uncertain.

Mercer pressed on. "If a part of us stays when we turn feral, a part that seeps through, then maybe becoming feral isn't the end. Maybe it's just another kind of edge."

Rissa's hands tightened, uncertain. The words hung in the air, not quite hope, not quite surrender.

Kalen glanced toward the blinds, morning bleeding in pale stripes. Elena's fingers brushed her necklace, her face unreadable.

Outside, the generator beat on, too loud, too steady, and full of questions no one wanted to answer.

The air inside the old warehouse was colder than outside. The lights buzzed overhead, and the smell of decay and antiseptic clung to everything.

Kalen stood near the doorway, arms crossed, watching Elena move through the row of makeshift containment cells. Each one was nothing more than reinforced partitions, steel bars welded from scavenged material, insulated lines running along the floor. The faint pulse of the dampener grid throbbed through the concrete like a slow, mechanical heartbeat.

Five cells. Four ferals.

They weren't thrashing or clawing. They sat or stood in their corners, heads low, bodies trembling faintly as the suppressors held them. The air shimmered where resonance met containment.

Kalen's throat felt dry. "You've been spending a lot of time down here."

Elena didn't look up from the clipboard she carried. "Someone has to find a solution before this whole planet turns."

He stepped closer to one of the cells, the green one. The figure inside was thin, clawed hands resting in its lap. Its eyes flicked up at him once, quick and unfocused, before sliding away again.

"They look tired," Kalen said.

"They are," Elena replied quietly. "Sedation doesn't erase exhaustion. It only blunts it."

Kalen's eyes shifted to her. "You said earlier that you've been studying them. What are you finding?"

Elena exhaled, setting the clipboard down on a nearby table. "Patterns," she said. "In the resonance surges, in their vitals, in the emotional flux readings. It's inconsistent, but there's something underneath it, like memory. Echoes of what they used to be."

"Memory," Kalen repeated under his breath.

She nodded. "When the dampeners are stable, the resonance waves flatten into rhythmic pulses. It's not random. It's almost… responsive."

Kalen frowned. "Responsive to what?"

Elena hesitated. "Emotion. Voices. Familiar frequencies. When I talk to them, the readings fluctuate."

He blinked. "You're saying they recognize you."

"I'm saying they react," she said. "And sometimes, the reaction looks a lot like recognition."

Kalen stared through the glass at the empty cell.

"She's the one from last night," Elena said. "A rage-red. The perfect specimen to study."

Kalen looked at her sharply. "These were people once."

Elena didn't answer right away. She rested a hand against the reinforced glass, the faint reflection of turquoise light rippling across her palm. "I think," she said slowly, "that maybe being feral isn't the end. Maybe it's something in between, like the body adapting faster than the mind can follow."

Kalen's voice dropped. "You think they can come back."

"Not all," she said softly. "But maybe some."

The vibration of the dampener deepened for a moment, as if agreeing, or warning them both.

He turned toward her. "If that's true... what now?"

Elena looked up from the glass. "You've lived closer to the edge than any of us. You've felt it, the color, the pull. If anyone can tell the difference between losing control and transforming, it's you."

Kalen stared at her hand on the glass, then at the faint silhouette beyond it. "So, what do I need to do?"

Elena's gaze lifted to meet his. "I need to get a reading on you when you're on the cusp of changing. If you can come back, why can't they?"

Kalen lingered in the hush; his outline etched against the blue-lit glass. "We need certainty," he said at last, his voice low, bruised with regret. "If there's even a sliver of hope for redemption, I can't keep destroying what might still be saved. Emily would never forgive me for that."

The tension in the room thickened, pressing against their ribs.

Elena's eyes met his, unwavering compassion and resolve woven into one. "I understand," she murmured, her words both a promise and a challenge. "Let me gather the team. We have the tools. Tonight, we'll chase the truth to its end."

Chapter 26

The morning's mist clung to the tall windows of Mayor Calder's office, tracing faint trails down the glass. The city below blurred into a shifting sea of color; the light that slipped through the sky was cold and flat.

Briggs stood with his hands folded behind his back, gloves still on, the smell of wet leather and oil clinging to him. Calder sat at the desk, shoulders tight, a stack of reports to one side and a cup gone cold. The room held the quiet of business waiting to be made urgent.

The door opened. Thane came in, uniform neat, face closed in that way men keep when they're measuring what they can still live with.

"Thane," Calder said before he could take the weight off his shoulders. "You asked for a word."

Thane didn't waste time. "There was a breach last night. We contained it. But the curfews, the ration cuts, the checkpoints, I think people are fraying. If we keep tightening, they'll break."

Calder's jaw tightened. "You left your post," he said bluntly, eyes on Thane. "You were assigned to keep that time-bomb out of trouble. Why did you abandon that duty to chase ghosts in the lower district?"

Thane's hand flexed once along the seam of his coat. "I did my duty, Mayor. Last night, what the people needed most was to be seen, not shut away behind more bars. If we keep squeezing, we create the very danger we claim to guard against."

Briggs watched the exchange, watching the small movements that told him everything: the tilt of Thane's head, the way Calder's fingers tightened on the desk. The man in front of him was tired, yes, but tired men break sharp and fast.

Calder's voice was flat steel. "Order keeps this city together, Thane. You know that. We cannot open the gates because a few tired souls complain. Your assignment is to protect the line."

Briggs stepped forward, voice even and smooth. "Look at his eyes, Calder," he said softly. "He disapproves of your methods."

Calder's gaze flicked up, troubled. For a second the mayor looked older than his title. The hesitation was a crack.

Thane squared his shoulders. "I didn't come here to argue, sir. I came to report the truth. The people are fraying. You can squeeze them until they break, or you can find a way that keeps them together without suffocation."

Calder's hand drummed once on the desk. "Dismissed," he said finally, too quickly.

Thane hesitated only a moment before he nodded and left, boots sounding hollow in the corridor.

The door closed. Briggs let the silence sit a breath, tasting it for what it might be. He turned toward the window and watched Thane's reflection leave the glass.

"You saw it," Briggs said, addressing Calder as much as the empty space Thane had filled.

Calder rubbed his forehead. "He's loyal. He'll come to his senses."

Briggs smiled, small and patient. "Or he'll be the first to find someone to join. Men like him, good men, snap when the ropes that bind them are no longer honorable." He moved closer to the desk. "Keep him close. Make him feel trusted. When he lashes out, you make an example."

Calder's shoulders dropped, the weight of choice settling back on him. He nodded once, slow.

Briggs regarded his own reflection in the glass. "I'll be gone for a while," he said quietly. "I need to secure the supply routes down south. I'll bring back additional troops soon, just as a precaution."

"Protection," Calder echoed, voice thin.

"Protection," Briggs confirmed. He set his gloved hands on the desk for a moment, the reflection of his face superimposed against Calder's in the window. Two men, two positions: one worrying he'd been left to hold a city together, the other already calculating how to keep it that way.

"Keep things calm while I'm gone," Briggs said. "The next few days will decide which side of the wall still stands."

Then he left, the echo of his boots swallowing the last of the office's quiet. Outside, the colors swayed steady, indifferent to the wars men chose to start beneath them.

Briggs emerged into the brightness of morning, spotting them gathered ahead, figures cloaked in hoods, their boots planted firmly on the stone like markers staking a claim. Vale stood at the front, a long scarf tucked into his coat, eyes flat and sharp. Around him the hunters formed a loose ring: lean, ready, the kind of quiet that smelled like old woodsmoke and danger.

Briggs kept his voice low as he crossed the short space between them. "Everything's set in motion," he said. "Calder's agreed to tighten the lines. Thane's been nudged back into place, enough to keep him watching, not acting. Your window opens soon."

Vale didn't smile. "We move now?" he asked.

"Not tonight," Briggs replied. "Not yet. We go back to the bunker. Final preparations. Check your gear, sweep your sectors, and be ready to take positions when I give the word. We don't waste chances."

A low murmur ran through the group, approval, readiness, the small sound of men made steady.

Briggs glanced once toward the city walls, where the light still burned faint. "Rourke will be forced into our grasp when this is done," he said, the words flat as a verdict. "He won't have any choice. Either he helps us gain control, or we break whatever's left of him to make an example."

Vale's jaw tightened at the name. "You expect resistance."

"Expect everything," Briggs said. "Prepare for a crowd, prepared lies, and a few who would rather die than be governed. You make the crowd look like the danger. We make the law look like salvation."

Vale nodded once, short and hard. "We'll be ready."

Briggs watched as the group filed into the SUV, shoulders hunched against the rain, boots scraping on the slick pavement. One by one, they climbed inside, the doors thudding shut behind them. He lingered a moment longer, feeling the city tighten around him like a fist, then slid into the front passenger seat. The engine rumbled to life, headlights reflecting a shifting spectrum of colors from the aurora onto the pavement, chasing each other through the mist as the city watched in uneasy silence.

Chapter 27

They were in the library workshop when the knock came, single, polite, the kind that asked permission before it took a life. Elena and Kalen both looked up. The knock came again, softer.

Thane's silhouette filled the doorway. He didn't step inside at once; he waited on the threshold like a man who didn't want to risk the room's balance with his weight. His coat was damp, sleeves rolled, the faint dust of the city on his boots.

"Kalen," he said. No salutation, no orders.

Kalen rose. "Thane."

He closed the door behind him but didn't sit. He kept his hands folded, voice low. "I came because I can't watch it keep happening."

Elena's pen stopped moving. The clipboard lay face down between them like a small, private altar. Kalen felt the room tighten.

Thane looked at both as if measuring for a scale. "Mayor Calder's prescriptions are tearing the city apart," he said. "I've seen the curfews, the ration cuts, the checkpoints. People fear us now more than they are of what's out there."

He paused, eyes flicking to Elena to gauge reaction. "I'm not sure how much longer I can act like this is okay."

Kalen waited. Elena's jaw was a line. She didn't speak. They both watched Thane, feeling him out as if he might be bait.

"You're cautious," Kalen said finally. "Understandable."

Thane's mouth tightened. "I'm cautious because I have to be. I've been listening. I've been watching. I need to know if what I think is true, if there's a plan in motion that can save people instead of suffocating them." He looked at Kalen then, carefully. "That said, what can you tell me?"

For a moment Elena and Kalen exchanged that look they always shared, same thought, two ways of measuring risk. They could say nothing. They could push him away. Or they could admit enough to know he wasn't an enemy.

Kalen let out a breath. "You're right, Thane," he said. "There's chatter. Leadership forming. It's not just talk anymore." He kept his tone even, offering just the frame of it, not the wiring. "They have been trying to move quietly, gather people who can be trusted."

Thane's shoulders eased fractionally. He nodded once like a man taking a temperature. "I already have intel," he said. "Command channels, whispers. I've been told an uprising is imminent." He paused, searching their faces.

Elena looked at Kalen. He could see the decision in her eyes, the exact place where curiosity and caution met. She gave a micro-nod.

Thane's gaze dropped to Kalen's hands for a heartbeat, then lifted. He stood there a second longer, as if weighing the future against the present. Then he came straight out with it, voice steady and raw. "Listen, Rourke, whatever you've got cooking, I'll help. If it's in service to the city and its people, you have my word."

The words fell between them, small but heavy, an oath given in the quiet. Kalen felt something shift, as if a quiet current had finally found a channel.

They didn't celebrate. There was no cheering, no grand promises. Just the small, terrible relief of another person stepping to the same side of a line.

Thane glanced toward the door, then back at them. "I'll keep my movements clean. I don't go public until I know this won't burn more people than it saves."

Elena's fingers found the edge of the clipboard and tightened.

Thane's words lingered in the air, quiet but solid.

Elena broke the silence first. "What fronts are you willing to fight for?"

Thane frowned, caught off guard. "What do you mean?"

"I mean we're fighting more than one war," Elena said. "The city's starving. The mayor's locking us in. Briggs is building his army in plain sight. And now…" She hesitated, glancing at Kalen. "We have reason to believe the ferals may not be as mindless as everyone thinks. So, we're balancing all of that and trying to hold the city together while we learn what's actually happening to us."

Thane's brow tightened. "You're telling me you think they can be reasoned with?"

"No," Kalen said quietly. "We're saying we don't know yet. And until we do, we can't keep killing what might still be people."

The words hung heavy in the room.

Thane looked between them both, studying their faces as if waiting for one to blink. "You're juggling politics, rebellion, and science," he said. "That's not a battle; it's a death sentence."

Elena's tone didn't waver. "Maybe. But if we only pick one, we lose the others by default."

He was silent for a long moment. Then he nodded slowly, the decision turning behind his eyes.

"Alright," he said. "I'll play my part. Whatever front I'm needed on."

Elena watched him carefully. "We'll hold you to that."

Thane gave a small, humorless smile. "I expect you will."

He turned toward the door, Elena stopping him before he left. "Be back here by curfew, we have an experiment to conduct, and we could use your help if anything goes wrong."

Thane looked back at Elena, "I'll be here." And left the workshop.

They left the harbor before nightfall. The outer districts fell away behind them, giving to the peninsula's spine, where the road thinned, and the air grew strange.

The farther they went, the quieter it became. No echo of machinery, no hum of dampeners, just the distant breath of the water and the sigh of wind through rusted towers swallowed by moss. The storm clouds hung lower here, heavy and bruised, pressing what little light was left into narrow, shifting bands.

By the time they reached the clearing, the air had changed completely. It felt thinner somehow, less dense, less suffocating.

Elena stopped to check her meter. The readings flickered like a dying pulse. "We're far enough," she said. "No interference. No eyes. Just us now."

They chose the tree at the center of the clearing. It was ancient and scarred, its trunk veined with black metal where lightning had fused bark to storm. Kalen stood against it while Thane wound the chains tight around his chest and wrists. The cold bit deep, metal cutting at skin that already remembered restraint.

Elena moved with focus, not hesitation. Each sensor she attached gave a soft, precise click, temple, chest and spine. They each gave tiny pulses of light that bloomed under her fingertips.

"Last chance to back out," she said.

"I have to do this." He quietly muttered.

She nodded once, stepping away. Rissa stood by the generator case, Silas and Mercer formed a loose half-circle, and Thane stayed closest, the syringe of amber sedative steady in his hand.

Elena's gaze swept them all. "Everyone clear-headed? Once this starts, you don't get to waver. If anyone's emotions spike, it could push you past the threshold."

Rissa nodded first. Mercer's jaw tightened. Thane gave only silence, but his grip on the syringe spoke for him.

Satisfied, Elena turned to Kalen, lifting a syringe filled with pale blue fluid. "The amplifier will accelerate the process. You'll hit the threshold faster, but—"

Kalen cut her off with a shake of his head. "No."

She blinked. "No?"

"If I'm ever going to control it, I can't rely on a needle to wake it up. It has to be me."

Elena's lips parted, then closed again. Slowly, she lowered the syringe. "Then it's you and whatever's left inside," she said softly.

Kalen exhaled, breath steady despite the cold. "Get clear."

Kalen closed his eyes. The world began to narrow, his heartbeat in his ears. This was what he'd feared all along, what the storm might turn him into, His thoughts began to focus. Every breath felt borrowed, every memory alive. He wasn't afraid of what he'd see. He was afraid of feeling nothing at all.

He reached inward. Finding the Drawer tucked deep inside. It creaked open.

The first memory drifted out like smoke. Lily's laughter, bright and unbroken. She was spinning through their small apartment as morning light caught in her hair. He could hear her socks slide on the tile, the sound of her giggling just out of reach. His chest ached at the warmth of it, at the simple cruelty of remembering joy.

The glow under his skin flickered, soft at first.

The next memory slipped free before he could brace for it. Emily in the kitchen, sleeves rolled, sunlight slanting through broken blinds. She'd been humming a small, tired tune that didn't belong to hope but kept it alive anyway.
"We'll make it work," she'd said. *"We always do."*

The words hit him like shrapnel. His jaw clenched; light crawled up his throat. For a moment, everything held still. Time hung suspended. Echoes murmured in the distance, copper tang clinging to his mouth, every breath heavy with tension, the moment balanced between thunder and release.

Then came the ruin.

The scream. The roar of wind and tearing metal. The air turning blue. Lily's voice crying for him in the dark. His hands, bloody and shaking, digging through rubble for something that no longer answered back. The smell of ash. The taste of iron. The moment everything good had burned.

The light erupted from him, blue veins across skin, heartbeat pulsing like thunder.

Elena's voice cracked the distance. "Kalen, breathe! Don't let it take you."

Her voice grew quiet. "You're not the only one afraid of what you'll become."

Sorrow answered in his chest, cold and steady. But the drawer was wide open now.

He felt it instantly; the drawer wasn't big enough anymore.

Faces. The dead. The countless. The weight of every failure he'd carried. They poured out of him, each one stoking the resonance higher.

The air turned electric. The ground trembled. Lightning tore open the clouds, bleeding white fire through the sky.

Kalen screamed. The sound broke through the forest, raw and primal and too large for breath. The chains snapped, glass links shattering into the dirt. Blue light flooded the clearing, freezing a ring of glass around his feet.

Rissa threw her arm over her eyes. Mercer held her steady.

"Kalen!" Elena's voice barely carried over the storm. "Hold on—"

The scream broke into silence. For one fragile second, the world held its breath.

Then the storm changed.

The wind stilled. Frozen shards hung motionless in midair, caught in the pulse of light that poured from him. Through the haze, two figures began to form, blurred, wavering, impossible.

They sharpened.

Emily stood just ahead, her hair lifted by the still air. Lily's small hand clutched hers. Both were wrapped in soft, shifting blue light.

Kalen froze; breath caught in his chest. For a moment, the world narrowed to the impossible sight before him, grief and longing tangling in his throat. He felt the ache of memory, the fragile hope that maybe, just this once, the storm would give something back instead of taking.

He took a trembling step forward, afraid to break the spell.

Kalen's breath hitched. "Emily…"

She smiled, calm and kind, the way she had before everything ended. "You still talk like you're alone."

Lily's voice was clear and small, the same that had once cut through his worst days. "Daddy, don't cry."

Kalen fell to his knees. Pieces of the chain lay around him like discarded serpents. His claws receded, trembling hands half-himself again.

"You're not real," he whispered.

Emily stepped closer. "Does it matter?"

The storm bent around her voice.

"I promised I'd protect you," he said. Tears glowed where they fell, blue against the mud. "I failed you both."

Emily's voice softened. "You didn't fail. You loved us. You fought for us. You're still fighting."

"I don't know how to stop," he choked out. "The pain…it's all I have left."

"Don't stop," Emily said. "Carry it. That's how you keep us."

His chest heaved. The glow brightened again, then faltered, flickering like breath in a storm.

"If I let go, I lose you," he said. "If I hold on, I lose myself."

Emily knelt before him, her hand hovering near his cheek. "You're not lost, Kalen. You're finally learning to live with what's happened, learning that acceptance is a struggle, not surrender. The hurt doesn't vanish, but it doesn't have to consume you either."

Lily stepped forward, tiny fingers finding his hand. Her touch felt impossibly warm. "We're here, Daddy. We're always here."

The storm quieted to a hum. The trees no longer bent, they listened.

Kalen's voice came out raw. "I want to come home."

Emily smiled faintly, eyes bright. "You are home. Right here. Right now."

He looked at them both, light and life made from memory, and something inside him gave way. His body stilled. His claws vanished. The glow steadied, deepening to a pale, luminous white-blue color of sorrow accepted.

Emily's voice trembled through the quiet. "Let go of the guilt. Keep the love. That's how you survive."

Lily's voice joined hers, soft as wind through glass. "We love you, Daddy."

Light burst outward, not violent now, but warm and pure, flooding the clearing with radiance. The chains melted where they lay. Emily and Lily's forms began to fade, their edges dissolving into mist and light.

"I'm not done," Kalen whispered. "Not yet."

Emily's voice lingered, fading with the light. "That's why we're proud."

Then they were gone.

The clearing held its breath. Rain fell again, soft as dust. Kalen stayed on his knees, trembling, the white-blue glow still moving under his skin like veins of light.

No one moved.

Then Rissa broke from the tree line, sliding to her knees beside him. Her hands glowed faint white as she pressed them to his arms, sealing the burns where metal had cut deep. "Stay still," she murmured. "Just breathe."

The healing light spread through him, merging with the faint luminescence of his own.

Elena stepped forward, pale and shaken, her voice half a whisper. "He did it. He actually…" She couldn't finish.

Thane stood behind her, the unused syringe still in his hand. His expression was unreadable. "No," he said quietly. "I think he embodied it."

Kalen opened his eyes. The white-blue light shimmered. He looked up at them all, voice rough but sure. "I'm not done yet."

The wind had died. A gentle mist curled around the roots and trunks. The world seemed to listen.

The clearing stayed silent for a long time after the storm passed. Kalen sat with his back against the tree, breathing in shallow, even pulls. His skin still glowed faintly under the new white-blue light, soft and alive, pulsing in rhythm with his heartbeat.

Elena crouched nearby, datapad trembling in her hands. The graphs still flickered across the screen, half corrupted, half incomprehensible. She stared at the readings, lips parted, voice barely above a whisper. "This can't be right…"

Rissa stayed beside Kalen, still monitoring his vitals, the soft white of her healing fading from her palms. "He's stable," she said. "Barely, but… he's stable."

Silas stood apart from them, pacing the edge of the clearing. Every few seconds, he'd look back toward Kalen, then to Elena, like he wasn't sure which scared him more. "You all witnessed it. That wasn't just some surge, this was something else entirely. Not just resonance. Something alive."

"Energy," Rissa finished quietly.

Elena's voice was distant, analytical. "No... not just energy, something beyond that. His resonance changed states. The energy bent inward instead of scattering. It's like he reached an emotional singularity, grief balancing itself." She looked up from the pad, eyes wide and unsteady. "He stabilized a transformation through acceptance."

Thane stood with his arms crossed, the unused syringe still in his hand. "You're saying he didn't lose control because he *evolved*."

Elena nodded slowly. "Or redefined it. If these readings are even half right, he achieved the same emotional frequency as the storm."

Mercer let out a low whistle. "So he just proved we've been killing people who could have come back."

The words settled like weight in the air.

Kalen stirred, his voice rough but steady. "Maybe not most of them," he said. "But some." He looked up at them, eyes burning faintly with that quiet light. "We can't go on acting like we have all the answers about what's happening."

Elena exhaled, lowering the datapad. "Once we get back, I'll need to compare this to the city's resonance grid. If their sensors caught even a fraction of that surge…"

Thane finished for her. "Calder and Briggs will have questions. They'll want control."

Mercer crossed his arms. "And they'll use what happened here to tighten their grip on Veil Harbor. They'll call it containment. Safety."

Rissa frowned. "You're already thinking about politics?"

Silas turned on them, frustration cracking through the quiet. "We just watched him do something impossible, something that shouldn't exist in the first place, and survive it. You're telling me we could reverse what's happening to the world, and you're worried about who's in charge?" He pointed to the frozen ring of glass around Kalen's feet. "Forget Veil Harbor. Let's get out of here. Find somewhere we can figure this out before someone else decides to chain him up again."

No one answered right away.

Finally, Thane spoke, voice low but certain. "Because if we leave, Briggs wins."

Silas's glare cut toward him. "Briggs? You think that snake matters compared to this?"

Thane stepped closer, his tone like stone against steel. "You don't get it. He's not just a man anymore, he's a movement. He's convincing the settlements that emotion is the disease, that control is the cure. If we vanish now, he owns the story. He'll turn this," he gestured toward Kalen, "into proof that he's right."

Mercer nodded slowly. "He'll weaponize the fear. And Calder will hand him the city on a platter."

Elena looked between them, her voice sharpening with clarity. "And Veil Harbor isn't just a city anymore, Silas, it's a fulcrum. If Briggs consolidates here, every other enclave will follow his doctrine. We can't let that happen."

Rissa's tone was soft but certain. "If we run, the world likely becomes exactly what we're trying to stop."

Kalen flexed his fingers, feeling the faint hum beneath his skin, the pulse of grief turned to resolve. "Then we stay," he said quietly. "We protect the truth until we can prove it. Then we fight for it."

Silas's jaw tightened, his anger cooling to exhaustion. "And if we can't?"

Elena met his eyes. "Then we make sure no one else dies in ignorance."

For a moment no one spoke. Only the soft rain and the low buzz from the equipment filled the clearing.

Thane finally slipped the syringe into his belt. "Then we're agreed," he said. "We need to move before the city's scanners pick up what just happened. Whatever that surge was, it didn't go unnoticed."

Elena turned toward the horizon where the mist was beginning to lift, revealing the faint silhouette of Veil Harbor's walls.

"Then let's get back," she said quietly. "We have no time to waste."

Rissa helped Kalen to his feet. The glow beneath his skin dimmed but didn't fade.

He looked at each of them, Elena's steady focus, Thane's wary calm, Silas's restless fire, Rissa's quiet hope. For the first time, he didn't feel alone inside what he'd become.

He nodded once. "We can't undo what happened," he said. "So, let's make it mean something."

Chapter 28

The old library workshop still carried the scent of leather and aged wood, with a faint trace of burnt circuitry haunting the beams overhead. In the corner, the generator throbbed with a weary pulse, struggling to disguise its impending failure. Elena's hands shook once, then steadied as she sealed the last weld on the gauntlet's housing. Blue crystal veins pulsed through the metal like veins under skin.

Kalen sat on the edge of the worktable, wrist wrapped in new bandage, still feeling the echo of the ring test from two days ago. His bones no longer buzzed, but something inside him did, a quiet certainty that refused to sleep.

Outside, the city's power grid flickered between districts, patches of light breathing in and out across the skyline. It looked like Veil Harbor was dreaming of staying alive.

Elena wiped sweat from her brow and set the gauntlet down beside him.
"It's ready," she said. "Channel's aligned, feedback damped. You'll feel everything that comes through, but you'll get to choose what to do with it."

He slid his hand inside. The fit was close, cold at first, then warming until the crystal seams caught his pulse.

Light crawled along the ridges in soft rhythm, blue, then white, then blue again. For the first time since the pit, the current didn't fight him; it listened.

Mercer leaned over the map spread across the table. The lamplight caught in the lines of his face, carving out wear and command.

"Curfews just increased citywide," he said. "The mayor's folded. Food rations cut again. People are scared, and scared people make noise."

He tapped the harbor district. "That's where we hold. Church at Saint Ronan's keeps the wounded under cover. Everyone else funnels through Dock Five. No heroics. We keep the pulse steady until dawn."

Rissa checked her rifle, the movement precise, practiced. "The underground's ready. Dock crews, market runners, even half the old guard. They've had enough talk; they want something real."

Silas perched on a crate, twirling a stripped screw between his fingers. "Real's about to hurt. Hunters were seen in the east quarter, three squads. Vale's leading one."

The room went still for half a breath.

Thane came in last, coat damp from the rain. He didn't speak. He didn't need to. Everyone could read the warning in the way he held his shoulders.

Kalen asked anyway. "Movement?"

"Convoy on the bridge," Thane said. "Heavy transport. No insignia, but the pattern's military. Briggs's kind of military."

The name landed like pressure.
Elena's jaw tightened. "You're sure?"

"Sure enough," Thane said. "He's back."

Elena slammed the wrench she'd been holding onto the table. The sound cracked the quiet.
"Of course he's back now," she said. "We were days from stable containment. The feral transition trials, if we stop them, we lose every data window we've got. Every person still half-wild out there? They stay that way."
Her voice shook, not from fear but from fury. "We built this to stop people from dying like animals, and now we get to watch it happen again because one man can't stand a world he doesn't control."

Mercer's reply was low, deliberate. "If we stay underground, the trials won't matter. There won't be anyone left to treat."

Elena pressed her palms to the table until her knuckles whitened, breathing hard through her teeth. "Doesn't make it feel any less like failure."

Kalen watched the light from the gauntlet pulse across her fingers. "It isn't failure," he said quietly. "It's triage."

That broke the silence's edge. Mercer exhaled through his nose, the closest he ever came to agreement. "Then we move," he said. "No one else dies in cages."

No one argued. They moved through the silence like gears catching, each to their own ritual: checking seals, counting ammunition, tightening straps that had already been tightened. The noise of preparation was its own language, the kind that measured trust in inches.

Kalen flexed his hand inside the gauntlet. The metal breathed with him, the light syncing to every heartbeat. He felt the storm under his ribs shift, slow and deliberate, like an animal turning over in its sleep.

Rissa looked up from her weapon. "You good?"

He nodded once. "Good enough."

Mercer folded the map and slid it into his coat. "We hit the harbor core at dawn tomorrow. Elena runs the grid. Rissa handles perimeter. Silas, backup on power. Thane keeps comms alive. Kalen—"
He met his eyes. "You hold the line. If Briggs wants the city, he'll have to walk through you."

Kalen didn't answer right away. Outside, thunder rolled somewhere beyond the docks, too slow to be weather. He lifted the gauntlet, the glow painting his scarred fingers in blue fire.

"Then we make sure he doesn't."

Rain bled down the glass. In the distance, sirens began to rise, faint and far apart, like a heartbeat learning its rhythm.

The rain hadn't stopped, just thinned into a fine, needling mist that turned the streetlamps to halos. Veil Harbor looked half-drowned, the gutters running silver with runoff and the smell of rust.

Kalen stood under the broken awning of the library's side entrance, watching the city breathe in uneven rhythm. Somewhere deep in the industrial wards, a transformer blew; the sound rolled through the skyline like slow thunder.

Rissa slipped up beside him, rifle slung low. "South watch says the docks are filling. Curfew hit and everyone panicked. Market runners, families, soldiers who don't know whose orders count anymore."

"They'll move toward the church," he said.

"Yeah. Everyone does, sooner or later." She kept her eyes on the skyline. "They think if they get close enough to you, it means something."

He didn't know what to do with that, so he didn't answer. The city lights flickered again, and for a heartbeat he could almost see the pulse running under the streets, the hidden rhythm of the storm's energy trying to stay alive beneath all the dampeners.

Behind them, the workshop door creaked open and Elena stepped out, coat thrown over her shoulders, hair damp from steam and rain. She looked like someone who'd forgotten what rest was.

"Comms are unstable," she said. "The storm is too dense here, too many frequencies."

Thane's voice came through the doorway, low and steady: "That convoy's not just soldiers. Military transports, yes, but I counted two containment trucks."

Elena froze. "Containment? Here?"

"Painted over Ministry markings. You can still see the edges under the new plates."

Her jaw set hard. "He's restarting his experiments."

Kalen felt his stomach twist. "He wouldn't risk that inside the city."

Thane's eyes stayed on the street, rain sliding off the brim of his hood. "I know his type. He won't stop until he gets what he wants."

The mist thickened, the light cutting through it in warped cones. Down the block, a cluster of citizens hurried past a checkpoint where militia held rifles angled low, not hostile, not friendly, just waiting.

Rissa cursed under her breath. "This place is one spark from burning."

Elena turned toward Kalen, voice sharp with something close to desperation. "If he activates those trucks, the resonance field will cascade. Half the city could go feral before we even reach them."

Kalen looked back toward the harbor, where the cranes rose like rusted bones against the glow. "We have to move first. I'm not sure what those pillars are for but it can't be good."

Mercer's voice carried from inside the door. "We don't move blind. We map the grid first. If Briggs is rerouting energy through the coils again, we'll walk straight into his choke point."

Elena's hands were shaking, not from fear, but from the weight of too many choices. "If we don't move, we lose every chance to stop him before the first test fires."

Rissa cut in, quiet but fierce. "And if we move too early, we lose everyone else. Why can't we catch a break."

The argument didn't rise; it just deepened. Everyone knew there was no right answer.

Kalen watched the mist drift across the ruined boulevard, the light bending through it. He could feel the city's pulse faltering. The gauntlet on his arm warmed, responding to the vibrations under the pavement.

"Listen," he said. The word came out softer than he meant. "Whatever he's doing, it's already started. Every second we wait, he digs in deeper."

Elena met his eyes. There was no anger left, only tired understanding. "Then tell me where to start."

He pointed toward the docks, where the glow of generators stained the fog orange. "The harbor core. That's his anchor. We break that, we cut the feed."

Rissa exhaled. "Then we'd better get moving."

Mercer stepped out from the doorway, pulling his hood up. "We move in two hours. I'll signal the underground to start clearing the lower streets. Keep it quiet until we hit."

They dispersed without another word. Boots splashed through puddles. Gear clicked. Rain softened every sound until it felt like the city itself was holding its breath.

Kalen stayed a moment longer under the awning, eyes on the shifting glow over the harbor. Thunder rumbled again, closer this time, though the sky hadn't flashed.

He whispered, "One way or another, it will end here." The air seemed to answer. The storm that had been sleeping above Veil Harbor began to stir.

By midday, Veil Harbor felt like a city waiting for a verdict. The rain stopped, but the air carried that dense quiet that comes when something larger than weather is deciding what happens next.

Kalen moved through the market lanes, boots splashing in shallow puddles, nodding to dock workers who watched him with wary hope. The militia patrols were tighter now, rifles slung low, eyes scanning faces for the first hint of trouble. No one spoke above a whisper.

A market runner slipped past a checkpoint, shoving a loaf of bread into a child's hands before vanishing into the fog. At the edge of the square, a soldier hesitated, his rifle lowered. He looked at Kalen, then away, and for a moment it was clear he wasn't sure which side he was on.

Someone painted a symbol on the wall behind the ration line, a blue line, a broken circle. The paint was still dripping when another hand added to it, quick and nervous, widening the mark into something clearer. Two children pointed. A woman covered her mouth to hide a smile.

Kalen reached the church, and with one final reassuring breath, he walked inside to the waiting resistance.

Inside the church, the air was heavy with candle smoke and damp clothes. Elena and Rissa checked supplies, lanterns, bandages, what little water they had left. Silas lingered near the doors, trading quiet words with the old guard.
"If this is the end of the world," he murmured, "at least the pews are comfortable."
No one laughed.

Rissa knelt beside a wounded boy whose veins still shimmered faintly blue. His mother stared at the stain spreading through the bandage. "He was only near the docks," she whispered. "Just walking home."
The boy's eyes rolled. Rissa's voice stayed calm, but her hands shook as she held the compress.

Mercer came in from the rain, coat dripping. He unfolded a scrap of paper, read it twice, then fed it to the candle flame. "Hunters at the power station," he said quietly. "Vale's leading them."

A ripple went through the room, not fear exactly, but recognition. Briggs had already moved his first piece.

Thane crossed the nave without a sound, giving orders in short phrases, redirecting patrols, sending runners with messages small enough to hide in a palm. When he reached the doors, he paused and looked up. The clouds were thick with green and violet threads, the kind that meant the storm was close enough to taste.

Elena bent over the radio again, static hissing in her ear. "Nothing yet," she murmured, though her eyes kept sliding to the windows. "If he's on the bridge, we'll see the reflection before we hear the engines."

The church was too quiet. Families huddled in pews. Children drew those same blue symbols on scraps of paper and pressed them to the walls when their parents weren't watching. Old men whispered about the convoy crossing the bridge, the words passing from mouth to mouth like a secret curse. The tension was everywhere: in the walls, in the way people flinched at every creak, in the way no one quite breathed until a siren finished its call.

Kalen sat near the altar, the gauntlet heavy on his wrist, its glow pulsing in time with the storm outside. He watched the families, their small movements, the way they clung to one another. He felt every promise he'd made settle like weight across his chest.

The silence pressed. We're running out of time, he thought. Every hour we wait, someone else turns, someone else disappears. He could feel the resonance under his ribs start to hum, a steady, dangerous rhythm. He breathed slow, forcing it down. Stillness hurt more than fighting ever had.

Elena joined him, voice low. "Grid's holding. No surge yet. Briggs is close, but not here."

He nodded, jaw tight. "Keep everyone calm. We move when the signal comes."

Mercer leaned close, voice a dry whisper. "The underground's ready. Dock Five's clear. If Briggs locks us down, we move fast."

Rissa checked her rifle, eyes on the windows. "They're scared," she said, "but they're listening. If you speak tonight, they'll follow."

Kalen looked out across the nave. The lanterns burned low, casting long, trembling shadows. "I'll speak when it's time," he said. "Not before."

Outside, thunder rolled, closer now, slow and deliberate. The lamps flickered.
Every heart in Veil Harbor waited, caught between fear

and recognition, ready to decide which one to listen to when the storm finally spoke.

The bells of Saint Ronan's groaned in the wind, their hollow notes rolling through the rain like breaths pulled from the sky.

Inside, the church was packed wall to wall with bodies slick with sweat and rain, faces lit by the thin, trembling glow from within.

Color rippled through the crowd, blue along arms, gold in eyes, red in clenched fists. The light was faint at first, the pulse of it uncertain. But it grew with every heartbeat, painting the walls in shifting hues until the whole nave seemed to breathe.

Kalen stepped to the altar, the gauntlet on his wrist thrumming like a second pulse. He looked out at them, the broken, the waiting, the ones who'd lost everything except the strength to stand. For a long moment he couldn't speak.

When he finally did, his voice was rough, low, honest.

"There isn't a single person here who hasn't lost something to the storm, not one of us who can't feel that pressure inside, pressing out, trying to break through."

The eyes in the room glanced at the floor, remembering.

"At first, I let the pain and anger inside me claw at whatever was left of my conscience. I built walls, not to protect, but just to keep everyone out, to isolate myself in the quiet comfort of self-pity. For too long, I let bitterness shape what I saw in the world, pushing away those who tried to reach me."

He paused for a moment, watching a tapestry of colors light up the room.

"Somewhere along the way, we let those walls become barriers to keep the world out instead of tools to reshape it. And now, look at us, gathered here, not to hide, but to decide who we want to be."

Kalen met eyes with Rissa, a genuine smile spreading across her face, hope flickering to life. He continued, "We've survived by adapting, by enduring what we had to, but we can't trade our hearts for safety, or our convictions for scraps of comfort. We fight not just to exist, but to stay true to ourselves, to keep our light burning even when the storm tries to snuff it out. This is our chance to choose what kind of world we build next."

He turned a slow circle, the crowd catching its reflection in him.

"We've been told to stay small. To keep our heads down. To survive quietly while the sky decides who deserves tomorrow.

But survival isn't living. Breathing isn't living. Living
is *choosing.*
And if choice is the only freedom we have left, then
it's worth dying for."

The air stirred. The colors brightened. A woman near
the front drew a blue line across her cheek with
trembling fingers. Someone else did the same. Then
another.

Kalen's voice found its weight.

"They built a world out of fear. They told us safety
meant silence, that order meant obedience. But there's
no order in chains, only quiet rot.
And fear? Fear is the oldest lie there is.
Fear says you can't. Fear says you're alone. Fear says
you have no choice. Well, I've lived long enough
inside that lie to know one thing:
fear dies the second we stop listening."

The crowd shifted closer. The glow climbing the walls
reached the ceiling, swirling in slow motion, blending
color into light.

"We can't rebuild what was. The old world's gone.
Maybe it needed to be. But what comes next, what we
build now, has to mean more than just surviving the
storm.
It must mean feeling again. Caring again. Trusting
each other enough to bleed and still keep standing."

His voice cracked, but he didn't hide it.

"I don't have all the answers. I'm scared, same as you.
But I know this: the world out there doesn't get to tell
us who we are anymore.
We get to decide that, right here, right now."

The thunder outside rolled closer, deep and slow, as if
the sky were leaning in to listen. The colors in the
room began to merge until faces were no longer
separate, just shapes in a shared light.

Kalen raised his arm. The gauntlet flared.

"Maybe the storm will swallow us. Maybe the next
dawn never comes. But if this is where we make our
stand, then let it be the place where fear finally breaks.
Let the world remember that we were here, that we
chose to build again.
Inch by inch. Breath by breath. Together."

He pounded his fist against his chest. "Together!"

A voice echoed him. Then another. Then the whole
church.

"Together!"

The sound became a pulse, the color a wave. The light
blazed upward, blinding white, bursting through the
stained glass in a rain of molten color. Outside,

lightning tore the sky open and struck the spire like a vow.

Kalen stood at the altar, chest heaving, tears cutting lines through the soot on his face. "Out there, they want to use this storm to control us, to enslave us," he said softly. "Let's remind them that humanity can still exist, even when we're no longer quite human."

The bells of Saint Ronan's swung again, this time not from the wind, but from the roar that rose beneath them.

The city was awake.
And for the first time in a long time, it was alive.

The chant still thundered through Saint Ronan's long after Kalen fell silent.
"Together!"—the word shook the walls, rolled down the nave, and broke out into the rain like a wave that had finally found the shore.

The bells above swung wild, their deep bronze throats booming over the roar of a thousand voices. The stormlight that had filled the church spilled into the street, color washing over stone, over glass, over faces that had forgotten how to lift their eyes.

Kalen stepped through the shattered archway, the night bursting open around him.
Rain hissed against hot stone. The air crackled with

energy. Behind him, the crowd poured out, their footsteps a heartbeat rolling through the square. The broken circle symbol glowed on walls and doors, drawn in ash and chalk and blood. Lanterns rose, blue and gold, until the whole city seemed to burn from within.

He turned slowly, taking in the sight. The fear that had lived in these streets for months was gone, washed clean by something louder, rougher, alive.

Rissa pushed through the crush beside him, rain streaming down her face. "You did it," she said. Her smile was fierce, almost defiant.

Kalen shook his head. "We did."

Mercer came next, coat torn, soot streaked down his cheek. "The whole grid's lighting up," he said. "They'll know."

"Good," Kalen answered.

Elena's voice crackled from the handheld radio at his belt, static biting through the words. "Power fluctuations across the docks. I'm reading multiple surges. Someone's trying to lock it down."

Kalen looked east. Beyond the smoke and rooftops, the horizon flared white, not lightning, spotlights. The low thump of engines followed, steady and cold.

Rissa cursed. "They're coming."

Kalen didn't flinch. The gauntlet on his wrist glowed once, a slow pulse, steady as a drumbeat. Around them, the chant swelled again, louder now, no longer uncertain. The echo of it traveled through the streets like a living thing.

Somewhere far off, a gunshot cracked. The crowd froze for half a breath. Then, as if answering itself, the chant rose higher, drowning it out.

Mercer's voice was quiet. "You just woke the city."

Kalen watched the rain shimmer against the stormlight, the color bending back toward the church like the world itself was breathing in. The bells above and the distant sirens began to ring in the same rhythm.

He drew in one deep breath, the kind that carries both faith and finality.

Thunder rolled across Veil Harbor, heavy enough to shake the ground. Lanterns flickered. The light in the clouds tightened, as if the sky were bracing.

The first convoy lights appeared at the edge of the river. The storm's answer had come.

Chapter 29

The convoy came on like a slow idea.

Engines low, lights hooded, tires whispering over the last slick boards of the river bridge. Rain fell in long, even threads, the kind that didn't bother to drum, just pressed. Veil Harbor lay ahead in a hush that wasn't peace so much as exhaustion. Here and there, color still clung to windows and puddles, stray afterglow from the church's outcry. It ran off the stone in pale veins and died in the gutters.

General Darren Briggs stood braced in the open door of the lead transport, one gloved hand on the frame, coat tugged backward by the wind. He watched the city without narrowing his eyes, the way you watch a wound: not for what hurts, but for what needs cutting.

"Two minutes," said the driver.

Briggs didn't answer. The rain gathered at the crease of his brow and slid off like everything else. Behind him, the column stretched across the span: trucks with sealed housings, signal vans with their antennae furled like sleeping herons, the flatbed bearing the regulator case that thrummed through the wood of the bridge. Men rode quietly, mouths set. They had learned not to fill silence around him.

Emotion has risen beyond tolerance, said the voice inside his head, no louder than a breath, no warmer than glass. *Correction is required.*

"Correction," Briggs said, almost under his breath. "Yes."

He stepped down as the tires kissed stone. The shore took the weight of the column; it took the weight of him. Soldiers flanked the street, helmets down, visors up against the rain, not snapping to attention, not calling out. Their respect was not noise.

"Perimeter," he said.

Vale met him at the harbor, rain slick on the black of his coat. He nodded once and lifted two fingers. Orders moved down the line with the grace of practiced memory. Teams peeled off into the alleys without clatter. The world closed around them and did not complain.

Briggs walked.

He did not stride; he did not stalk. He moved with the care of a surgeon crossing a field to a table. Water made mirrors of the ruts. In them, his face appeared and broke apart and came back again.

Veil Harbor had always been stubborn. It did not beg. It did not weep. It only resisted until whoever pressed on it got tired. He had not been born with the flaw that tired easily.

A banner lay torn across a broken bench: a circle, closed now, drawn in blue. Someone had pressed a palm to it and smeared the paint with the heel of a hand. Footsteps ran over the mark and away in ten directions. He placed his boot through the ruin of the circle and kept going.

Compassion misapplied is recursion, the voice observed. *It reproduces its failure infinitely.*

"Compassion," Briggs said, as if testing a tooth. "We have tried that."

There was a memory he'd long kept buried. The image of a metal bed lingered—his wife's lips vivid in the lamplight as she struggled for breath, the sickness in her chest, something deeper than fever. Beyond the walls, the storm battered the window, relentless, as if determined to finish what it had begun.

He had held his ground between his family and the world outside, palms raised, taking a stance like a man called to testify. But there was no one left to bear witness.

He walked past a door hanging by one hinge, past a bar whose sign had let go of its last screw, past a stall where a rack of fish lay silver in the rain. No one came out to meet him. The city had already met him once. From an alley mouth, two figures watched, one with a bandaged forearm bright beneath the rain, the other clutching a coil of wire. When his gaze touched them, they became brick and shadow again.

At the base of the municipal steps, Vale set his hand on the rail, waiting for a nod that came without looking.

"Coils?" Briggs asked.

"Primed," Vale said. "We have lines on the grid. The regulator is stable enough. The east bank will be the first to feel it."

"Good," Briggs replied. "We start at the wound's edge and move in."

He didn't glance back at the bridge. The river would hold. It always had. It would even hold the weight of what he was about to do.

The doors of City Hall swung open, drawn back by a soldier. Inside, the light was sharp white, unwavering, unconcerned. He stepped across the threshold as if crossing into the answer of his own command.

Begin sanitation, the voice murmured, almost kindly.

"Soon," Briggs smiled. "We will do this cleanly."

The corridor's echo did not belong to footsteps. It belonged to years. Old paint, scrim of dust, a line on the plaster where some previous glory had hung. The generators in the basement spoke an even hum into the bones of the building. The sound pleased him. It was a future speaking through a wall.

He took the corner into the mayor's study alone and closed the door behind him with a soft click of habit. The room smelled of lemon oil and paper. Rain silvered the tall panes and made the city appear through ripples, as if Veil Harbor were underwater and men were looking down at it from a boat.

The regulator case sat on the long table like a coffin with no lid. Six housings. Six dials. The faintest suggestion of breath in the way the filaments glowed. He placed his hand on the metal and felt heat through the glove. It felt like the first time he had pressed a palm to a fever and known how it would end.

"You weren't wrong," he said, not to the regulator. "You never are."

Incorrect. I am frequently wrong, said the voice. *But I am never sentimental.*

Briggs almost laughed. The sound reached the corners of the room and came back improved.

"Is that the difference," he asked softly, "between gods and men?"

I am not a god, the voice said. *I am a conclusion. You came to me because you were already there.*

He let the quiet sit. The rain made each window a lid. The city waited under them like a patient on a table.

"When the sky broke," he said, "we were given too much proof of what feeling can do when it outruns mind. Love made men carry their families into the storm because they could not watch them die in the dark. Rage set neighborhoods alight so that no one had to live under another's roof. Mercy kept the sick on our pillows long enough to take the rest of us down with them. We told ourselves these were virtues. They were accelerants."

Emotion is energy, Sovereign replied. *Unbounded, it becomes heat. Heat becomes fire. Fire consumes. You require a system that holds energy without combustion.*

"And you are the system," Briggs said.

No. You are. Your hands. Your voice. Your willingness to be despised for being correct.

He stood with his fingers resting lightly on the levers. The room looked like a chapel only because he had decided it did. The dials could have been candles if candles admitted they were instruments.

"When I was a young man," he said, "I believed in failure. I thought we were allowed it. I thought there was time to learn by breaking things and then forgiving ourselves. And then the world ended slowly and did not forgive. I adjusted my theology."

He breathed out like a man praying and did not use that word.

"Stillness," he said. "The hour before the surgeon cuts. The silence at the top of the inhale before a diver goes under. The rest between movements where the audience holds its breath. That is the only mercy I have left. I will give it to them. I will make them hold their breath together until the fever breaks."

They will hate you, the voice said. *They will carve you out of their stories.*

"They can," Briggs said. "Stories are the softest thing we have. I prefer stone."

He thought of the church. Stones had a way of remembering better than worship. If the building had an opinion about the hour, it would hold it. He did not resent the people who had filled it with light. It had been pretty. But pretty was the last expression of sickness in a terminal course.

On the far wall, a mirror held a second city. In it, the skylight had a crack he hadn't noticed in the glass. He watched rain find that line like a pilgrim finding a road.

Vale knocked once and waited before entering. He put a roll of maps on the table and unscrolled them with hands that did not twitch.

"Grids," he said. "Traffic. Residual flares. The docks still breathe."

"Not for long," Briggs said.

Vale looked at him with the flat black of a man who has stepped beyond asking if this is right. He had asked once. He liked the answer and taken it as a standing order.

"You will announce to the men," Briggs said. "No anomalies in conduct. No theater. No voices raised. If you are required to fire, you fire once. Anything unfinished is an insult to what we are doing."

"Yes, sir," Vale said.

Briggs waited until the door closed again. The regulator case hummed through his wrist bones. Everything in the room had moved a fraction closer to a single note.

The organism anticipates correction, Sovereign said. *The field is crowded. The probability of collateral conversion is high.*

"Collateral," he repeated. "We will call it that. And I will remember every face. I'm not as pure as you. I am old enough to carry names."

Then carry them, Sovereign said, untroubled. *They weigh nothing in the sum.*

He thought of the boy whose face he had seen in a file three days ago, veins lit with borrowed light, asleep with his mother's hand on his chest. He had written two words in the margin of the report, too late, and closed it.

He set his palm flat on the table until the heat came up through the nerves and made a small trembling he refused to give a name. He had always trusted his hands to tell him when it was time.

It was almost time. He let his hand hover above the nearest lever and, only once, felt the urge to lift it back into place, to give the city one more breath. The impulse passed like a ripple through glass. He did not indulge it.

The mayor entered like a song from another season, brisk, bright, a little too pleased with its own melody. His slicked hair shone under the white light. His shoes clicked on the parquet as if floors were still a thing that listened to men like him.

"General," he said, going straight for the window. "Do you hear them? They roar and think it makes them real. It makes them visible." He spread his fingers on the glass, an old man's vanity in the way he framed the city in his hands. "But noise tells on you. It shows your position."

Briggs did not turn to look. He seldom warmed men by facing them.

"Noise is what happens before understanding," he said. "It is not the understanding itself."

The mayor laughed softly, like a man remembering applause. "You and I understand each other," he said. "You bring the discipline. I bring the legitimacy. Together we move this ruin back into the shape of a city."

"Shape," Briggs agreed. "Yes. That is the word."

The mayor poured two drinks from a heavy cut-glass decanter. The bottles had survived because men like him had carried them out of basements when houses flooded.

"To quiet," he said, holding one out.

"I don't drink." Briggs looked at the glass. He had once. The memory was so old it had good manners not to tug.

The mayor took both, then set one untouched on the sill and sipped the other, eyes half-closed.

"They will love us for this," he said. "They will not say it. But watch, watch how quickly a man will sleep when you take the decision out of his fists."

Briggs said nothing. He adjusted one dial by a notch.

The vibration in the floor deepened. It could have been a trick of storm pressure. It was not. The regulator's filaments brightened until the room's white altered, less pallor, more intent. Through the panes, the city seemed to draw in its light and hold it close to its ribs.

"They are making marks," the mayor said into the glass, fogging it briefly with the warmth of his breath. He wiped the circle away with his sleeve. "Children with chalk. Men with ash. As if drawing something makes it live. You will teach them the difference between a picture of a door and a door."

"Pictures are better than doors," Briggs said.

The mayor glanced back, startled into a first honest look. "How so?"

"Pictures do not admit weather," he replied. "Doors always leak."

The mayor blinked at that as if trying to decide if he had been complimented or corrected. He settled on compliment.

"You speak like scripture," he said. "They will write you down."

"I prefer stone," Briggs said again.

From somewhere lower in the building, a hallway door slammed and then apologized. The vibration arrived a half-second later, the way thunder follows heat. Vale, back with the whisper of movement that meant decisions had been made and obeyed, took up a position near the table. He did not touch the holster when he stood there, but his hands hung near it the way a mechanic's hands hang near tools that have learned to work with them. His trigger finger lay straight along the frame; the knuckle whitened, then eased. He breathed once, shallow and controlled.

"Bridges sealed," Vale said. "Units in place along the river. The power station yields to remote."

"Yields," the mayor echoed. "Wonderful verb."

Briggs looked at him then, finally, and with nothing in his face but attention.

"You are pleased," he said.

"I am restored," the mayor corrected, and for three words he almost was, the man he had been in a sash on the day a ribbon was cut on a water plant that had functioned for two summers. His smile slid over to Briggs and clung there. "You see, General? They can be brought to heel with care."

"Care," Briggs repeated, making a weight of it. He let the word sit between them until it found its level and then he brushed it aside with the back of his hand. "No," he said. "Not care. Calibration."

He stepped from the table to the window, not close enough that the mayor could mistake it for companionship. The rain had thinned to a fine grain. In the grain, light gathered and let go, repeatedly, as if the city were practicing breathing.

"You are about to do something historic," the mayor went on, speaking to the glass as if the glass would bear witness. "You will end a riot with a single note. That is art."

"Art is indulgence," his voice lowered, "this is medicine. Hold still."

The mayor swallowed the last of his drink and set the tumbler down too hard. Crystal rang around the room, an honest sound that didn't know it wasn't welcome. He opened his mouth, perhaps to say that history would put their names beside each other on a plaque.

The hum rose a fraction. Briggs glanced at the nearest dial and made no corrections.

Field density increasing, Sovereign said. *Conversion threshold: observable.*

Briggs did not nod, but something in his jaw acknowledged. He watched the river's surface quiver in a pattern that had nothing to do with wind. In the alley nearest the steps, a man turned his head sharply as if a thought had brushed his ear.

The mayor's posture changed by a finger's width. It is possible to see the exact moment a man realizes the story he is in is not the one he cast himself in. Briggs had learned to look for it so he could spare speeches.

"What is that?" the mayor said. It came out merrier than he meant, because panic often puts on its old coats.

"Resonance," Briggs stated. "Aligned."

The mayor touched his throat without meaning to. His fingers came away clean. He smiled and almost relaxed. Then the light under his skin turned silver, as if a small coin had been pressed beneath it long ago and had decided to show itself at last.

Briggs stepped back from the glass and returned his hand to the levers. The room did not get smaller. It simply admitted less air.

"We will proceed," he said.

Vale's answer was the smallest of movements. The mayor's hand tightened on the sill until the knuckles blanched and then, in a soft, private motion, his legs forgot how to conspire with his spine.

Rain went on falling in the careful way of a thing that could not be hurried. The regulator case shed a little heat into the study until perspiration found the line of Briggs's temple and stopped there. He did not wipe it.

"General," the mayor said, and in his voice, there was a child who had not been in the room a moment before. "Is this, this is normal, yes? The feeling in the chest?"

Briggs did not lie. "It is expected."

"Good," the mayor relaxed, and smiled like a man at a bad dinner who has decided to be pleasant.

Under his skin, a fine cobweb of light stitched across his jaw and down into his necktie. The tie darkened as if it had been dipped in mercury. He lifted two fingers and watched the tendons stand out like wires.

"Vale," Briggs said, in the same tone he might have used to ask for a pencil.

Vale's hand fell to his side, not yet to the weapon. He would wait for the word he knew would come. Briggs admired restraint wherever it showed itself. It cost more than courage and bought more in return. Vale's eyes flicked once to the mayor, then to Briggs, asking a question with no air in it. The answer was the set of Briggs's jaw.

The mayor found breath enough for one more confidence. "They will love us," he said again, and might have said it a thousand times then if the note in the floor had not deepened into something that asked men to be quiet while the doctor came in with clean hands.

Briggs laid his fingertips across the metal. The levers were cool. The room smelled of metal and lemon and rain and something that lived in hospitals.

"Now," he said.

Vale did not move. The mayor did. He rose onto his toes as if the floor had come up beneath him and stalled, mouth open in a sound that had not been invented yet. The silver in him brightened until his color had to step out of the way. He turned toward Briggs with bright eyes that did not know what they were looking at.

"Now," Briggs said again, not to Vale this time.

Proceed, Sovereign breathed.

Briggs closed his hand around the first lever and found it where it had been waiting all along. He did not pull.

Not yet. He let the weight of it settle into his grip, the way a surgeon lays a blade against skin to feel the temperature of what will open. His thumb hovered the width of a breath. Doubt rose and thinned, a filament stretched to breaking. He pressed it flat.

Outside, somewhere very far and very near, the city held its breath.

The buzz from the coils had become weather. It filled every room, a vibration rather than a sound. Dust rose from the floorboards and hung suspended in the light like waiting rain. Vale stood by the console, one hand hovering near the regulator as if it might bite.

Briggs measured each breath. He felt the building's frame answering him, steel, stone, air, all caught in the same chord. The mayor's reflection jittered in the windowpane, silver veins crawling through the image like cracks in ice.

Sovereign's voice rang out in his head. *"All variables converge. The equation holds."*

Briggs whispered solemnly, "Then let the world be still."

The click of the first lever was small, almost polite. The lights dimmed once, twice, then steadied in a pallid, lunar glow. The air went thin. Even the rain slowed, falling in perfect vertical lines.

Vale glanced over, waiting for a command that would finish the thought. Briggs gave a single nod.

Outside, the sky began to draw itself inward, clouds folding around six rising columns of light that speared upward from the districts. The city had been given its signal.

The resonance built until it pressed against the skin. Paper lifted off desks, maps curled, the smell grew sweet. The mayor stumbled to the window, murmuring something about beauty and control. The silver tracing his veins brightened; his silhouette in the glass blurred. Across the square below, a scarf rose from a woman's shoulders and hung in the air as if remembered there.

Briggs did not look away. He saw the reflection bend and collapse back into light. For a heartbeat, the entire room was white, too bright for color, too complete for sound.

When vision returned, the mayor was crumpled on the floor. Half turned, color fading. Vale's sidearm hung loose in his hand, barrel smoking. The single report still echoed somewhere in the rafters. His wrist trembled once, no more than a shiver of air, then steadied. He did not look at the man. He looked at Briggs, waiting to be told what this meant.

Outside, the six beams widened, touching at the center of the sky. A pulse of silver radiated outward through the clouds and down into the harbor. Every building, every flooded street caught the sheen. The noise of the city vanished, replaced by a single low note that rolled out over the water. Lightning climbed the spire and never struck; the rain forgot how to fall and hovered like breath waiting to be released.

Briggs whispered, "Peace."

Sovereign's reply came as a vibration through the walls. *Correction complete. Entropy contained.*

He stepped closer to the glass. Veil Harbor was pale now; color drained to the uniform tone of moonlit metal. Far below, people had stopped moving; the pulse held them at the edge of breath. In the far harbor, a faint blue thread winked once inside the silver haze and went still, the way an ember pretends it has given up.

In the eastern distance, beyond the curve of the piers, a darker shape detached itself from the storm, a craft descending through the mist. The old rescue chopper, retrofitted with dampener shielding, its rotors throwing halos in the rain. The engines beat a steady, deliberate rhythm that sounded less like flight than inevitability.

Vale followed Briggs's gaze. "Extraction?"

"Yes," Briggs agreed. "But not until I have Rourke."

Chapter 30

The sound that took the hall wasn't a sound.
It was the toll of a bell, air tightening, walls learning
how to be quiet. Lanternlight thinned to a skim, color
stepped back from faces like a tide that had somewhere
else to be, and the whole church seemed to lean a
fraction as if the city itself had braced for an impact
already inside it.

Kalen didn't fall.

The pressure slid through him hunting for edges. It
found the old fractures, Emily, Lily, and pressed. The
gauntlet woke under his skin with a soft blue pulse,
brightened, then settled against his bones like a
steadying hand.

Breaths stalled all around him, caught in throats,
trapped behind teeth. A woman bent over a wounded
man with a strip of linen in her fingers and froze mid-
knot, eyes wide, not panicked so much as paused. The
bell rope trembled once, a vein under a thumb, then
remembered how to be rope and went still.

"Down!" Rissa's voice made it through, rough and
close. She herded three people behind a pew with the
flat of her hand, then took a half-step toward the
transept, rifle low, shoulders set as if the floor had
moved under her and she'd decided to move with it.

Mercer swayed and caught himself with a palm on the shattered rail of the choir. His veins lit once, gold, too bright, and went dark, like a coal choosing not to burn. He blinked hard, jaw clenched, waiting for everything inside him to choose one direction.

Silas wasn't in sight. Kalen saw a flash of orange near the side aisle and the sudden, unfunny stillness of dust that should have been drifting. Then a cough, wet and stubborn, fought its way out from behind the fallen plaster.

The pressure dropped one more notch.

Somewhere behind them a boy screamed. Not fear, just wrong. The scream had that skittering, metal-on-metal edge Kalen had learned to hear too late. He pivoted, vision narrowing to the aisle: a man two pews down, eyes mercury-bright, mouth twisted off its hinge. The man moved without wasting ground, hands hooking, feet wrong, and came over the pew recklessly.

Rissa met him. Stock to throat. Elbow to temple. Clean and ugly. Enough to break a charge without breaking the man. The feral fell, rolled with inhuman grace and tried to rise again on his shoulder; Rissa stamped the movement flat and kept him there with her knee.

"Second!" someone cried.

Kalen turned. A teenager at the altar rail, fingers hooked into the wood, tendons like wire. Light crawled the veins in the boy's hands, brightening and dulling in waves as if something was trying to find a rhythm and kept finding the wrong one. His pupils had gone wide to swallow the world.

Kalen didn't shout. He stepped forward and let the sorrow he carried lift to the skin the way tide lifts a boat. He didn't drive it outward. He kept it where it belonged: centered, held, with room around it for other people to breathe. The gauntlet warmed, blue veins in its metal matching the thin, pulsing lines under the boy's skin.

"Look at me," Kalen said softly, as if the boy had asked him to come closer and he was answering a favor. "This way. Don't fight the pull. Let it have what it wants and then ask for it back."

The boy wasn't listening; the thing inside him was. Kalen felt it pressing, blind and hungry, like a creature that mistakes doors for open ground. He widened his stance, let his own chord broaden until the wrong note the boy was holding sank against it and slipped. The pressure in the room tamped down a fraction. Somewhere to his left a woman sobbed the rest of a breath she'd forgotten how to take.

"Good," Kalen whispered, not to the boy but to the part in him that was falling toward a cliff and slowing. "That's it. Come on. Come back."

It cost. The edges of Kalen's vision salted with black, and the hot sting at the back of his nose told him what he'd see on his sleeve if he wiped it. His fingers numbed from the knuckles in, and the gauntlet's veins flickered pale, then blue, then pale again. He held anyway.

The boy's hands unclenched. The light in the veins dulled from bright blue, the same color threaded in the gauntlet. The kid's jaw loosened. He made a sound like someone remembering water after a long drought and folded to his knees. His shoulders shook. The wrongness bled off him in weak waves that broke and went nowhere. He was alive and ashamed; both were better than the other thing.

"Who else?" Rissa asked without turning her head.

"Here? Three," Mercer answered, voice low, already counting off with two fingers. "City?" He listened to echoes from the doors, knuckles rapping code, a runner's whisper cutting through the seam of the jamb. "Two dozen. Pockets. Docks, market lanes, the cannery edge."

"Not a purge," Silas said from the rubble, voice coming up with a little laugh that didn't try to be brave and was braver for it. He shoved a slab aside, wriggled out with one boot and a curse. His cheek was covered in blood. His grin showed the tooth he always managed to chip on days like this. "Just a reminder we're mortal."

Kalen let the chord in his chest soften before it collapsed. The room's note eased a little. The air learned how to pass through people again. A lantern that had thought about dying thought better and coughed back to life. The bell rope quivered, thought about moving, and refused.

A hand caught Kalen's sleeve. The woman with the bandage strip stared past him at the boy he had brought back. She lifted the linen. It took a moment before her fingers remembered the knot.

"I've got him," she said, voice shaking. "Go."

He nodded and stood slowly. His knees had a new opinion about how to work. He gave them time to argue and win. He wiped his nose with the back of his hand and didn't look at the blood. When he finally did, it was only a smear, not a leak. He could live with that.

The light in the room had changed. It hadn't died, not like the stories from other cities when the sky went white and stayed there, but it had gone thin. Silver ached at the edges of things, the way cold makes a room feel bigger by showing all the space air takes up.

Out beyond the cracked stained glass, rain debated direction. For a second, a thin line of blue cut through the silver over the square like a vein seen under skin in the right light. It winked and was gone. He filed it away like a tool he didn't know how to use yet.

"Silas?" Kalen called, knowing that voicing his name meant he couldn't walk away and leave him there.

Silas flapped a hand from the floor and sat up. "Reporting for duty," he said, and then winced because duty had bumped a bruise. He tilted his head left and right until something in his neck adjusted into place. "I hate architecture."

"Stay still," Rissa told him, which meant don't be a hero until I tell you when. She tightened a strip of cloth around the unconscious feral's wrists and looked up at Kalen. "Can you hold the room again if it spikes?"

"For a little," Kalen said. Honesty had stopped being polite a long time ago. "Not everyone at once."

"Then we don't ask that," she said. "We ask what we can pay for."

A runner staggered in from the side door, damp and bright-eyed. He hadn't lowered his hood against the weather; he'd lowered it against the light. He tapped a rail with two knuckles: a dock signal, quick and clipped. Mercer answered with three and a palm. The runner breathed once and swallowed.

"Market Lanes have four turned," he reported. "Old pier has two. Dock Five is burning hotter than we can measure, but it's still holding together. The sump at the cannery is humming, and something's off with the wiring down there."

"We felt it here," Mercer said.

Silas pushed to his feet with Rissa's hand on his elbow and propped himself on the end of a pew. "We've got, what, twenty ferals out there?"

"Maybe," Mercer said. "Maybe a few more by the time we're told it. Not a wave. Not yet." He looked to Kalen when he said it, not for permission but to put the words into something that wouldn't lie to him.

Kalen crouched beside the teenager he'd pulled back. The boy had his hands over his eyes like they were the only doors he could close. Kalen rested a palm on the kid's shoulder, light, and felt the tremor under skin that had not decided what to keep.

"What's your name?" Kalen asked.

The boy murmured his name into his hands. Kalen didn't press him to speak up. He simply echoed the name once, making sure he got it right, and gave a nod as if the world hadn't just tried to strip away his identity with something he never wanted.

"Can you sit by the rail?" Kalen asked. "Stay with her." He touched the woman's sleeve; she nodded as if she lived to be given work. "If your hands start to sing again, you grip this." He tapped the boy's palm, then the wooden rail: solid, dumb, honest. "Not me, just this. It won't move."

The boy nodded. His breath found a rhythm. It wasn't pretty. It didn't need to be.

Another cry tore across the room. Not feral, fear this time. Someone hadn't found their people in the right line of light. Rissa moved toward it with her rifle low, the way a shepherd moves toward a cliff. Mercer stayed at the center and let his presence anchor the room to the floor. He didn't speak; he didn't need to. The place steadied around him because that's what he did: turn air into shape.

Kalen's chest ached where he held the sorrow. It wanted to spill the way a bucket wants to pour when you carry it wrong. He adjusted his stance, let the weight sit where it should, and some of the ache let him go.

"Elena?" he called, not really expecting a reply. He looked at the sensor cart beside the altar, it gave a brief flicker before going dark for good. The grease pencil marks she'd scrawled resembled a diagram of something painful to the touch. Her kit was splayed open at the foot of the hall, one tool angled eastward as if dropped in haste but still pointing, remembering its purpose even abandoned.

"She was on the grid," Rissa said without looking away from her work. "Near the station. She'll have moved when it sang."

Silas wiped at his cheek and inspected the result. "Bad news, I'm handsome," he reported. "Good news, I can fix that." He glanced up toward the broken window and squinted. "You see that?" he asked. "The blue?"

Kalen didn't say yes. He didn't say no. He filed away that Silas had seen what he'd seen.

The pressure in the room eased another notch. Not gone, just settling into a posture it could hold. People breathed in twos and threes. Rissa's voice drifted along the pews: count, confirm, wrap, move. Mercer's hands moved without jerk or flinch: lift, steady, give. Everything that could be done inside the walls would be done. The next thing would happen somewhere else.

Kalen walked the length of the aisle slow, letting the smell register the way smells become memories: lemon oil from the pulpit where someone had decided to care about the wood even now, wet wool, metal, a thin thread of antiseptic, the damp, brittle scent of old hymnals whose pages stuck when the weather turned. Every face he passed was lit in the same uneasy silver, the color that had crept under the storm since it learned their names.

By the doors, Rissa straightened. "He's breathing," she said, meaning the feral she'd dropped. "Wrists, ankles. We'll decide what to do with him when we're not choosing between dying and moving."

"Agreed," Mercer said.

Kalen nodded and looked past them through the doorway. The square outside had the washed-out look of film left in sun: puddles silvered over, stone a pale reflection of the sky. Movement was wrong, too deliberate. Not a parade. Not a stampede. People finding their feet and not trusting them yet.

A second runner slipped through the side door and put two fingers to his throat. The gesture was Dock Five's; the eyes were a man who had seen something he hadn't asked to live through.

"Cannery edge," he said. "Basement hum's high. People close to the wrong end of it are slipping." He swallowed. "We can hold them if something pulls back from the edge."

Kalen let the weight inside him settle another degree. He could pull. He could hold. He could not do it for a city. The truth fit his mouth like a splinter. He left it there and spoke around it.

"Where?" he asked the runner.

The man tapped the map Elena had drawn in grease pencil. His finger landed on a circle under the cannery. "Here," he said. "The pressure is growing stronger and stronger."

Silas leaned over the broken sensor and whistled. "Sub-relay," he said. "Right where you'd put it if you hated us." His grin came quick and thin. "Which is flattering."

"We can reach it easily," Mercer added. He said it as memory, the map lived in his body, even if the paper said otherwise.

Rissa shot him a look that meant agree to the truth before we get crushed by it. "We go," she commanded. "Small and fast. If he plays this note again, we'll have twice the number in the wrong shape, and I don't have enough knees to kneel on all their chests."

Kalen let the image bring the decision together. Elena had drawn the route with a pencil and faith. The field would cool; when it did, the snapped-back emotion would be a lash if nobody cut the line. The blue flicker had shown up twice, the same color as the breath he could hold steady if he didn't try to swallow the whole sea.

He looked at Mercer. "You with us?"

Mercer's mouth twitched, ashamed for a breath by something that had his name on it and passed. "I was always with you," he said. "Even when I wasn't."

"Silas?"

"I'm always in for a good time," Silas smirked, "let's do something stupid."

"Rissa?"

Rissa slung the rifle on her shoulder and checked the strap. "I'm in," she said, "we trust you."

Kalen drew in air that tasted like blood and prayer. He turned back to the nave, to faces that had looked to him when he'd stood on a piece of stone and told them the storm couldn't tell them what they were. He didn't give them a speech. The city had speeches. It needed a cut.

"If you can walk," he said, pitching his voice to the room's edge, "you help those who can't. If you can't, you breathe and hold the person next to you steady. When you see the blue mark," he pointed to the chalk on the door, "you gather and wait for a hand to take you. We'll send the hand."

The woman with the bandage strip nodded without looking up from her work. The boy, his boy now, for as long as it took, kept his eyes on the rail like it was the last honest thing in the world. It might have been.

Kalen took one more look at the broken window. Rain had made up its mind: down, clean and straight. And in the silver smear above the square, just as he turned away, the thin blue line flickered again, smaller, stubborn.

He touched the stone of the doorway as he passed under it and felt the building answer: old, tired, unwilling to crack. Rissa went first into the rain, shoulders squared. Mercer followed, steady, a hinge for the air to turn on. Silas hopped the last step like it was a joke he was telling the ground.

Kalen paused with one boot on the threshold and looked back at the nave. The bells hadn't rung; no one had asked them to. He heard them anyway, phantom and low, the part after the strike where a city remembers it can be loud without losing itself.

"Hold," he said to the room, and to himself, and to whatever waited under the cannery.

Then he stepped out into the square, and the door fell quiet behind him.

Chapter 31

Light came through the rain as a thin gray, enough to carve edges but not enough to name colors. The city wore the blast like a bruise.

Rissa took point, rifle down, eyes working corners before the rest of her body agreed to follow. Mercer moved at Kalen's shoulder, a quiet gravity that bent the street toward discipline.

Silas ghosted rear guard with a limp he refused to admit to; every few steps he flicked his baton against his palm like he was reminding both it and himself that they were real.

Thane joined in beside Mercer, coat darker from the rain, expression unreadable. He moved like a man who'd seen both sides of the coin and no longer trusted currency.

The symbol on the nearest door, the blue line through a broken circle, had been repainted in the night. Newer strokes overlapped older ones, some careful, some furious, some the small, stubborn scrawl of a shaking hand. The mark had weight now: not a secret, a direction.

They kept to alleys where they could. They weren't running aimlessly; they were trying to reach the substation before Briggs's Hunters locked down the district. Storm glass still lined the cobbles from windows that had exhaled their strength. The air hummed low, one long note the city hadn't let go since the blast. It lived in the teeth and the joints and the stitch at the back of the skull.

"Two blocks east, cut south by the boardwalk," Mercer murmured, more to the map in his head than to them.

"Eyes up," Rissa whispered, and palmed a side-door latch before moving past it. The room beyond held nothing but a cot, a cracked basin, and the warm ghost of someone who had left before they arrived.

They passed a row of stoops where people had dragged chairs out into the wet not to sit, but to make the world remember their shapes. An old dockhand stood, veins faintly lit, a bandage around his wrist where someone had kept his hands from making the wrong decision. He didn't speak. He watched them go with a confident nod.

At a corner, a young woman with a shaved head knelt beside a boy who wouldn't wake, whispering a rhythm for him to borrow. Kalen would have stopped, he had learned the hard way what happened when you believed you could carry all of it, but Rissa's hand on his sleeve kept him moving.

The city had learned silence, but not how to keep it. From somewhere in the houses came a low, shared hum, no words, just threads of sound running toward each other until they braided and thinned again. Once, someone laughed too loudly. It broke and turned into a sob that didn't quite reach the throat.

"Feral sign?" Silas asked under his breath.
Mercer shook his head. "Too quiet for that."
"Too quiet's when they're closest," Rissa said.

They crossed what should have been a road and found only a trench half-filled with rain. Blue lights licked the water's skin when the wind pushed it.

Kalen's gauntlet warmed. He flexed his fingers inside the metal and felt the articulation answer smoother than it had any right to. The blue thinned and thickened along the lattice, tracking currents in the air the way a bird tracks weather you can't see.

"Reading?" Mercer asked, a quiet tilt of his head.
Kalen lifted his hand and let the metal listen. The pulse pulled east, then down, as if the city had veins that ran underground and something had stuck in one of them.
"Substation," he said.
"Or a trap," Rissa said, as if both were the same duty.

They cut south, then east again, keeping to walls where the silver still hung and the blue hadn't burned the corners bright. A set of steps spilled onto a lane with a view of the harbor's outer edge.
Far beyond the piers, the sky wore six pale columns like dowels holding up a sheet: Briggs's lattice,

dimmer now, stuttering in a rhythm that wanted to be regular and wasn't.

Silas nudged Kalen's shoulder with the back of his hand. "You feel that stutter? Like it's breathing wrong."
Kalen did. The city's big note had a hitch, an offbeat that said either the machine was failing or the man behind it had a hand on the dial and a plan.
He didn't waste breath on which he preferred. "Keep moving."

Door symbols thickened as they neared the east district. Blue chalk on wood. Blue paint on brick. A cloth strip knotted to a latch. The symbol had become a way to touch without breaking.

At the mouth of a narrow court, two rebels stood watch with lengths of pipe, faces tight but unafraid. One recognized Kalen and straightened not with awe, but relief so sharp it made the eyes look raw.
He raised two fingers, Dock Five's quick sign, and pointed east. Then he drew a small circle in the air and broke it with his thumb. *Trouble.*
Kalen nodded, touched the man's knuckles with his own, and moved on.

"Can't we just talk like normal people, instead of all these hand gestures?" Silas called out as they came closer to the substation.

Rissa didn't look back, just kept her eyes on the blue-lit cracks ahead. "Normal gets you noticed," she said quietly. "Hands keep you living."

"I suppose," Silas said, eyeing Rissa as they ran by. "Whatever that means."

They reached a low ridge of factories: tin roofs, broken teeth of skylights, the smell of wet oil in the lumber. The substation sat beyond them. Even at this distance, the air above it had a wobble. Blue splintered up from the sump grates in fine lines, brightening and dimming, trying to find a tempo. Silver rode the edges, thin as a knife.

Mercer studied the layout. "East access," he said. "Over the culvert. We don't take the center ramp unless you want to be a story about what not to do."

Silas peered down and made a face. "Smells like an old battery licked a dead fish."
"That tracks," Rissa said. "We'll stink of it either way. Keep your teeth together if it spikes. Hold it together."

They moved lower, keeping brick under their palms, feet placing themselves. Twice Rissa froze them with a finger's lift, once for a feral shape far off on a rooftop, watching but not choosing; once for a pair of figures guiding three more across the open, all five lit faintly blue and leaning into that light like wind.

At the culvert, the water ran slow and mean under a grate buckled by heat. Kalen crouched, pressed fingers to metal already cold again, and felt the pulse run up his arm.

He stood with a slowness born of caution, not age. "She's close."

Rissa's eyes flicked to him, then to the wobbling air above the substation. "Alive?"
The gauntlet answered before he did, a thin bright line racing the filigree and settling where his pulse lived. He didn't smile. He let the relief sit like food on a lean day.
"Working," he said. "Which is the same thing right now."
"Then she's got minutes, not hours," Mercer said. "If the lattice coughs again…"
"The city is lost," Rissa finished. Her mouth made a grim line, she knew what was at stake.

They crossed the culvert one at a time. Thane lingered behind them until the last step, scanning the roofs. "If Briggs still has hunters moving, this is where they'll find you first," he murmured.
"Then keep them looking the other way," Kalen said. Thane's eyes met his. "Always."

Halfway down the run to the substation gate, the city shifted.

"Together," Silas said, too quiet for anyone who wasn't close to hear, and this time he didn't say it like a joke or a prayer. He said it like a password you use to unlock yourself.

They reached the outer fence. It had been cut earlier. Inside, the ground had been chewed into by rain and boots. Blue bled from hairline cracks in the concrete and ran to a junction box on the wall that shouldn't have had that much life left in it.

Rissa checked the corners, then tipped her chin. "On me."

They slipped through.

The smell hit first, followed by the hum. It wasn't noise. It was pressure, a pulse that made every rib ring like glass. Blue light breathed from the floor grates in uneven waves, rising to meet the ceiling in a shimmer that had no center. It looked alive but unsteady.

Rissa entered first, rifle raised. Mercer followed, sweeping the far wall with his flashlight until it struck movement.

"Elena," Kalen breathed.

She was crouched at the base of the main control column, sleeves rolled, face lit by the reflection of a thousand small failures. The console before her looked like it had been rebuilt a dozen times and reprogrammed by instinct more than logic. Every gauge bled blue light from its cracks. Elena's fingers trembled as she rewired a coil the size of her forearm. Sparks jumped from wire to wire, arcing across her skin, but she didn't flinch.

Kalen started forward. "You're—"

"Alive," she said, voice rasping. "Barely. Don't touch anything. It's like surgery on lightning."

He froze mid-step, letting his eyes travel over the tangle of cable and tools at her feet. The gauntlet on his wrist pulsed in rhythm with the room. He realized the grid was breathing the same pattern as his heart.

Rissa knelt opposite her. "What are you holding together?"

"The grid," Elena said. "Or what's left of it. When Briggs triggered the amplifier, it didn't just broadcast a field, it reversed polarity in the lattice." Her voice cracked. "He tried to erase resonance, but he left a harmonic behind. It's spreading."

Silas frowned. "In English?"

"She means it's a feedback loop," Mercer said. "The city is feeding off the energy now, not the storm."

Elena nodded weakly. "The backlash alone if the circuit is cut will be too much for all of us."

A tremor rolled through the floor. Dust drifted from the overhead beams. Outside, a gust pushed the rain sideways, bending it in arcs that pulsed blue white for a heartbeat before turning silver again.

Kalen crouched beside her. "You've been here since it hit?"

"I didn't want to leave it alone," she said. "It's trying to stabilize, but it doesn't understand balance yet. It's like it's… feeling its way through grief."

The word hung there, *grief.* It was what they'd all been living inside since the storm began.

Kalen brushed his thumb along the gauntlet's edge. The metal responded with a soft hum that made the coils nearest Elena shiver. The blue glow steadied for half a second before resuming its frantic pulse.

Rissa's gaze darted to him. "What was that?"

"It responded to me," Kalen said quietly.

"Don't get poetic," Silas muttered. "If it heard you, that means it can answer."

"It already is, in its own way," Elena said. "If the resonance is evolving, it's looking for anchors. It's building itself around them. Kalen's one. Maybe the only one."

Kalen studied the trembling light in the column. It looked like the same color that had burned through him when he'd first found control, blue threaded with something deeper, something that wasn't color at all.

"What happens if I connect?" he asked.

Elena met his eyes. "You could stabilize it, or it could eat you alive. Either way, we'll know what's left of the storm."

The hum climbed in pitch until the air itself quivered. Rissa's rifle strap buzzed against her shoulder. Silas clapped his hands over his ears.

"Kalen," Elena warned. But he was already moving.

He reached out, slow and deliberate, the gauntlet glowing brighter with each inch. The light spilling from the column bent toward him as if magnetized. When his palm met the control housing, the entire substation went white.

The floor dropped away. The noise stopped.

He was standing somewhere that wasn't space, just distance, folded and waiting. A network of blue threads stretched in all directions. Through concrete, through air, through memory. Each strand pulsed with fragments of emotion: anger, fear, hope, envy, love. Every echoform in the city was there, connected by a living filament of light.

For a moment, Kalen wasn't alone in his skin. He could feel them, thousands of hearts beating, uncertain but alive. And beneath it all, the faint static whisper of something else: a current colder than the rest. Briggs's residue, still embedded, trying to pull everything back toward silence.

He heard Elena's voice somewhere distant. "Kalen! You're bleeding. Let go!"

He didn't. He steadied his breath and did what Mercer had taught him: control, not fight.
He pushed his sorrow outward, not as grief, but as clarity. The blue network pulsed brighter, rejecting the silver threads that still crawled through it. For a heartbeat, he saw Briggs's lattice shudder and fracture. The vibration in the city changed pitch, softening from command to conversation.

Then the vision snapped.

He fell back hard, the gauntlet smoking. The world returned in bursts of sound. Rissa's voice swearing, Elena shouting for tools.

Silas grabbed his shoulders, eyes wide. "You with us?"

Kalen's vision steadied. "Yeah." He looked at Elena. "This storm is something we can't contain."

Elena's hands shook as she adjusted a readout. "We try anyway. We have a right to fight."

Mercer looked toward the eastern windows. The rain had stopped. Beyond the glass, faint beams of silver flickered in the clouds, six pillars, trembling like broken fingers trying to rise again. "He's not done."

The blue light around them dimmed, like the world itself was drawing a breath.

And then, far off in the distance, thunder rolled, heavy, wrong. The floor trembled, and a heartbeat later, a flare lit the horizon. The eastern sky erupted in light as the first pillar exploded.

The shockwave rolled across the city like a shout. Glass shivered in its frames. Dust lifted off rafters. Every head in the substation snapped toward the windows.

Silas blinked hard. "Please tell me that wasn't the grid deciding it hates us."

Mercer frowned. "No. That was shaped." Shaped meant intentional. Shaped meant someone fired on it.

A distant hum rose, not resonance, not storm, not anything Veil Harbor had ever claimed as its own. If one pillar fell, the others would follow, and the storm would have nothing left to hold it back.

Rissa's breath caught. "Hear that?"

Kalen already did. A low rhythmic thup thup thup, growing louder. Not thunder. Not wind. Rotor blades.

Elena ran to the shattered window frame, bracing her palms on the sill. "East," she said, voice thin. "Look."

They saw them before they heard the second blast. Six dark shapes punched through the cloud cover. Then fire. Another pillar bloomed white and came apart in a clean burst of light, detonating as if cut from its base.

Silas staggered back. "Someone's hitting the columns on purpose."

Mercer drew a slow breath. "That flight pattern is military. Federal."

The third pillar erupted. The shock reached them late, flattening the grass outside the station. Kalen felt the vibration in his chest strengthen, the storm inside him reacting like an angry animal.

Elena whispered, "They're taking out the entire array."

Rissa's jaw locked. "Question is who."

The helicopters broke fully from the cloud bank – then, sleek and armored, rotors braced by storm metal ribs that glinted under the aurora. Blackhawks, but heavier. Reinforced.

The fourth pillar vanished. Then the fifth. The eastern quarter dropped into darkness.

One helicopter peeled off and dropped into a low hover above the main square. Its searchlights swept rooftops and empty market lanes. The loudspeaker crackled.

A voice carried across the city, steady and clipped, the tone of someone reading a verdict. "Attention Veil Harbor. This is the United States Army."

Silas whispered, "I can't believe I'm hearing this."

The voice continued. "General Darren Briggs, stand down. You are under arrest for treason, unlawful martial seizure, civilian endangerment, biotechnological terrorism, and unauthorized deployment of resonance class weaponry."

Elena's hand covered her mouth.

Rissa stared upward. "They actually came for him."

Mercer's voice sounded like stone grinding. "Too late to stop what he already started."

More helicopters descended toward the piers, landing in staggered formation. Soldiers fast-roped down, boots hitting pavement in tight coordinated squads. Their visors reflected the storm light, their movements clean and practiced.

Gunfire cracked in the distance. Not at them. At ferals.

Troops advanced street by street, pushing into alleys and clearing intersections. Bursts of white pulse fire flashed from their rifles, calibrated to immobilize instead of explode.

Elena's eyes widened. "Counter resonance weapons. Briggs must have completed the prototype before he defected."

Mercer muttered, "Or stole it."

Another squad formed a perimeter near the substation entrance.

Kalen stepped back from the window. "They're sweeping the city. Closing in on his position."

Silas looked at him. "If Briggs is still inside City Hall …"

Mercer finished, "Then they'll pin him. Hard."

The last pillar blew apart in a bloom of white across the western skyline.

Veil Harbor fell into an unnatural quiet. The storm overhead flickered in confusion, as if pieces of itself had been ripped away.

Rissa checked her mag. "He's not going to let himself be taken. He'll make for the docks. Or the bunker."

Elena grabbed her pack. "Then we need to move too. Before the Army finds us first."

Kalen stepped toward the doorway, rain pushing sideways across the square.

"Briggs won't run," he said. "He'll aim for control."

Mercer nodded. "Which means he's planning something else."

Silas flicked the broken dust off his sleeve. "Fantastic. We get to race the Army to a mad general."

Rissa jerked her chin toward the stairs. "Then move. He doesn't leave here."

Chapter 32

Every step towards City Hall felt heavier. The pillars had fallen; the lattice was gone.
But Briggs wasn't.

Thane rejoined them outside the old library steps, coat torn, his radio hissing fractured strands of military code.

"They're sweeping the eastern blocks," he said. "Not us, them. Briggs's last hunters are being pinned down by the Army. They're calling it 'containment protocol.'"

Rissa glanced toward the low clouds, where faint pulses of light throbbed like a heartbeat behind the storm. "Containment of what?"

"Whatever's left of him," Thane said.

Kalen watched the skyline. City Hall loomed half-lit, broken glass flashing blue where the stormlight caught it. They needed to reach the council chamber— whatever Briggs was building, whatever was feeding him, they had to shut it down or understand it before it finished consuming him.

They crossed streets that weren't streets anymore, flooded lanes where colors wove and ebbed like breath. Survivors watched from doorways, hollow-eyed but alive. Someone reached out, brushing the edge of Kalen's coat, whispering the word that had survived every translation:

"Together."

He nodded once and kept moving.

City Hall's entrance stood half-collapsed, marble cracked under heat and memory. The Army's bombardment had shaken the upper floors; smoke bled through seams in the roof.

Thane cleared the stairs first. "He has to be up here."

At the landing to the council chamber, Thane stopped. He knelt beside a dead hunter—armor cracked, silver light gone dull.

"He turned halfway," Thane murmured. "Then the pulse hit. Froze him like this."

Rissa crouched next to him. "Still think Briggs is saving anyone?"

Thane didn't answer. He rose, jaw tight. "He doesn't know how to stop. Men like him never do."

Elena's voice lowered. "He's drawing on the feedback from the lattice collapse. He's using himself as the conduit."

"How is any of this even possible?" Mercer asked.

"At their core, emotions are frequencies," Elena said, glancing at each of them. "Any of them can be accessed—though not easily. Clearly Kalen isn't the only one who's learned how."

She turned the handle slowly and pushed open the door.

Briggs stood near the shattered window. His uniform was shredded, skin streaked with blood and silver light. The storm had already taken half of him—veins along his throat glowed like molten wire, his left hand pulsing with a steady, unnatural rhythm.

He turned when they entered, eyes catching the blue shine from Kalen's gauntlet.

"So," he said softly. "You survived the correction."

"Barely," Kalen answered. "You didn't."

Briggs's mouth twisted toward something like a smile. "You think this is ruin? This is ascension. The city breathes through me now."

"It's choking," Kalen said.

Briggs laughed—raw, uneven. "You sound like her." He meant Elena. "All feeling. No vision."

Rissa moved to flank him, rifle steady. "Funny thing about vision," she said. "You lose it right before you die."

Briggs raised his hand.

The air thickened. Light warped. Gravity seemed to hold its breath. Rissa's shot fired wide and dissolved midair, the bullet turning to vapor before reaching him.

"Enough!" Kalen shouted, stepping forward.

Briggs's head snapped toward him. "You don't give orders here. I gave you a world worth saving."

He moved faster than his broken body should've allowed. His strike hit Kalen like a hammer made of resonance, flinging him into the wall. The gauntlet flared, absorbing half the impact, then cracked apart.

Mercer dragged Rissa down as another wave tore through the room. Sparks rained from the ceiling. Elena ducked behind the console, shouting, "He's pulling from City Hall's grounding field! If he keeps that up, the whole structure goes!"

"Then stop him!" Rissa barked.

"I'm trying not to die!" Elena shouted back.

Kalen pushed himself upright.

Briggs's glow was spreading—crawling up his neck, down his arm. His voice split into two tones: the man and the storm speaking over each other.

"Do you hear it?" Briggs whispered. "The silence finally learning how to speak?"

"I hear you breaking," Kalen said. He stepped forward, peeling the ruined gauntlet from his arm. "And I'm done listening."

The clash hit like a storm contained in a single heartbeat.

Blue against steel.
Light folding, screaming.
Glass shattered outward; rain burst through the windows.

The entire floor trembled.

Briggs swung harder now, more storm than man. Kalen countered, movements tighter, angrier, blue light singing with every blow. When their palms collided mid-strike, the floor cracked beneath them.

"Still think you're saving them?" Kalen shouted.

Briggs's eyes blazed white. "I am them!"

He drove a surge into the floor, shattering the console. Lights flickered once, then died. Sound collapsed into wind.

Briggs staggered for the first time. The glow under his skin flickered—unstable. The storm was consuming its host. He stared at his trembling hands, then at Kalen.

"You're right. We will take our revenge."

Kalen froze. "Who... what?"

Briggs lurched backward. "You think this changes anything? I still have control." A grin crept across his face. "Sovereign and I will bring peace to this planet."

A deep concussion rolled beneath the building. The floor shook. Thane's voice crackled over Mercer's comm:

"Army's closing. Helicopter inbound to the docks. Different than the rest."

Briggs's eyes snapped toward the shattered window.

Stormlight flared against the incoming rotors— spiraling down toward the harbor.

"You can't stop inevitability," Briggs said.

"I don't have to," Kalen replied. "Just you."

Briggs ran. He burst through the broken window, coat whipping behind him as he vanished into rain and wind.

"Helicopter's on final approach, ten seconds!" Thane shouted over the comm.

Rissa bolted, but Kalen grabbed her arm. "No. He's mine."

She nodded once. "We're right behind you."

Kalen ran.

The stairwell was half-collapsed, smoke and sparks spilling through the gaps. He dropped down the last flight and shot out the front doors, the sound of rotors pounding the air like a second heartbeat.

Wind tore the world sideways, rain and dust spiraling. The helicopter hovered above the docks, floodlights washing the pier in blinding white.

Briggs staggered toward it, one arm raised against the downwash. The light inside him flared—violent, uneven.

Kalen stepped into the storm.

The wind caught them both, rain, light, the echo of everything broken on the way here.

For a second, the world narrowed to two voices:

One trying to control the storm.
One trying to let it breathe.

Briggs saw him and laughed. "You can't kill what the world needs to survive!"

"Then maybe it doesn't need you!" Kalen roared.

The helicopter's floodlight burned them bone-white. Briggs hesitated, the storm inside him guttering like a candle trapped in its own draft.

"This is mercy," he said, voice shaking.

Something alive flickered behind the wreck of his eyes.

Then he turned and climbed into the aircraft.

The rotors screamed higher.
The helicopter lifted through the rain—
and vanished into the cloud.

Chapter 33

The docks shook with noise that did not belong to water. Searchlights raked the fog. Soldiers shouted coordinates over static. Engines throbbed above the pitch of wind. Salt spray hammered the planks sideways, cutting grit into their faces.

Thane was already shouting into a radio, trying to hold back the line of troops spilling across the pier. "Stand down! He's taking off. Do not fire. Repeat, do not fire."

No one was listening.

Elena fought her way through the floodlights, scanner flickering in her hand. The readout spiked every few seconds, each spike matching the rhythm in Kalen's chest. "He's here," she said. "Right here."

"Kalen!" Rissa shouted, but he was already moving.

He ran, feet hammering the boards, the sound lost inside the mechanical roar. His pulse matched the rotors, faster and faster. Elena's voice followed him, thin against the wind.

The aircraft made a slow circle.

Kalen skidded to a stop twenty feet away, breath torn out of him by the downdraft. He raised a hand against the spray, trying to see through the blades and the blur of light.

For an instant, the storm parted. Briggs stood in the open doorway, one hand braced on the hatch, the other gripping a figure pulled from a cargo crate bolted to the floor. A small frame. Gagged. Wrists bound. Eyes wide.

Kalen's knees buckled.

"Lily!"

The name tore out of him as if something inside had broken loose. Elena froze, breath faltering; she recognized the child instantly. "Lily…"

Briggs's smile did not move, but something in it sharpened. Kalen felt the world tilt, pressure rising, storm leaning in, waiting. "You left her for the world I had to rebuild. Consider this a lesson in follow-through."

The helicopter lifted higher. Wind and grit drove Elena back a step, and she grabbed Kalen's arm. "No, Kalen. Listen to me. You have to control this."

But control had already torn free. Red haze was crawling at the edges of his sight. He had spent so long fearing what the storm might turn him into.
But becoming something wasn't the danger.
Losing himself was.

The sound hit first, a deep rising thrum that was neither wind nor engine. It came from Kalen himself.

Blue light burst from under his skin, spilling through every crack of him until he was nothing but outline. The pier vibrated beneath his feet, boards rattling like teeth. Elena shielded her eyes.

Kalen could not feel his body, only the flood, the endless cold of it.

Then the scream came.

A voice detonated inside his skull. Enormous. Familiar. Terrifying.

That man will die for this! Cinder had returned.

Kalen staggered, hands clawing at the air. Blue aura flared upward, ten feet, twenty, bending the rain into spirals. A heartbeat later, red fire erupted through it, fighting for space. The two colors orbited each other, colliding with sonic cracks that sent waves across the harbor.

Stop fighting me. The voice was no longer outside him. It filled every inch.

Kalen dropped to one knee. The red surged, furious and alive. The blue tightened around it like a lung. Each pulse was a question and an answer. The air shook.

Helicopters above lurched sideways from the shockwave. Glass along the shore fractured and fell in sheets.

Red for the fight that had kept him alive. Blue for the grief that had kept him feeling. White for what waited when he stopped choosing between them.

The light twisted together until there was no border left. Only brilliance, hot enough to bleach the world, alive enough to remake it. The storm folded inward, silence drawing breath, and then the colors collapsed into one searing hue: white-gold, pulsing like a heartbeat that belonged to both of them.

Kalen stood in the center of it, every edge of him burning, every emotion awake. Pain blurred into clarity. Cinder was no longer an intruder. He was a voice in the same breath. Kalen did not fight the fire. He reached for it.

The roar of the engines faded, leaving only wind and the hollow thrum of a city trying to remember itself. He stood where the color had bled out of the night, his chest open, his heart burning. Pain gave way to clarity. The two voices inside him found the same breath. The ground trembled under his boots, the air tightening, the pulse of something immense waiting to be unchained.

He lifted his head. His eyes burned, one red, one blue.

Sit back, Cinder growled, heat rolling through his skull. *My turn to drive.*

The world tilted. Color roared through him.

Kalen raised his face to the heavens. His voice cut through the wind, steady and alive. "No more fighting, Cinder. Show me your true power."

For the first time since the sky had burned, the world did not move. It simply waited.

Epilogue

The air still hummed. It always did now, low, electric, endless. Color threaded the clouds like veins under skin, shifting slow as breath. The city beneath it glowed from its own scars, alive but never quiet.

Saint Ronan's Square no longer existed. The church's bones jutted like black teeth from a mouth of rubble; the barricades had cooled into slabs of glass. Yet voices moved through the wreckage, hoarse, stubborn, rhythms reknitting themselves one task at a time.

Rissa worked the longest line, where the med stretchers made a crooked path across the square. Her white light was thin and steady, a candle cupped against the storm. She touched a shoulder, a cheek, a small hand, and the tremor in each person eased a notch. Twice she swayed and had to grip the edge of a broken seat to stay upright; twice she stood back up because someone had already stepped forward with a question in their eyes.

Silas limped three blocks of debris with a crew of volunteers and two soldiers who kept trying to tell him to sit down. The sling across his ribs creaked when he hauled a doorframe off a crushed stairwell. "On three," he said, and grinned anyway, because the grin made people move. "One, two—seven." The door lifted.

Someone laughed through their teeth and didn't stop until the coughing did.

Mercer parked himself near a shattered rail, rifle laid across his knees, gaze flicking between the perimeter and the low clouds that bent light wrong. His aura was a dull red-gold ember now, the color of something that refused to go out. He watched south more than he watched anywhere else. No one asked why.

The Army's command tents pulsed with generator glow. Storm-rigged transports idled in the street, their armor welded from coil plating and road signs. Kinetic blasters thrummed in a rack like singing tuning forks. Officers spoke in clipped vox: corridors cleared, pockets of ferals contained, grid hazards flagged. The words "trial" and "tribunal" whispered through the canvas like moths that couldn't find a light to die in.

Veil Harbor had changed overnight in ways that metal and muscle couldn't touch. The old trees along 4th Street wore threads of pale light in their bark that pulsed in slow answer to footsteps. Rain that wasn't rain lifted off puddles and drifted upward, winking into the air like reverse ash. Low walls and shopfronts held echo-scars, smears of color that sometimes replayed what had happened there if you passed too close: an arm raised, a face turning, a burst of laughter that broke your heart because it wasn't here to make anymore. Two children with gray-tinged eyes discovered if they hummed together, they could brighten the lamps strung over the aid tents by one shade. A feral in restraints calmed, just for a breath, when Rissa set her palm over his and let her white thread through his pulse.

No one announced any of this. They just noticed and kept moving.

By afternoon, a message crackled through the battered radios that made heads lift without anyone meaning to: "No sign of General Darren Briggs. Helicopter wreckage located south along the coast. Negative on bodies."

Silas stopped listening, then shook it off like rain. "Gotta love mysteries with teeth," he muttered, and levered another beam.

A medic zipped a bag over a form laid out with care under a tarp near the courthouse steps. The helmet had been set beside it, and the visor cracked clean through. Vale's gauntlet rested on the chest as if he'd remembered to fold his hands. A private placed a ration biscuit on the tarp like an old rite and crossed herself. No one spoke to fill the silence he left.

Toward dusk, when the clouds brightened for a while and then thought better of it, Rissa gathered with Silas and Mercer at the boundary where the Army's lights flickered into the makeshift streets. They ate without tasting much and checked the names scrawled on a blackened strip of wall: FOUND, ALIVE, MISSING. Kalen's name wasn't there. Rissa traced it with a fingertip against the soot anyway, as if absence could be circled and contained.

"He's out there," Mercer said finally, not looking at them.

"Yeah," Silas said. "And when he gets back, I'm gonna hit him in the mouth for leaving and then hug him until he can't breathe."

Rissa's tired smile flickered. "You won't be the only one."

They stood for a while under the humming lights, the city breathing around them, the air charged enough to lift the hairs on their arms. Then they went back to work, because that was the only thing that made the waiting feel like action.

Elena had slipped away after the last coil of wire ran out and the last amplifier fragment gave up a single blue sigh and stayed dead. She crossed the south blocks alone, past the places where color clung like lichen and the places where it refused to come back at all. Past a storefront that now hummed when you stepped over the threshold like it remembered music, past a row of trees that leaned a fraction toward the sound of a whispered name.

The pier creaked under her boots. The lake beyond it shifted like a mirror filled with ink and veins of light. Every wave carried fragments of red, gold, and blue that never sank.

She sat at the end board where the wood was smooth from old years and new storms. She set the cracked communicator beside her and waited for a blink that didn't come.

Elena didn't speak for a long time. There was too much inside.

When she did, the words came small and exact, like she was laying them in a row so they wouldn't break on their way out.

"You didn't have to go alone."

The lake kept moving. The clouds above breathed their slow color. The pier answered under her with a soft knock like an old house remembering a footstep.

"I know why you did," she said. "I know you think it had to be you. It's always you when someone says it has to be." She breathed, steady and shallow, "But we were still here. You don't get to decide you've finished carrying us because you're tired of the weight."

Her mouth tipped in a shape that might have been a smile if it weren't so tired. "We're going to find you," she said. "When you burn out or burn through or finally remember how to stop. We'll be there. And together…" She swallowed, knuckles whitening on the communicator. "Together, we'll finish this."

Elena rose when her legs began to ache the way grief did when it remembered it was also a body. She faced the city. The air tasted like wet iron and ozone and the memory of rain that didn't fall anymore. Somewhere above, the storm turned over in its sleep and showed another color.

She stood for a long moment, listening to the hush that followed her own voice.
The city below answered in small sounds, wind through scaffolding, water shifting against stone, the distant creak of a world still trying to remember its rhythm.

Behind her, Veil Harbor shimmered under the sleepless sky. The storm never truly left; it only learned to rest. Its colors were quieter now, folded into the seams of things. Streetlamps breathed faint violet between heartbeats. Windows caught reflections that moved before the people inside did. Even the air felt sentient, tasting of salt and static.

Elena watched a pulse of light travel across the harbor's surface, not lightning, not reflection, but something alive, drifting like a vein of color beneath the water. It curved toward the shore, then sank without a ripple. She knew what it meant. The resonance was spreading.

Elena tilted her face to the wind. It smelled of rain, but also of iron and something faintly floral, like the storm itself was blooming. Somewhere out there, beyond the drowned roads and the forests that still smoked blue at night, Kalen was moving through that new growth, carrying the storm with him, or keeping it at bay. She didn't know which. She only knew that she would find him.

She turned toward the city lights. They blinked once, all together, a long, slow pulse that rolled through the streets like a heartbeat.

For a breath, she thought she heard her name threaded in the wind.

Elena...

Not a voice. A resonance. A memory of warmth pressed into the air.

Her throat tightened, but she smiled. "I hear you," she whispered. "You're not done, are you?"

Far above, the clouds stirred, faint crimson bleeding through green. A new front was forming on the horizon, slow and deliberate, like a giant drawing breath. Lightning stitched along its belly without sound.

Elena watched until the light faded behind the ridgeline. Then she lifted her collar against the wind and started back toward the heart of Veil Harbor, each step echoing softly on the flooded stones.

Behind her, the water rippled once more, glowing faint amber, just for a heartbeat. Far beyond the city's edge, in a ruin swallowed by trees, a figure paused mid-stride as the same pulse brushed his chest.

Kalen lifted his head to the sky.

The storm answered.

And the world kept changing.

END OF BOOK 1

Thank You for Reading

Stories only come alive when someone feels them, and if you made it this far, it means this world meant something to you. That alone means more than I can ever say.

If you enjoyed *The Storm That Broke the World*, Book 1, the best way to support the series is to leave a short review on Amazon. It can be one sentence — just a few words — and it makes a massive difference. Your review helps new readers discover the book and keeps this world growing.

Thank you for spending your time here.
Thank you for feeling this story with me.

— Tim

Acknowledgments

To everyone who carried me through the making of this book, thank you.
To my amazing wife, and my 3 children for being there for me every step of the way.

To my friends and family for every moment of support.
And to every reader who understands how deeply we feel the things we carry—this story is for you.

Your encouragement kept this world alive.
Your belief brought it to the finish line.

Thank you.

About The Author

When I started writing *The Storm that Broke the World*, I didn't set out to build a world where emotions had color or power.
I was trying to make sense of how deeply we feel—and how those feelings shape everything around us.

The story began with a single question:
What if emotion itself could be seen?
What if every hidden part of us—our anger, our grief, our empathy, our love—was visible, uncontrollable, and impossible to fake?

From there, *The Storm that Broke the World* became more than a story about survival. It became a reflection of what it means to be human in a world that constantly tests it.
Kalen's grief, Elena's hope, the storm that changed them—they're all pieces of the same struggle we live every day: trying to hold onto ourselves when everything is shifting beneath us.

The **color system** grew out of that idea.
Red became defiance. Blue became memory. Gold became love—the most dangerous and beautiful force we have.
It wasn't about superpowers or fantasy—it was about

emotion itself as energy, the way it connects us and destroys us at the same time.

Writing *The Storm that Broke the World* was like watching light break through fog: painful, messy, and strangely healing.
It's a story about loss and forgiveness, about how we carry the people we love long after they're gone.
But above all, it's about **what happens when we finally stop running from how we feel—and start using it to build something new.**

If the book leaves you with anything, I hope it's this: Even in the ruins, even when the world feels colorless, there's always a spark waiting to come back to life.

Stay Connected

Want early looks at Book Two, special announcements, and behind-the-scenes content?

Visit: **www.echoofthestorm.com**
Follow on TikTok: **@stormthatbroketheworld**
Follow on Facebook: **The Storm That Broke The World**

Your support keeps this world alive.

www.ingramcontent.com/pod-product-compliance
Lightning Source LLC
Chambersburg PA
CBHW051941240626
47153CB00005B/1582